RIGHT OF REPLY

ALSO BY JOHN HARRIS

The Lonely Voyage
Hallelujah Corner
The Sea Shall Not Have Them
The Claws of Mercy
Getaway
The Sleeping Mountain
The Road to the Coast
Sunset at Sheba
Covenant with Death
The Spring of Malice
The Unforgiving Wind
Vardy
The Cross of Lazzaro
The Old Trade of Killing
Light Cavalry Action

JOHN HARRIS

Right of Reply

COWARD-McCANN, Inc.
New York

c, 2

to

ROBERT LUSTY

whose idea it was

Note

Although this book tells a story similar in many respects to the attack on the Suez Canal in 1956, it is not intended in any way that any individual or unit shall be identified with anyone involved in the Suez affair, or that the story should be a reflection on the present-day Services.

When the British assemble a
force to defend their base na-
tionalized by an African country,
they arouse opposition from their
own country and from their allies.

Part One

1

'*In these tense days,*' the notice on the wall said, '*the eyes of the country are upon you and, knowing the onerousness of your task, I am sure you will be patient, ardent and above all strong. Britain relies on you.*'

The message was from the Prime Minister of Great Britain, the Right Honourable Arthur Starke, and, addressed to all members of Hodgeforce as part of a big morale build-up, a copy had been attached to the wall of the guardroom of the 17th/105th Assault Battalion—as it had in every unit orderly room and all messrooms and canteens of the great base camp at Pepul. It had been properly printed, with a nice line in decorative edging, and proclaimed its ringing message just above the head of Private Kevin Lawrence Bowen as he worked over the fire bucket which, traditionally, as a petty military criminal, he had scraped and polished until he could see his blunted, pale face in it, even the thatch of stiff ginger hair, yellow fox's eyes and freckles that blurred the outline of his features.

He had already painted the bucket red, and scraped and polished it and shone it again—a task designed especially to bore him to tears by the unsympathetic Sergeant Patrick O'Mara, of the Royal Military Police, who was an expert at such things.

Outside, the wind that came from the sea was warm and sticky and, on its passage through the mangrove swamps that surrounded the largest part of the camp's perimeter, it had picked up the curious smell of the mangroves, that odd mixture of acid gas and rotten vegetation.

Dark masses of thick-trunked cotton trees leaned over the base, shutting out the yellow moon and making it a chequerboard of blacks and ghostly whites. Beneath the trees, the splintered leaves of the banana plants rasped in the hot wind and, beyond them, the sky, carved into segments by the curving boles of palms, was pricked by starlight.

Outside the camp boundary, the mud and wattle huts of the village of Pepul, huddled among the foliage, were thrown out here and there in silhouette by the faint light of an oil lamp or the glare of a fire, and what few stone buildings there were picked up the moonlight on their whitewashed fronts and tossed it back in a silvery glow. The aromatic air of the Equator was heavy with the acrid scent of woodsmoke and the ancient heady smell of Africa.

Not that Ginger Bowen cared much about the acrid scent of woodsmoke or the ancient heady smell of Africa. And, while he was very well aware of the onerousness of his task, he felt neither ardent nor patient, nor even particularly strong. And, just at that moment, he couldn't have cared less whether Britain relied on him or not.

In a mild puzzled way, he felt he had become familiar with all the emotions of a cold-blooded murderer before the act. The sound of the bull-frogs, the crickets and the mosquitoes made music with the cheep of bats and the screech of the owls, and from time to time he heard the rats making love in the undergrowth and the noise of a beetle roaring round the room like a flying bomb. The thermometer on the wall registered eighty-eight and the heat stood in the shadows with the suffocating menace of an assassin. His shirt was black with sweat and he was suffering from prickly heat, which he felt was a personal imposition not inflicted on the other men about him in the camp.

He had no wish to be where he was. In fact, he wasn't at all sure why he *was* there. All he knew was that two months before he had been an unwilling recruit at one of the few remaining training camps in England, and eleven months before that, before the new National Service Act which a hard-pressed Britain had been forced to bring in again, had caught him up, a bricklayer's labourer—still unwilling—in a Sheffield wire-works.

Ginger Bowen's unwillingness was not brought on by his unexpected presence in Africa. It was a built-in unwillingness

2

that had been with him most of his life. Where it had started, he didn't know—even if he'd ever thought about it—perhaps somewhere on the cheerless council estate that covered the tilted acres of a wind-swept Yorkshire hillside, perhaps in the out-of-date school that successive governments had been promising for generations to replace and never had, perhaps in the cramped home, noisy with television and transistor and disputatious voices, where he'd been brought up. Wherever it originated, the fact remained that Ginger's unwillingness was a real thing, as real as the blunt and shapeless nose in the centre of his face.

It wasn't that he was devoid of humour—rather the contrary—it was simply that the welfare state and the permissive society in which he had lived had never fitted him for doing anything else but what he pleased.

He put aside the bucket at last and stood up, flexing his fingers and staring at the green polish marks on his hand with disgust. Then he carefully put away the rags he'd been using and folded the dusters as O'Mara always insisted, and picked up the bucket.

'Ah, the good Ginger!' O'Mara looked up as he put the bucket down in the entrance to the guardroom. 'See that it's filled with water, old boy—and, mind, not a splash on the outside. Any fires that now occur will be put out all the more efficiently for the work you've put into that bucket.'

'Nail a plank across it, Sarge,' Ginger protested, not without friendliness. Over the months, both in Africa and in England, through all his numerous arrests and detentions, Ginger had got to know Sergeant O'Mara well and bore him no ill-will. There was, in fact, quite a lot of mutual trust and liking between them, in spite of the fact that more often than not they were firmly on opposite sides of military law.

'You know what they say,' O'Mara said gaily, enjoying the leg-pulling. '*Excreta tauri cerebrum vincit*. Bulsh baffles brains. And if your cup of happiness, Ginger, has been soured by the gall that led Lieutenant Jinkinson to shove you on the peg, then perhaps the rumour that we're leaving here soon might bring roses to your cheeks.'

'Leaving?' Ginger looked up, interested. 'When?'

O'Mara gestured. 'When the boys back in Westminster run

3

out of ideas what to do next,' he said. 'That's when we come into the picture. Didn't anybody ever tell you? War's a failure of diplomacy. And warriors like us are the dogsbodies they drag out when the politicians can't think of anything else to say.'

Ginger gave him a disgusted look and went to fill the bucket at the stand-pipe at the back of the hut. Beyond the camp boundary, he could see the road into Pepul, open to all but criminals like Ginger, and along its fringe the huts where the native women sat, selling mangoes or bananas from the wide calabashes between their feet, and the tailors huddled over their ancient machines, slaving away in the yellow glow of kerosene lamps. From among the foliage behind, came the drab plink-plonk of a tuneless melody in fragments of broken sound from an instrument made from a biscuit tin—and like an accompaniment across the stifling air the thud of a drum through the crowding trees.

Listening to it, Ginger wondered what malignant fates had conspired to land him in this god-forsaken part of Africa. He was aware in the casual manner of a man who never reads anything but the sports page of his daily paper that some sort of emergency existed. He was aware that a British base at King Boffa Port in Khanzi just to the south had been sum-marily nationalised by Khanzians still revelling in the fact that they had tossed aside the yoke of one of the decadent new African states, whose corrupt politicians had undone all the good that a hundred years of British colonial rule had done, so that all the provinces in their dominions were now trying to do exactly what they had done themselves twenty years before. The fact that the Khanzians had happily ignored the treaty made with Britain by their erstwhile rulers, Malala, and closed the base, had been sufficient to rouse in a Great Britain still smarting at no longer having either Empire or foreign bases a feeling of bitter resentment which had been supported by the African rulers of the land where Ginger now unwillingly resided, who were for once eager to uphold Britain's rights because they marched in step with their own.

The result was that the somewhat ramshackle base at Pepul, some two hundred miles to the north of King Boffa Port, had been hastily built up with a view to forcing the new owners of

King Boffa Port to stand by the treaty and hand their loot back to Britain.

All these somewhat confused international politics were way over Ginger's head, however. Since Macmillan's 'wind of change' had swept across Africa, the newly independent states changed their names as often as they had changed rulers so that no one, least of all Ginger, was any longer certain where they were or what they were currently titled, and Ginger was quite indifferent to whether Britain got her base back or not. He was unmoved by the cries of treachery that certain elderly Members of Parliament who could still remember Britain's greatness were sending up. He was untouched by all the haste and urgency that existed around the new base, all the scurrying hither and thither of Mokes and Landrovers and Champs and Donkeys containing high-ranking officers, all the departures and arrivals of aircraft on the hastily enlarged airfields at Pepul and Korno to the north, all the urgent and uncomfortable conferences between British and Malalan commanders that went on incessantly in the newly-erected huts of the operations block and in the white concrete parliament buildings of Machingo, the capital of Malala, just to the south. Ginger was untouchable.

It never occurred to him that, but for the crisis, he might have spent the rest of his days in the provincial English city where he was born. On his trip to Malala he had seen Gibraltar, Dakar and Casablanca. He had smelt the exciting smell of Africa, that strange mixture of charcoal and vegetation that could always stir the hearts of old Coasters. He had seen the sea in half a dozen moods. He had experienced blazing dawns and roaring sunsets that he would never have experienced in Britain. He had seen the moon like a huge orange in the sky, and stars that seemed so close and so glowing bright he could almost touch them. He had seen the Slave Coast—the old White Man's Grave—and palm-fringed beaches so shimmering they looked like bleached ribs in the sun, and the brilliant green of jungle foliage covering the harsh red land.

He had travelled as he would normally never have had a chance to travel. And it had left him only with a numb horror that the National Service Act, which had had to be introduced when the crises of the Seventies had forced military preparedness on Britain, had scooped him out of his little niche in Yorkshire and forced him to live in a wider, higher and more colourful world than he was used to.

As he put down the full bucket and went inside the guardroom again, Sergeant O'Mara looked up.

'Do you know, Ginger,' he said cheerfully, 'you never told me. What was it for this time?'

Ginger grinned and his lumpy face warmed and crumpled in a way that always amused O'Mara. 'Out without a pass,' he said shortly.

'Girl?' O'Mara asked.

'Yeh.'

'Was she worth it?'

Ginger's grin widened. 'She was *that*.'

'Who is she?'

'Sulfika Achmet's her name.'

'Nig?'

'White bints out here don't look at *me*,' Ginger said. 'One of coffee, two of milk.'

'On the knock, or just a friend?'

'Bit of both, I suppose.'

O'Mara grimaced. 'All you'll get out of that lark,' he commented, 'will be a bad reputation and kinks in your spine.'

He bent over the transistor he was toying with, his head cocked as he tuned it carefully.

'How about a bit of music, Sarge?' Ginger asked. 'Makes my load lighter.'

O'Mara shook his head. 'Not this time, Ginger,' he said. 'I'm trying to get the Prime Minister. I don't suppose you're aware of it, you probably couldn't care less if you did know, but it *might*—it just *might*—interest you to know that he's about to address you. He's making a broadcast to the nation to explain why we're here and what he intends to do about us.'

The radio crackled and a solemn voice filled the little guardroom.

'This is him, Ginger,' O'Mara pointed out. 'Talking to me, Ginger—and to *you*.'

Ginger paused to light a cigarette as the sonorous steady voice, with all its politician's tricks of emphasis and inflection, forced him to listen.

6

'. . . the first and most urgent task,' it was saying, 'is to uphold the rights of Malala in its dispute with the provincial government of Khanzi. We do not wish to use force—God forbid!—but when Malala became a sovereign state twenty years ago, it was part of the agreement she made with Britain that she could call on us, in the event of aggression or disorder, to support her. That is what we seek to do, and all we seek to do.' The fact—unknown to all but a few technicians—that the performance was not as spontaneous as it seemed but had been well rehearsed and put on tape at Downing Street earlier in the day in no way detracted from the Prime Minister's performance.

Ginger drew on his cigarette, his eyes blank and opaque. The sombre phrases could hardly have been said to have caught his attention.

'It is sad,' the heavy voice continued, 'to find the provinces of a former member of our great Commonwealth at logger-heads with each other, but it is still our duty to separate them. We are concerned, we are anxious to assure the world, first with protecting the rights of Malala and secondly with taking care of British nationals at King Boffa Port where the disputed base is situated. These and these only were in our thoughts in preparing *Operation Stabledoor*. We pray it will never have to be used.'

O'Mara lifted his feet to the desk, his face expressionless, and Ginger leaned on the doorpost, his mind already far away in the Moyama Bar in Pepul, where Sulfika Achmet would probably be queening it with his friends, her olive face alive with laughter, her slender body sinuous under the gaudy lappas she favoured. Ginger drew a deep breath at the thought, and, drawing his hand heavily across his face, he coughed harshly in an effort to shatter the uneasy picture.

'If the United Nations . . .' the slow voice nagged at his attention again just when he was enjoying the memory of Sulfika's soft golden skin and the way the light from the oil lamps caught her shoulders and breast '. . . if they were to take over the physical task of restoring order in the area, no one would be more pleased than Her Majesty's Government. But some sort of police action there must be. Treaties solemnly made cannot thus be summarily broken, and agreements must

7

be upheld, both by us and by those who made them with us. Otherwise the globe will descend into anarchy. We have therefore asked the American ambassador at Khanzi—we ourselves have no embassy there as we have never recognised the state—to inform the so-called President of Khanzi, Colonel Scepwe, that unless they are prepared to withdraw from the base in King Boffa Port, we are prepared in the end to resort to force to take back what belongs to us . . .'

O'Mara's face was sombre as he listened. He was an intelligent enough man to believe that the Prime Minister's self-righteous words were a little suspect. The issue as he saw it unclouded by ambition and half-truths, was simply that Britain had lost a base and that she was determined, by threats if not by force, to get it back. She was finally taking a stand against the cheerful plundering of the remaining parts of her Empire, to which—harassed by well-meaning pacifists and racialists, by the anti-imperialistic groups in the United Nations, and by the United States who gaily stepped in whenever she withdrew—she had hitherto been obliged to submit. The whole point of the force gathering at Pepul was that it was a pistol pointed at the heart of Khanzi. Every new man who was jammed into the crowded tents and hutments, every new aircraft that roared down the hastily prepared runway, and every new ship that anchored in the creeks and bays nearby, increased the threat; and all the nonsense that the politicians talked about going to the help of the Malalans was just a lot of cloudy oratory to obscure the real point.

O'Mara mopped at his face, not at all sure what to make of it all. He looked up at Ginger's unprepossessing form as he listened. Under the clauses of the new National Service Act, which had been brought in unwillingly by a Government eager not to offend the trade unions, no man in a profession or a trade, or training for a profession or a trade, could be called up, with the result that only the left-overs like Ginger could be used—and most of them, though they were cleverer than Ginger, weren't half so likeable. Regulars like the sergeant were in the habit of sweating blood to rouse enthusiasm in people like Ginger and, as pay had recently been cut for all but those with over ten years' service in an effort to stave off Britain's growing economic problems, enthusiasm was not an emotion that was easy any longer to find in the Forces.

As the country's Chief Minister stopped speaking, O'Mara switched off the set and sat for a moment, staring at it. Whether the severe cut in Servicemen's pay which had taken place a mere three months before the present crisis had blown up was a wise move was now something very much to be doubted. With eleven years' service behind him, the sergeant was not affected, but he'd heard Ginger sounding off more than once about it, and he had a feeling that in the uncomfortable and crowded camp a feeling of greater fury than Ginger was capable of expressing was hardening into resentment. The Government, he thought, might have got away with it if it hadn't been for the crisis.

He looked up and saw Ginger still standing in the doorway, waiting to be dismissed.

'Well, Ginger,' he said, his smile returning. 'Did you listen to your First Minister?'

Ginger shook his head. 'No,' he said frankly. 'Not really.'

'Perhaps you ought to have. It might have a great effect on your future. It looks very much to me as though we might be going to war.'

Ginger's sweating face didn't alter much. 'Whacko,' he said, a slow grin spreading across his features.

'You like the idea of being incinerated by an atom bomb?'

Ginger shrugged. 'They won't use an atom bomb for this,' he said confidently.

'No, they won't,' O'Mara agreed. 'But somebody—probably the Russians—might decide it's more than just an attempt to get a base back, and they might make a stand. There might even be a line-up, and then—*then*, Ginger—there *might* be an atom war. After all, it only wants some bloody fool somewhere to pull the trigger.'

'Ah, well,' Ginger grinned, 'it might come down on you, Sarge.'

O'Mara shook his head, with all an old soldier's contempt for an unwilling recruit.

'Shove off,' he said. 'And see you're here tomorrow—*on time!*'

As he watched Ginger disappear into the darkness outside, his brows came down in a frown. Ginger was careless, lazy, stupid and unwilling, and the sharpest punishment never impressed on him the necessity for listening to what he was told to do. It would be a bad day for England, O'Mara thought, if she ever had to depend on men like that. Yet Pepul camp, he knew, was full of Ginger Bowens—*and worse*—rounded up from a dozen camps all over the country at the urgent request of the Government in its efforts to raise an army.

The sergeant flung his cigarette away angrily. What he knew, what his officers knew, what the general down in the capital knew, but what the politicians back in England, without their intimate knowledge of the workings of the military mind, did *not* appear to know, was that the demand for soldiers to make up depleted units had resulted only in commanding officers taking the opportunity to get rid of as many of their troublemakers as possible.

They'd all since arrived in Malala, and Pepul was full of them.

2

In Machingo, the capital of Malala, Lieutenant-General Horace Hodges, D.S.O., commander of Hodgeforce and, when the chain of command was carried to its last link, Ginger Bowen's commanding officer, wiped away the perspiration round his neck and slowly began to pack his pipe with tobacco.

The hotel suite he'd been given for the use of himself and his staff during the conferences in the capital was modern and cool, with sleek Swedish furniture, angular lights and drapings in muted colours, but all the modernity in the world couldn't hide the fact that the room was far from spotless and that the streets outside, for all the square concrete buildings that had been flung up in the last twenty years, were a little unkempt and shabby. Of all the places he could have wished to be sent, Malala was probably lowest on Hodges' list.

He didn't even particularly like the Malalans as a race, and he found their senior officers inefficient, self-important in their newly designed uniforms, and far too full of military clichés to be easy to get on with. Circumstances had forced a Malalan Deputy Commander-in-Chief on him and he was already at the point when he couldn't think of General Ditro Aswana without feeling ill. A political appointee, Aswana had jumped from major to lieutenant-general almost overnight during the Young Officers' Revolution.

Hodges sighed, realising he was not alone in his dislike of the Malalan troops. Judging by the number of fights that occurred at Pepul, it seemed that the British troops shared his distaste for their allies.

He finished loading his pipe and lit it slowly, savouring the taste of the tobacco. He was a squarely built man, tall but broad enough to make his height seem considerably less, and looked not unlike Wavell in the way he stood, rigid as a monolith, with his head up and his feet planted solidly on the ground.

He turned to his Chief of Staff and indicated the radio set he'd just switched off.

'So much for the Prime Minister,' he said slowly. 'What did you make of it, Stuart?'

Colonel Leggo stiffened by the table where he was studying maps, and turned quickly. He was young enough to be Hodges' son and he looked vaguely like him, except that there was nothing about him of the unmoving stolidness of Hodges. Leggo looked as though he were of finer grain and quicker intelligence, but probably of less staying power in a crisis.

'Excuses, sir,' he commented shortly. 'It ought to be accepted by now that no coloured race's going to accept domination by a white race simply because the white race's stronger militarily. I thought the Americans and the French had discovered that in Vietnam. I thought it had been drummed home in England by Suez.'

The general nodded. 'Makes a difference, though, doesn't it,' he said, 'when the white race has a coloured ally? Still'—he shrugged—'I suppose Malala's terms of independence did say that Britain could intervene in case of trouble, though I don't expect anybody thought that it would be *this* sort of trouble.' He sucked at his pipe for a moment, filling the air with clouds of blue smoke. 'That was twenty years ago, too, and things are different now. The Americans have been blowing hot and cold for weeks and there's been a hell of a divergence of policy between us and them.' He scraped another match and sucked flame into the tobacco for a moment. 'It'd be a tragedy for us if *this* half-baked affair brought *that* friendship to an end.'

Leggo dabbed at his forehead with a handkerchief. He had been aware for some time that his general was not relishing the task ahead of him.

'Particularly'—Hodges seemed to read his thoughts and went on to explain the way he was thinking—'particularly as Malala doesn't have the best of reputations either in Africa or Europe. Let's face it, even when they were part of the Empire, they weren't the steadiest of troops and when they were granted independence it was practically the only place outside India where there was trouble.'

'Braka seems pretty well in the saddle now, though, sir,' Leggo pointed out, thinking of the long thin African with the beard and horn-rimmed spectacles with whom they had been conferring only that afternoon.

Hodges had moved to the window to stare down into the street and through the new buildings opposite to the corrugated iron roofs among the palms in the old quarter of the city. Immediately, the heat struck him, in spite of the hour, and he felt the sweat start out down his spine and under his arms.

The brightly hued chattering people below him seethed outside the flare-lit open-fronted shops where the Syrian traders squatted, their corpse-faces impassive but their restless eyes not missing a single move of the black hands over the goods they sold. A Creole clerk went past, one of the new Africans in his smart starched suit of dazzling drill and white topee, staring down his nose at a Hausa trader in a dusty pyjama-cloth robe and shabby gold-embroidered smoking cap who brushed against him as he hurried by. Pushing arrogantly past the trader's calabashes, the clerk elbowed his way between the labourers with their strident banjo voices and slapping feet and the mammies with their Madras head kerchieves and the hideous Mother Hubbards, which had been forced on them generations before and had not yet entirely disappeared.

The melon-slice grins over the baskets of fruit and the paper-stopped ginger-beer bottles brought a smile to Hodges' face because he loved Africa for its colour and its rawness and its noise, though he had little liking for the new Africans like the Creole clerk, who had swept away all the old tribal loyalties and dignities without replacing them with anything better. The thought reminded him abruptly of Leggo's comment on Braka.

'Do you think so?' he asked. 'Do you *really* think he's consolidated himself?'

He was thinking of the private instructions he'd received from the Foreign Office before he'd left England. 'Watch Braka,' they'd said. 'We're not sure he's very safe.'

Neither was Hodges. They'd been greeted warmly enough, apart from a few banners in the streets and a brick bouncing on the car bonnet, which Braka, all affability and smiles, had explained away with the suggestion that the sight of white faces was still inclined to incur African wrath. There'd been willing co-operation, however, in the setting up of the base at Pepul where Malalan soldiers had been marched out of their camps and the green and white flag had been replaced by the Union Jack. There had been a formal handing over and a review of British troops, and a great deal of speech-making by Braka and a lot of hot air about friendship, ties with Britain and the need to honour the sanctity of treaties. It hadn't cut much ice with Hodges. He knew from the Foreign Office that Braka had been influenced less by noble sentiments than by the several million pounds which had been hurriedly placed at his disposal to bolster up an unstable economy.

Hodges frowned, uneasy in spite of himself. Ever since he'd joined the Army as a young soldier in 1940, he'd dreamed of an independent command, but now that he *was* in command, he wasn't so sure that reality had come up to his dreams. When he'd had his dreams, there'd *been* an army, but now his command consisted of a few companies from two or three first-line regiments—all of them under strength because the clause in the National Service Act which let out craftsmen provided only the sort of men this type of regiment wouldn't have touched with a barge-pole—and a hotch-potch of other battalions, hastily brought up to strength by intakes from depots all over the country, entirely devoid of pride or a feeling for tradition, and transported by over-age vehicles scraped up from every vehicle pool in the United Kingdom and a few more places besides.

He thought of his orders and how they were framed. '*You will enter King Boffa Port and, in conjunction with Malalan troops, will undertake operations aimed at re-occupying the base there. If necessary, Khanzian forces will be engaged and destroyed. Casualties on both sides to be kept to a minimum.*'

Hodges considered the signal for a moment. Leggo had not yet seen it, but Hodges had spent several days considering it. Once he received the preparatory signal, it only required the code word, 'Dash', to put the whole thing in motion, but the idea implicit in the last sentence was that he was to do the job without anybody getting hurt. In the climate of rising temperatures and cooling personal relationships in Africa, someone at home had got cold feet at the last moment and they were asking him now to drive a military machine with all the brakes on. They preferred to call the operation a police action instead of war, but the academic difference in terminology meant only that the politicians had felt that, because of political expediency, the planning should be done in London and had changed the arrangements a dozen times, with the result that Hodges' initiative was now constrained within a narrow limit. He was to fight a battle under a directive which said 'Thou Shalt Not Kill'.

He pushed his uneasy thoughts aside and picked up a photo interpretation laboratory file, marked with the red seal of Intelligence. The photographic enlargements inside showed a view of King Boffa Port taken from a big R5. As it had floated with blunt-ended wings on the thin upper air at 40,000 feet, the pilot checking his instruments and flicking the lever that had started the cameras whirring in the slender body of the machine, it had shown on the Khanzian radar screens as nothing more than a blurred blip.

'How old are these, Stuart?' Hodges asked.

'Two months.' Leggo lifted his head to reply.

'Is that the best they can do since they took the job from Admiral Hoosey and gave it to that damn' lackey of the Prime Minister's? Ask for fresh ones.'

Leggo nodded, turning to his maps again, his fingers tracing across the sheets the coloured blocks of the harbour installations and mole at King Boffa Port. He looked up sharply.

'Are the swing bridges strong enough for tank regiments' new Senators, sir?' he asked.

'So the Planning Committee says,' Hodges affirmed.

'And are we to expect the lock gates to be in operation?'

Hodges shrugged. 'Planning Committee says no,' he growled. 'I say yes.'

'Do you really think the Khanzians can work the harbour installations on their own, sir?'

'I'm damn' sure they can,' Hodges rapped. 'The Egyptians worked the Suez Canal. There's not much difference.'

Leggo nodded. 'That's true,' he said. 'And we know they've

got Russian experts to help them.' He wiped from the chart a droplet of perspiration that had fallen from the end of his nose. 'I'm not sure I like the way the Russians have been sending arms to Africa, sir,' he said. 'Some of 'em might have reached Khanzi.'

Hodges grunted. 'Russian arms are the least of our troubles, Stuart,' he said. 'My worries are much closer to home. Let's have a drink and a look at those returns.'

Leggo handed him a pink file, then turned away and poured him a whisky and soda while Hodges stared at the papers, frowning.

'Lot of sickness in the 4th/74th,' he said sharply, the regimental titles offending his eye as he read. Since the Army had been expanded again, all but the crack regiments had lost their regional identities and had reverted back to numbers, and now, with the linking of regiments, nobody was certain where traditions and loyalties lay.

'Perhaps it's this climate, sir,' Leggo said, handing him the glass. 'A lot of 'em haven't been out of England before. They've had no chance to get acclimatised.'

'Neither did we in 1940,' Hodges grunted. 'But the sick returns never looked like this.'

'Lots of youngsters, sir,' Leggo pointed out. 'They don't measure up as well as the older chaps.'

'Never did,' Hodges grunted. 'Trouble is, there aren't *enough* "older" chaps these days. Only too-young recruits and too-old reservists. The Army's not been the place for a man to consider a profession for some years now.'

'We didn't do too well at Suez, sir,' Leggo admitted.

'We did damn' well against the Nazis, though,' Hodges snapped.

Leggo stared at the general's back and said nothing. Leggo was one of the new wave of officers who were coming to the fore and, though he was very fond of Hodges, he sometimes thought the old boy harked back a little too often. Modern soldiers just wouldn't wear the kind of conditions he'd experienced in the Nazi War. What had sufficed in 1940 these days only stirred up trouble.

Hodges turned over a sheet. 'Crime's up,' he commented.

'Mostly trivial stuff,' Leggo explained.

'It's the small stuff that shows what they're made of,' Hodges snapped.

He was fond of Leggo but sometimes he thought the younger officer was a bit too conscious of creature comforts. Too much concern with comfort, he considered, had helped to make the Army a soft one. There hadn't been much comfort in the desert in 1940 and there'd been very little wrong with *that* army.

He opened a folder inside the file. The first thing that caught his eye was a bitter report from his parachute brigadier, complaining about the aircraft they were having to use and the fact that half his men were in need of practice drops; and a similar one—even if not quite so bitter—from the tank brigadier. Trying to prepare for a war that was not a war in an atmosphere of peace that wasn't quite peace had revealed a state of military unpreparedness that was staggering.

He made up his mind abruptly and tossed aside the file. 'Call a conference of brigade commanders when we get back tomorrow, Stuart,' he said abruptly. 'I want to talk to them.'

'Yes, sir.' Leggo had his head down as he made a note on his pad and the general couldn't see the wry look on his face. 'Any agenda?'

'No.' Hodges spoke sharply. 'I just want to put the breeze up 'em a bit. There's too much sickness and too much crime, and not enough work being done. Too many can't-be-doners and better-notters among the regimental commands. They've got to pull their socks up a bit. We'll spring a surprise inspection on 'em when I get back. That ought to make 'em jump. Calhoun wants a bit of stiffening and I think Dixon could do with a rocket up the backside. He's got it in him but he's too damn' lazy by a long chalk. He's fine on computer stuff but not so hot on the two-legged animal. I didn't want him anyway. I wanted Tom Southey.'

'What happened to Brigadier Southey, sir?' Leggo asked.

'He got diverted at the last moment—together with the brigade's ack-ack guns. Ship's engines failed. They said it was sabotage and sent me Dixon instead.'

'Been rather a lot of that, sir,' Leggo observed.

Hodges grunted. 'You don't have to tell me,' he said. 'This thing's been a nightmare. We're badly armed and under-trained. Dixon's short of ack-ack and field artillery, and most of Calhoun's weapon carriers are in Scotland with Tom Southey. Our transport's largely civilian, scraped up from anywhere we could get it, together with a few lorries we've raised in Malala and paid for at enormous cost, and we've no maps of Khanzi but a lot of old rubbish supplied by Braka. Where did they come from, anyway?'

Leggo gave a twisted smile. 'Bus routes or something, sir, I suspect.'

Hodges snorted. 'They got us here too damn' quick, Stuart. I've never seen such a shambles in my life. War Office might have pulled their fingers out a bit.'

Leggo's smile widened. 'They punctiliously informed you of your promotion to lieutenant-general, sir,' he pointed out.

'And signally failed to keep me informed of the changes in plan.'

Hodges' eyes fell on the file in his hand, and his mind moved restlessly over his problems. 'Stuart,' he asked suddenly, 'how many coloured men have we in Hodgeforce?'

Legge looked up, startled by the question. 'Around ten per cent, sir,' he said. 'I can make it more exact, if you wish.'

Hodges considered the figure. When the first of the coloured recruits had found their way into the Army it had been considered unusual but, more and more, as Englishmen aimed for the high wages offered by industry, the Army had had to fall back on the more willing coloured immigrants; and now, with the return of National Service, British-born Africans and Jamaicans had been swept into the Forces with their white comrades.

As it happened, they had turned out to be excellent soldiers with a liking for that army ceremonial which was anathema to most white men, but *Operation Stabledoor* had raised a problem with them that nobody seemed to have considered in Whitehall where they were merely names on a list.

'I wonder if they're all right,' Hodges said.

Leggo lifted his head again. 'All right, sir?'

'Dammit, Stuart, their fathers and forefathers came from this strip of coast! Even the West Indians! They *must* have some fellow-feeling for the Khanzians. I wonder if we can rely on 'em.'

Leggo thrust out his lower lip thoughtfully. 'I'd say you could rely on them as much as, if not more than, some of their white colleagues, sir,' he said after a pause.

'Perhaps you're right at that.' Hodges seemed to dismiss the thought. 'Let's get down to stirring up these battalion commanders. Make the conference the day after tomorrow when these blasted politicians have finished with me. They should have ironed out a few faults at Pepul by then, with the embarkation rehearsal.'

'Very well, sir.'

'You'd better fly up there yourself tonight and have a look at it. I can manage here with Lyall and Fraschetti. See the Senior Naval Officer and the Support Committee and the A.O.C. and find out how it's gone. You can fly back and report to me here.'

Leggo, who was none too eager to return to the discomforts of Pepul, just managed to refrain from pulling a face.

'Very good, sir. Anything else?'

'No, Stuart. And Stuart . . .'

'Sir?'

'Do me a favour and take that supercilious look off your face for a change.' Leggo's face set at once in an expression of smart attention. 'It probably doesn't worry you half as much as it does me, but I don't like what I see. I was at Suez, and I don't fancy being humiliated twice in a lifetime.'

3

The speech that Ginger Bowen and Sergeant O'Mara and General Hodges had listened to had put a stop to all television viewing back in England and, for that matter, in the half-dozen other countries to which it had been relayed by Telstar and the numerous other satellites which had gone up in the late Sixties and early Seventies.

The intense activity which the crisis had stirred up at the United Nations Headquarters in New York halted while the delegates listened, huddled round their radio and television sets in their hotel suites and common rooms, and for the first time the Chinese intervention in North Korea, where Chinese troops had rushed to the aid of a tottering government, had been pushed off the front pages. Suddenly no one wanted to hear how many people had been killed in the fighting there. For once the number of casualties and the names of burned villages held little interest.

In London, the Prime Minister's speech had been considered important enough to break into the evening's viewing at the peak hour, and on ITV had even elbowed aside the everlasting *Coronation Street*, which seemed to most people to have been running since the beginning of time. There had been an abrupt silence in most homes and in the pub saloons where it had been heard, as the Prime Minister's plump avuncular face had faded out, before the uneasy chattering had started again. Ex-soldiers, remembering the Nazi War and Korea and Vietnam and a dozen other minor bush fires, began to see all the hopes of world peace which they had so precariously entertained during all the bitter years since 1945 disappearing at last in a puff of smoke.

'We just dodged the bomb last time,' was the general feeling. 'We'll be lucky to dodge it again.'

There was a feeling of uneasiness running through the whole country. Nobody liked seeing one of Britain's last remaining bases being taken over by what seemed to be a gang of undisciplined Africans but, since 1945, the British people on the whole had got used to the idea and were able to accept it, if not with equanimity, at least without rancour. They had always managed to establish new bases somewhere before, with the use of money, promises, persuasion and a little American help; and the idea of departing from that method now came as a shock, because most people were aware that, thinly veiled beneath the Prime Minister's words and deftly hidden by all his high-sounding wishes to preserve the *status quo* and the sanctity of treaties, there was a definite threat to go to war against the Khanzians. He could call it 'a divergence of opinion' or 'a provocation' or 'a security operation only' until he was black in the face, it still stuck out a mile that bombs were likely to fall and that the world might be heading for self-immolation.

Opposition to what was taking place in Africa had built up swiftly in the high flat cube of the United Nations edifice in New York, and faced with a situation that could easily explode into a global nuclear conflict, the mood was sombre and laden with anxiety and expectancy.

Russia, at last aware of the danger of China and aligned with the West, had already warned that she was prepared to take sides against Colonial-type action, and the United States had said quite bluntly that she wasn't going to be a party to any aggression, no matter what the excuse. She'd had enough after Vietnam of other people's wars.

'Let it be known,' the American delegate had said quite firmly only the previous week, 'that my country regards with grave disquiet any action that might let dangerous elements loose in Africa. That continent has a right to work out its own future without interference from the white races, and the slightest interference with their sovereign rights will make them turn their eyes to where they might expect to find sympathy.'

Everyone knew he meant China. Everyone seemed to mean

21

China these days when they talked of people finding sympathy. While ever there was the slightest excuse for the Chinese or Russian Communists to fish in troubled waters, world bitterness and resentment would continue to flourish.

The Prime Minister himself was well aware of this and, travelling back in his car to Downing Street from his office in the House of Commons, where, with a few of his Ministers, he had listened to his speech, his mind kept drifting back to the reports he'd received from embassies and consulates all over the world, and to the hostility to his action which seemed to have arisen almost overnight in places where he'd confidently expected to find friends. It had taken him by surprise and he was bewildered and dismayed by the way the delegates to the United Nations had begun to discuss *Operation Stabledoor* even before it had taken place. Hodgeforce, which he had hoped to throw in quickly enough to present world opinion with a *fait accompli*, had become only *fait* without being *accompli*.

Remembering only too well the way the Rhodesian crisis had been allowed to drag on until Britain had seemed in the end completely to have lost control, remembering the way Nasser had got away with it in 1956 because action hadn't been taken at once, remembering even the way they'd dithered in the late Thirties and allowed Hitler to build up his forces when decisive action would have put paid to him once and for all, he had dispatched Hodgeforce as soon as the crisis had blown up, and it had very quickly been in camp within a short ocean voyage of where he intended it to go. Unfortunately, it had had to leave without a great deal of its transport, because it had been found difficult to raise sufficient from the depleted depots, and the men weren't of the highest quality. But there *were* several parachute and Marine companies and four companies of the Guards, and what mattered most, they were in a position in Pepul to exert some influence on world decisions, though the Prime Minister wasn't entirely happy about the way the Ministry of Defence had admitted that the additions to the force were all going out in dribs and drabs as long-forgotten equipment was dug out.

He was unable any longer to keep up his pretence of satisfaction. Though the Chinese had no right to quibble about what he was proposing to do when they were still engaged in putting down anti-Communist opposition in North Korea, the same attitude could hardly apply to the unconfirmed reports he'd had that Russian submarines were grouping in the sea area between Malala and Khanzi. Their presence might well be embarrassing if they decided to place themselves obstinately in the path Hodgeforce had chosen to take if it were directed at King Boffa Port.

He put his uneasy thoughts behind him, but immediately doubt assailed him again at the reaction to *Operation Stabledoor* that had sprung up even in England. Demonstrations had taken place in London, and students from the University and the Schools of Medicine, Art and Economics had turned up unexpectedly at Westminster with banners, so that the police had had to be hastily called out to remove sit-down strikers from Trafalgar Square and a flag from the War Memorial in Whitehall. He didn't worry overmuch about these manifestations of disapproval, however—youngsters these days seemed obsessed in their opposition to strife and someone occasionally had to have the courage to make unpopular decisions—but he *was* concerned with the trend of more mature opinion.

His next day's engagements, he knew, included an appearance at Rudkin and Hale where the by-election wasn't going as well as they'd expected. He had a feeling that the visit wasn't likely to be any too pleasant, because reports from the local agent indicated that there'd been a great deal more heckling than for years. It wasn't that the candidate was unpopular. It was simply that he found himself standing for a party whose foreign policy had suddenly become anathema to the constituents.

The Prime Minister sighed. He'd rather hoped he might dodge Rudkin and Hale, but he'd given his word and he had to put in an appearance because it seemed there was some danger of the seat being lost without him.

'It'll be all right,' he'd been told, 'if only you can go there and see them.'

It was going to be a long day, because there was also a lunch of the Oxford Chamber of Commerce, where they would inevitably expect him to comment on events, and a dinner in the evening of the Honourable Coopers' Company of London, where his speech was expected to be a major statement of policy. Although both the Chamber of Commerce and the Coopers' Company were likely to be smoother rides than the meeting at Rudkin and Hale, because his audiences would have many investments in Malala and Khanzi and would be anxious to see them protected, there would still be some with investments in America, where the reaction to *Stabledoor* had been most hostile, who would expect him to give *them* some comfort, too.

As the car turned out of Westminister into Whitehall, he shifted restlessly in his seat, aware of a feeling of having too much to do. He was far from being a lethargic man but somehow, just lately, he had often felt that his age was catching up on him.

The uproar in the Opposition press to *Stabledoor* troubled him more than he felt it ought, because, with politics centred on two parties only, he hadn't a great deal to worry about with a majority of seventy-nine. A report from his Party Chief Whip only that morning, however, had indicated that the National Opinion Poll had unearthed the fact that his Government's popularity had dropped by around fifty per cent. Reflected in votes, this might have meant at a General Election that he was hanging on to power only by the skin of his teeth.

'If they can only find out things as unpleasant as that,' he had retorted, 'then they'd better not find out anything at all.'

This fact, together with Rudkin and Hale and the knowledge that a small group of discontents under George Gordon-Grey, the Member for Upham and Harthill, were not prepared to go along with the Party line was of far more concern than the behaviour of a mob of students. He'd put the hostile movement among his back-benchers down at first as one of the minorities that were always emerging in the House, a ginger group that would just as rapidly disappear when the crisis had passed, but instead of disappearing it persisted in growing and even seemed to be attracting the attention of Lord Edbury, an elder of the House who, as a Minister in a previous Government, carried a surprising amount of weight despite his age, and was the sort of man dissatisfied back-benchers liked to put up as a figurehead.

The Prime Minister frowned, conscious of a vague feeling of contempt for his critics. Even allowing for a few dissident back-benchers, he felt quite certain that the vote of censure which the Opposition was clearly determined to bring would never be carried, but he sat up abruptly, nevertheless, his mind made up. Perhaps something ought to be done about the disaffection, he decided, before it became too powerful.

As it happened, however, a far more dangerous reaction was building up round the person of the Leader of the Opposition, the Right Honourable Spencer Carey.

In his office at his Party Headquarters, Carey had listened to the Prime Minister's speech with growing indignation—not so much because he felt it was wrong to stand up for what belonged to his country, but because of the hypocrisy implicit in the speech.

'If you have anything unpleasant to say,' he always maintained, 'say it unpleasantly.' And, like Sergeant O'Mara and General Hodges three thousand miles away in Malala, he regarded the oblique references to upholding the *status quo* and the preservation of treaties as just a lot of political eyewash.

'Trust him to talk of peace,' he said bitterly to his Shadow Chancellor, Derek Moffat. 'Whichever way you look at it, this is nothing more than an ultimatum. They've given Scepwe a limited period to get out, or we're going to throw him out.'

He moved to the window and stared out. He was a tall man, lean and good-looking in spite of the heavy-framed spectacles he wore. He had recently been elected over the heads of several longer-serving opponents to the control of his party, and though it had not held office since his election, after many years in opposition it was now beginning to flex its muscles for what it considered was the period of crisis when it might well reach power. Only the stubbornness of Arthur Starke and the large majority he could command in the House stood in its way.

Carey stared through the window, startled to find he could feel so bitter, and surprised that London, spread below him, could remain so normal with things as they were.

The weather was typical of an English spring—grey with a cold bite in the air—and the view over St. James was blurred by the damp. The lake was a flat sheet of glass below the towers and turrets of Westminster and the raw evening showed a suspicion of mist through the glow of the street lights, while the air was so still the smell of burning rubbish from the afternoon's sweeping seemed to infiltrate into the room from the park, heavy and acrid and reminiscent of quiet days away from London.

Carey studied the view for a second or two, only half hearing the muted roar of the traffic and noticing how much this area of London remained the same in spite of all the rebuilding, then he swung round again into the room and, picking up a pencil, jabbed at the air with it.

'We haven't the slightest excuse for sending this force,' he said. 'We haven't even Eden's laboured explanation on Suez that he was holding the Egyptians and the Israelis apart. It's sheer aggression and nothing else.'

There was no love lost between Carey and the Prime Minister, none of the respect that normally existed between the holders of two high offices, or of a man for a hard-hitting opponent. No one had ever seen the Prime Minister and the Leader of the Opposition walk out of the Chamber chatting together after a bitter debate.

'I've never heard anything quite so transparently dishonest,' Carey continued. 'What's worrying him is having to answer for another lost base at the next election. This is the third we've lost in the lifetime of this Parliament, and he's simply being forced into trying to hang on to this one. And, good God, the Chinese have already said that they'll help the Khanzians, and the Khanzians have said they'll accept help wherever it comes from.'

'Spencer,' Moffat reminded him in his educated Scots voice, 'the Chinese can't do anything. They're too involved in Korea, and what they're doing there gives them no right to criticise anyone.'

Moffat was a small man with a high forehead and a twisted back, which was the result of an injury at school. They liked in the House to call him 'Crookback', but he had the reputation for having an undevious and accurate mind that went as straight for the heart of any subject as an arrow from its bow.

Carey studied him for a moment. 'Put it another way,' he suggested quietly. 'What *he*'s proposing to do about Khanzi takes away any right *we* have to criticise the Chinese. And it's

26

sheer arrogance for him to assume that Scepwe's government's going to fall because we're assembling an army just outside their borders.'

Moffat shrugged. 'The by-election at Rudkin and Hale'll show what the country thinks,' he said.

'We should avoid making any political capital over it, though,' Carey said sharply. 'Nevertheless, I do feel the voters should realise what's in the balance. It could easily escalate into another world war.'

'Nobody's said *yet*, of course, that we're going to fight,' Moffat reminded him gently.

'No, but we are.' Carey began to tick off points on his fingers. 'Troops have been assembled and I know that currency overprinted "Occupation of Khanzi" has been issued.'

Moffat looked up quickly. 'Are you sure?'

'I'm sure. Never mind where I got my information, but I'm sure.' Carey stuck up another finger. 'Troops have been disembarking at Pepul for weeks. R.A.F. jets have flown out, the trooper, *Ascara*, has been ordered home and naval vessels on routes away from Pepul have received orders to proceed towards it.' He lifted another finger. 'Senior British civil servants have stopped getting the usual classified documents as if they've been struck off the lists and Josh Cambridge has been sent on unexpected leave. So have Vasey Pole and Andrews. All Khanzian experts, Derek. Every one of them.'

'Are you sure?' Moffat suddenly looked worried.

'I had lunch with Vasey Pole,' Carey pointed out. 'He told me. You know these civil servants. He feels slighted.' He lifted another finger. 'NATO and friendly attachés have reported being left in the dark by the drying up of channels of information normally open to them, and two months ago British ambassadors of African countries flew home for consultations. Finally'—he gestured once more—'Clifford flew out to Machingo last week. You know what Clifford is, Derek. He's an expert on psychological warfare. It all adds up. And what makes it all so sad is that we probably can't pull it off.'

Moffat stared. 'You mean Scepwe could beat us? Surely it would be all over before he could get moving.'

Carey smiled. 'Derek, this thing's being organised in a peaceful atmosphere devoid of the urgency of war. And what's worse, in a political arena. The stage management of a military operation, Derek, has to be first class. But, worst of all, he's had the greatest difficulty in getting Hodgeforce together. We didn't help.'

'What do you mean?'

'All our demands for economy in the last few years.' Carey frowned. 'We ought to have known they'd cut what they thought they wouldn't need.'

'They *didn't* need the Forces until now.'

Carey nodded. 'Until now, Derek,' he agreed. 'Reliance on nuclear weapons presupposes an empty battlefield. The threat of nuclear annihilation meant it was desirable to reduce battle-field densities, and that meant smaller armies.'

'You're talking like a soldier now. Or else you're elec-tioneering. Economies had to come.'

Carey ignored the jibe, his face heavy. 'Not in pay cuts,' he said. 'The teachers, the Civil Service and the police had unions to object, and *they* didn't get *their* pay cut.'

He put down his pencil and stared at his feet for a moment his hands in his pockets. He was a man with a burning sense of destiny and he could see lesser men holding the centre of the stage.

'I'm very unhappy about the whole thing, Derek,' he said slowly. 'And I feel I ought to *show* how unhappy I am.'

'What are your thoughts on coalition? There've been moves to encourage the idea. If things went against him, he might consider it.'

'I couldn't entertain it,' Carey said. 'I don't trust him.'

Moffat gestured with the file he was holding. 'Very well,' he said. 'What do you suggest? Questions have been going down all week. The Table Office are ringing a new one every minute.' He paused as Carey stared at the floor, thinking, then went on eagerly. 'There's one from Gordon-Grey and that's a good sign. I thought we might follow him up with a couple of our own. Make the first one fairly innocent and then hit them for six with a supplementary.'

'They'll do their best to prevent us bringing it up,' Carey pointed out. 'He's already refused a debate on the grounds of security.'

'He's taking a hell of a risk, Spencer.'

'He's taking the biggest risk of his career,' Carey agreed. 'And we've got to protest against it, Derek.'

'We've been a bit slow,' Moffat said wryly. 'The students have stolen our thunder.'

'Well, let's avoid *that* sort of nonsense,' Carey said sharply. 'Protest meetings are associated too much with all the oddities who come out over Easter.'

'There's still Gordon-Grey and a few on the other side of the House,' Moffat said. 'I've heard that Lord Edbury's prepared to join them. Perhaps they only need a shove. There may be more than we think.'

'How about a broadcast?' Carey said unexpectedly.

Moffat stared. 'They'd never give us the time,' he replied. 'They'd never have given it to Attlee in September, 1939— even if he'd wanted it.'

'They might have given it him in *July*, 1939.'

Moffat eyed his Party leader. 'What have you got in mind, Spencer?'

Carey gestured. 'At times of crisis, everybody forgets *Coronation Street* and turns to Auntie B.B.C. for the plain unvarnished truth straight from the horse's mouth.'

'We'd never get them with us.'

'Wouldn't we?' Carey threw down his pencil. 'Derek, we're all rather apt to forget how independent Auntie can be, especially as every government that gets in starts setting about her if she doesn't come to heel. But I've been going into this a little. There's no specific instruction to the B.B.C. in the Charter other than it has to be impartial in political matters. It's their responsibility to distinguish what's a Government broadcast of a non-political nature and what's a broadcast containing within it an element of political controversy to which the Opposition has the right of reply.'

Suddenly galvanised into enthusiasm, Carey got up from the chair and began to move about the room, gesturing as he talked. 'The decision taken by the B.B.C. at the time of the Suez crisis probably more than any other single decision, established in fact and in principle their complete independence,' he went on. 'We'd have to persuade them that that broadcast of his on Tuesday contained an element of political controversy, of course, and was not a Government offering.'

29

Moffat looked at his leader, his eyes bright.

'*Can* we persuade them?' he asked.

'I think you could set it out.'

Moffat moved towards the door, caught by Carey's enthusiasm. 'I'll get hold of the Chief Whip,' he said. 'We've got to do this quickly.'

'We'll have to let him know our intentions, of course.'

'He'll argue we have no right.'

Carey tapped the desk. 'I don't think he'll succeed,' he said. 'The situation's an exact parallel of Suez, and Gaitskell spoke against that when the ships were actually under way. If they started shooting, of course, it'd become something else entirely because we'd be at war and the B.B.C. couldn't agree. But while we're still at peace, we have a right to voice our mistrust and disagreement. Gaitskell established the precedent.'

Moffat stared at him, then he smiled. 'Didn't do much good,' he said in a flat voice. 'They still went into Suez.'

'Yes.' Carey nodded heavily. 'They still went in. But, at least, Gaitskell was able to say afterwards that he'd opposed it.'

'It didn't stop him losing the next election.'

'No.' Carey paused, his hands in his pockets, his eyes reflective. 'He never expected the electorate to do that to him. Still—I'm going to see the Governors of the B.B.C., Derek, and then you and I are going to get together and write out what I'm going to say. So start thinking about it. It's got to be good, even if we draft it a dozen times, and it's got to mean exactly what we want—no more or less. No fireworks either. In politics we always tend to reduce everything to a good slogan and, this time, there must be no backlash.'

He tossed a file across the desk. 'Those are constituency reports,' he pointed out. 'And it seems to me he hasn't got as many behind him as he thinks he has. And, whatever happens, Derek, we've got to register our protest.'

'Suppose the fighting starts—while *we*'re under way, so to speak?'

'Then we stand a chance of being branded as traitors. But that's a risk we've got to take.' Carey looked at Moffat and smiled. 'Sometimes, in a man's life, Derek, he's got to take a chance of being ruined just for the sake of a principle. It's never come my way before, but I think it's come now.'

4

The next day, while the conferences at Machingo were drawing to a close and while the politicians in England were manœuvring for their next move, the troops from the base at Pepul went on board their transports for the practice shakedown that had been ordered by General Hodges before his departure for the capital. Rumour had it that it had been insisted on by senior naval and air force officers in charge of the arrangements who were troubled by all the things that seemed to persist in going wrong.

The base at Pepul had filled too quickly with troops. Four companies of Guards had arrived, hacking down trees when they had been given a wooded strip to camp on, so that not one tent should be out of line; and a squadron of tanks, which had immediately been instructed not to move because of the damage they were doing to the frail roads round Pepul. Water was short, the firing ranges were full, a great deal of ammunition and stores had been misdirected to the Far East, and because of the increased traffic, the Malalan accident rate had gone up alarmingly.

Hodgeforce had been gathered together with a great deal too much haste and too much barrel-scraping, and had then been allowed to wait too long without orders, so that the erosive effect of inaction was already beginning to show. Reservists had begun to demand to be sent home while the National Servicemen did not show the care their older comrades did. There had been a nasty accident on the airfield next door when one of the Kestrel bombers, which had arrived from England carrying the bombs they would have to use if it came to a shooting war, had disappeared into fragments, together with her crew and ground staff, because of an error during a practice bombing up. It was said to have been caused by insufficient training and was only one of a series of accidents which had started when one of the great transport petrol dumps had gone up, killing seven men and destroying a dozen tankers, and stripping trees and flattening all the native houses along the perimeter.

While the sabre-rattling had continued in the capitals of the United Kingdom, Malala and Khanzi, therefore, and in an attempt to iron out a few of the snags that troubled the command, the people who were most concerned with the crisis—the men who in the event of fighting were to fire the shots and carry the loads—left their comfortless and overcrowded billets for a rehearsal.

The movement was carried out with a fair amount of efficiency, but to Captain Richard White, of Number 5 Air Contact Team, attached with his men to the 17th/105th Assault Battalion, it stuck out a mile that all was far from well with Hodgeforce.

A National Serviceman in the days of the first National Service Act, White had stayed on in the Army after the Act had been rescinded and had managed to work himself up to the rank of captain; and it was while he was secretly hoping he might even make major that, by a Government edict, the British Army had been cut by fifteen thousand men on the grounds of economy and White had been among those to go.

He had, in fact, just been in the process of fixing himself up with a job he was sure he wouldn't enjoy when the crisis had blown up and, before he knew where he was, like several hundred other Reservist officers, he had found himself reporting, as instructed in his papers, back to the depot he had just left.

There he had learned that, to give Hodgeforce the weight of a little experience, every officer who had ever heard a shot fired in anger was being flown in from the few remaining British bases about the world—Hong Kong, Germany, the Pacific; and that the transport belonging to his unit—over-age lorries, obsolescent tanks and even amphibious vehicles that had been scraped off every beach in England—one even with a notice board still attached to the side: 'Saucy Sue. Trips across the bay'—was still in process of being made to work.

The commander of the Air Contact Group had turned out to be completely in the dark about what was going on as he tried to expand his unit to three times its normal size. The wireless sets that White was expected to use turned out to be old-fashioned and heavy, and the fact that he himself, earlier in his service, had added modifications to the best of them and written an instructional pamphlet on its use, had rather knocked the bottom out of the harangue of the warrant officer who was explaining its advantage to him.

Six weeks later, in a charter aircraft that had recently been carrying holidaymakers to Spain and still bore the route maps in the pockets, he had flown to Malala where he learned he had been attached to a training battalion recently out from England that was composed entirely of National Servicemen and was commanded by a colonel who, only a week before, had held a command in Hong Kong.

From a point above where White was standing, Colonel Leggo watched the operation from his Landrover. He had flown up to Pepul the night before, jammed uncomfortably into the wireless operator's seat of a V31 bomber; and he now waited alongside the sea wall in Victoria Street, staring down at the sun-bright water and the beaches where the mammies normally operated the market around the fruit boats that came down from the creeks towards Machingo.

He was not alone. Since this beach where the troops now waited in patient lines was the only available strip of sand that fitted their purpose and was smack in front of Africa Town, the market quarter of Pepul, half the population had turned out to see the fun. Porters, screaming small boys in ragged shorts, and mammies in gaudy lappas and Mother Hubbards lined the wall with Leggo, watching what was going on and cheering and turning somersaults at every new hold-up.

Below them, against a wide stretch of new concrete slipway, two or three landing craft had dropped their ramps, and beyond them, the resurrected destroyer, *Banff*, lay by the end of the mole, along which a thin stream of khaki-clad men were filing, loaded down like pack animals with their radios, weapons and personal equipment.

It was quite clear already to Leggo that the slipway would have to be re-laid. It had been put down at Hodges' insistence by a Malalan contractor named by President Braka and, while it had been done quickly, with the labourers chanting their rhythmic deep-throated tribal songs as they had swung their picks in unison, it was quite clear now that it had been done too hurriedly and that the concrete was of indifferent quality. Rumour had it that a fair proportion of the purchase price for it had found its way past the contractor to Alois Braka himself, and already the concrete was crumbling under the heavy vehicles so that Leggo shuddered to think what would happen when the Senator tanks appeared.

He wrote a few words in his notebook, then took off his cap and ran his handkerchief round the leather band inside. It was already hot, with the breath-catching bite of an oven as the flaring rays of the sun glanced violently off the surrounding mountains. In spite of the early hour, Pepul harbour wore a jaded look, red with dust and drained of energy and, as the sun rose over the hills, the heat began to rebound from the smudged grey walls near the sea.

The port rose, white and red and glaring green from the Spanish steps to Hastings Hill, from Saba Town to Africa Town, from the flat Mohammedan area beyond Passy past the worn stone statue of Queen Victoria that still survived after twenty years of independence, for no other reason than that no one seemed to be able to raise the money or the energy to remove it. Farther to the east and west among the tall, tufted palms and the thick-leaved banana plants were the unpainted houses that abutted, dry and sun-drenched, like heaps of kindling wood, on the town centre. Beyond them, the dwellings of the poor, of hammered tin or mud, clung to the water's edge, their rusting roofs and their air of old junk making nonsense of all the boastful speeches of Alois Braka in Machingo.

Leggo watched the men filing past him from the open space where the lorries had deposited them, their shirts drenched with sweat, their faces gaunt with exhaustion. There was an air about them of sullenness and dislike that worried him and

34

he was just making a mental note to take the matter up with Hodges when he returned, when a shout behind him, startling in its familiarity, made him swing round in his seat in surprise.

'Stuart Leggo! What in hell are you doing here?'

Leggo's head jerked round, startled by the feminine voice which, even after six years, he still knew as well as his own.

Accompanied by an under-age interpreter in a pair of torn shorts through which his shining black bottom showed, the woman who spoke was standing in the doorway of the harbour police office and was staring at him as if he were a ghost. She was no longer a girl, but was still good-looking, in spite of the absence of any make-up and the fact that the heat had made her hair moist with perspiration.

'Davey,' he said. 'Good God! Fancy bumping into you! What are you doing here?'

She frowned. 'At the moment I'm making myself a pain in the ay-double-ess to the harbour police about my camera.' She indicated the slender young Malalan with two pips on his shoulder who was standing behind her. 'This guy's trying to take it away from me.'

Leggo lifted his long legs out of the Landrover and crossed to the police post.

'Sir!' The young Malalan clicked to attention and saluted as he saw Leggo's rank. 'My orders say no cameras. I must follow my instructions. Miss Davies must not claim exemption.'

The woman bridled. 'I represent *Now*,' she said sharply. 'One of the most influential magazines in the United States. Stuart, tell this guy . . .'

Leggo took her arm and pulled her to one side. 'Let's just talk for a moment first, old love,' he said gently.

Across the road he could see a bar, a small dark place with a few Africans sitting at the counter, and he pulled her towards it. Normally, his rank would almost have precluded him from entering, but the moment was urgent, and he didn't quibble. He pushed her gently into the shadows and pulled a stool forward.

'What'll you have? Whisky?'

'Beer. You know I never drink anything else but beer. I haven't changed. I'm still the same Stella Davies.'

35

Neither of them said anything as they waited for the drinks, though she lit a cigarette and puffed at it quickly, her eyes on Leggo, and when the beer was pushed across to them, she picked up her glass and took a deep draught of it. Leggo watched her, his eyes amused.

'You haven't changed,' he said. 'You still drink like a horse at a trough.'

Her angry face softened and he grinned.

'It's nice to see you again, Davey,' he said warmly.

Her expression melted once more. 'Honest?'

'Honest.'

'I'm not sure I believe you,' she said. 'You bolted like a rat up a drain last time.'

He laughed. 'I was scared. You scared me.'

She was silent for a moment, looking at her cigarette. 'I guess I was a bit younger then,' she said slowly. 'And growing a bit desperate. I'm not so young now and I'm not desperate any longer. I've gone past all that. It's much nicer.'

He wiped the perspiration from the back of his neck as he looked at her. 'Married yet?' he asked.

'Uhuh.' She shook her head. 'You?'

'Uhuh.'

They laughed together, then her face became serious and she leaned forward.

'What are you doing here?' she asked.

He shrugged, hedging. 'Duty,' he said.

'Was it duty that took you away from Hong Kong?'

'Yes. But I was glad to go. I was scared.'

'Are you *still* scared?'

'No. You're different.'

She stared at him for a second, a faint hurt look in her eyes, then she stubbed out her cigarette abruptly with a nervous gesture and changed the subject.

'Stuart, that camera: I was only taking a few pictures. Nothing to sweat bullets about.'

'I don't believe you, Davey. Once a newshound, always a newshound.'

She paused, staring at him, then her eyes fell again, and she reached for her glass. She took another gulp at it before she spoke, and he noticed that she deliberately avoided looking at

36

him and used her head to indicate the ships and the furious, sweating soldiers.

'What gives, Stuart?' she asked.

He studied her, his eyes shrewd, then he smiled. 'It's an exercise,' he said evasively. 'British and Malalan armies putting on a show together. First of its kind.'

Her voice showed her disbelief. 'Can't your country find anyone bigger than Malala to play soldiers with?'

He shrugged. 'We're rather keen on the Malalans at the moment. What are *you* doing here?'

'I was in Machingo. Story on Braka. Arranged months ago. Then I heard things were jumping up here. Thought I'd take a look.'

He smiled at her, urbane, handsome and calm. 'You were never a good liar, Davey,' he said.

She lifted her eyes to him and smiled. 'No, I never was,' she admitted. 'I'm interested in what's going on. What's *your* angle?'

'I'm Chief-of-Staff these days to the General Officer in Command here.'

She lifted her eyebrows. 'You've got on,' she said.

'Sheer ability.'

'What do you do?'

'Make sure everything goes smoothly with the exercise.'

'Exercise?' She looked sideways at him.

'Exercise,' he said firmly.

'*You* were never a good liar either, Stuart,' she said soberly. 'I knew it that time in Hong Kong.'

'I'm a better liar now than I was then.'

'O.K.' It was her turn to shrug. 'I'll try not to pump you. I thought you might be just the guy I was looking for. It isn't an exercise, of course, is it?'

'It's an exercise.'

Her brows came down in a frown. 'Stuart, for God's sake, come clean! Nobody else will. Neither in London nor New York. That's why I'm here. I've come to this place from King Boffa Port and I know what's going on. Down there, they're talking of war.'

He raised his eyebrows and smiled. '*We*'re going on exercise, Davey,' he insisted.

37

'Oh, God,' she gestured, 'you were always a stubborn bastard, Stuart! Perhaps that's why . . .' She paused and went on more slowly. 'All the other guys I knew were always willing to come running.'

'That's because you tended to dominate them, old love.'

'I couldn't dominate *you* if I tried. And you goddam well know it.'

He smiled and she tore her eyes away from him.

'What *is* going on, Stuart? Put it on the line for me. I'll give you my word I won't use a word of it. You can trust me, can't you?'

His smile faded and his face became grave. 'Davey,' he pointed out, 'officers can be broken for talking when they shouldn't. I'm in a position to tell you everything I know, but I'm not going to. Let's just say you can't have your camera back with the film in. You've got to get away from this harbour, and you've got to mind your own business.'

'This *is* my business.'

'You shouldn't be here. They had instructions to watch all immigration—both here and at the airport.'

She made a faint gesture of contempt. 'I didn't come this way *or* through the airport,' she said. 'I flew from King Boffa Port to Freetown, and a charter company there landed me up-country. I came here by road.'

He looked uncomfortable as old loyalties took hold of him. 'I wish you *weren't* here, Davey,' he said shortly.

She frowned. 'Stuart, don't kid yourself,' she urged. 'I'm only the first. Any day now you're going to have all the news-hawks in the world descending on this place. You've got to face the fact.'

He smiled again. 'Let's say that at the moment we've just got one or two—all British and well under control—and *you*. That'll do for now. But you can't take photographs round the docks, Davey. Nobody can. You can't talk to the troops. And you can't talk to me—except about old times.'

She stared at her drink. 'Stuart, you're a bastard. But, O.K., your job and mine don't fit together.'

'They never did.'

'I was always prepared to give mine up.'

He frowned. 'Let's not talk about that now,' he said quickly.

'I'm supposed to be out there now, working. Suppose we have a meal somewhere.'

'I'm not coming to your goddam mess again. Last time all I did was fight off your general.'

'My general's in Machingo this time and he's a nice old boy.'

'Let's eat at my hotel.'

'Very well. I've got to fly down to Machingo tonight. When I come back?'

'O.K.' She seemed suddenly nervous.

'Now let me get you a receipt for that camera.'

She shrugged. 'Oh, tell the guy to keep it! I'll pick it up later. I guess—' she paused—'I guess it shook me up a bit seeing you, Stuart.'

He followed her out into the sunshine and they found a patch of shade near her jeep, close to the fruit vendors and the white walls where lizards seemed to hang in the glare of the sun. As she climbed in, he waited beside her until she had started the engine. She sat for a moment in silence then she turned to him abruptly.

'Stuart, I wish I could . . .' She stopped again, ill at ease. '. . . Oh God, I know so much more about what's going on here than you think!'

He grinned, unperturbed. 'I haven't the slightest doubt about that, Davey. I hope none of it came from our chaps.'

'Your—chaps—aren't the only source of information in the world.'

'I guessed not.'

'At the hotel then. Ring me when you get back.'

As Colonel Leggo returned to his Landrover, below him, on the slipway, Captain White was conferring with another Reservist, Sergeant Frensham, on the things that had already gone wrong, with their own particular part of the embarkation.

His first days at Pepul had been spent licking his signallers into shape under the eagle eye of Frensham and, though the men were mostly newcomers, he had been relieved to find they weren't quite so bad as the men of the 17th/105th who, until a few days before, had been without a commanding officer. Between them, he and Frensham had taught them a little of how to behave in the event of being fired on, while Frensham had actually brought them up to some sort of pitch of efficiency as wireless operators, making them work blindfold and in traffic where, among unsuppressed vehicles and power cables and screened by tall buildings, they had had to slave merely to keep in touch with each other.

It had not taken White long, however, to find out that, thanks to the interference from London and the changed plans, whenever they disembarked wherever they were going—and White had long since hazarded a guess where that was—they were going to have to off-load tools and personal equipment before they could get at the wireless cable that was so essential for them to maintain contact between the forward troops and the aircraft that were supporting them.

What was more, it was clear that brigade and battalion commanders had been told not to communicate their instructions to anyone, with the result that only hints and nods were coming across, and junior officers were having to make up their minds on the merest suggestions. If such secrecy were kept up to the last minute, White realised, the less intuitive would find they were short of things when they badly needed them because they'd not been told in as many words what to expect.

He frowned, hoping to God the problems would be ironed out before too late, and glanced at a group of men of the 17th/105th Assault Battalion who were unloading a lorry alongside him. They weren't enjoying it and there was a certain amount of bad language flying about in the heat of the day.

Their officer, Lieutenant Jinkinson, was a very young man with over-long hair who had already had one or two brisk passages of arms with White, and, with Sergeant Frensham's loud and acid comments on the hamfistedness of the infantry-men adding a little more to the tension, he now waved to the N.C.O. in charge of the group and moved thankfully to the water's edge for a smoke.

It was still a matter of surprise to Jinkinson that one of his best men should be a pure Negro whose father had come originally from a village not more than a hundred miles to the south of where he now stood. Acting Lance-Corporal (Unpaid) Jesus-Joseph Malaki had grown up in England and, although his father had probably not had more than a few days of mission schooling in his life, Jesus-Joseph himself had gone to a modern comprehensive school, was intelligent and quick-witted and possessed a surprising dignity which none of the good-humoured jibes to which he was sometimes subjected could even begin to shake.

There was, however, still a vague unspoken doubt at the back of Jinkinson's mind because of an indefinable unsureness about him, as though he seemed unable to grasp the fact that he was accepted by the other men and felt the need always to prove himself.

While Jinkinson puffed energetically at his cigarette Captain White—since he felt he needed to know something about them—kept a quiet eye on his men. The efforts to get aboard *Banff* had become an unmitigated shambles and Sergeant Frensham's disapproval became more marked as he stood beside White and watched the attempts further down the mole to sort out the tangle.

A Malalan lorry driver, objecting to the presence of white troops on his doorstep, had placed his vehicle in the midst of the stream of tanks, guns, armoured cars, bulldozers, jeeps and trucks that was heading for the waterfront and left it there, and it had become obvious at once that the Malalan roads were far too narrow for the military traffic of *Stabledoor*.

There were a few Malalan soldiers from Korno lounging about as the move on board halted, built up, and finally became chaos, but none of them made any move to help. They wore jungle green with American-made weapons hanging off their shoulders, and grenades fastened to the pockets of their blouses. They looked inefficient and remarkably dangerous, and most of the British officers considered it fortunate that for the most part they were confined to the other end of the town.

Frensham scowled as the Military Policemen moved in, shouting and waving their arms, and turned his attention to the shipping.

'Don't think much of the task force,' he said. 'L.S.T.s that have been carrying civilian cargoes in the Middle East, obsolete army craft and all that remains of the mothball fleet.' He indicated *Banff*, her grey anti-radiation paint scarred and scabrous with rust along the water line. 'There's probably a notice on the stern,' he said sourly. 'Advertising trips round the bay.'

White studied Frensham for a moment. There was a question he wished to ask, and it was a delicate one.

'Sergeant,' he said, at last. 'How do the men regard all this?'

Frensham hesitated, because the question had taken him unawares and he needed a little time to think about it. He was no happier about *Operation Stabledoor* than White but he'd been a soldier long enough to keep his own counsel about his likes and dislikes.

'*How do the men regard it?*' he repeated, sounding faintly shocked.

White subdued a smile. He knew Frensham was trying the old soldier's trick of denying everything until he could come up with a good answer.

'Yes,' he said slowly, to give him more time. 'What's the chaps' reaction to this operation?'

Frensham had recovered a little by this time and felt he could say what had to be said. 'Well,' he observed, 'they don't talk to me a lot, sir.'

'Nor to me, Sergeant,' White pointed out. 'But at least you're in a position to hear the comments they make to each other, and I'm not. You must have formed an opinion.'

'Yes, sir, I have, sir.' Frensham saw it now as a fair enough question, and he tried to answer it honestly.

'I suppose, sir,' he said, 'most of 'em don't think much at all. Most soldiers don't. On the other hand, I suppose we've got more than our fair share of talkers—like everybody else in this operation.'

'Talkers, Sergeant?'

'Sir, the Army's so small these days that when they wanted to mount this operation, they just couldn't move units about. They had to make new ones. They scraped the depots a bit. Asked C.O.s for ten per cent of all effectives. You know that, sir.'

'Yes, I know that.'

'What would *you* have done, sir, if you'd been asked to supply ten per cent of your effectives? With no names mentioned.'

White grinned and Frensham went on:

'If you'd had ten wireless operators, sir,' he said, 'you'd have sent the one who could never manage to get to the shack in time to take his watch. If you'd had ten electrical mechs., sir, you'd have sent the one least likely to repair a pranged set. If you'd had ten of anything, sir, you'd have sent the worst. And you know, sir, as well as I do, who're always the worst ones.'

White's smile had vanished again. 'Yes, Sergeant,' he said soberly, 'I know who're the worst ones.'

'The troublemakers, sir. That's who. The sort who ought to be slung out and would be if it weren't so bloody hard these days to get recruits.'

White was frowning now. Frensham's difficulties were only an extension of his own.

'These talkers,' he said reflectively. 'What are they talking *about?*'

Frensham flicked a piece of fluff from his immaculate uniform. 'Cuts in pay chiefly, sir,' he said. 'Bad move that. Especially as it don't hit people like me and you.'

White nodded. 'You're being very helpful, Sergeant. But, actually, this isn't quite what I asked you. I asked how they regarded *this* operation. There's been a lot written in the newspapers. There's been a lot argued on the radio and the television. They must have seen and heard it. They must have formed their opinions. A lot of people are against it. Are *they?*'

Frensham frowned, pinned down on something he'd hoped to avoid. 'Well, sir,' he said, 'I wouldn't say they were *for* it.'

5

The following evening, with the sweat dropping off the end of his nose as he worked, Ginger Bowen was again in the little room at the back of the guardroom at Pepul, painting with red paint the fire bucket he had so laboriously polished the previous day.

He was almost alone, because Sergeant O'Mara was at the main gate busy with the ceremonials attending on the departure of General Hodges. Everybody in Pepul above the rank of major had been aware of the 'blitz' that had gone on throughout the camp, because of the urgent calling for details such as medical officers' reports, provost officers' reports, daily returns and so on, and the shaken look on the faces of the infantry brigadiers, Calhoun and Dixon, as they had emerged from the conference, had been reflected shortly afterwards in the faces of their staffs as the stirring-up process had been promptly passed on to them. Now, with General Hodges installed with a drink in the officers' mess waiting for a broadcast by the Leader of the Opposition from London, everybody in camp, sensing a new atmosphere about them, was suddenly on his toes.

With the possible exception of Ginger Bowen.

Ginger had taken part in the practice shake-down at sea, bent like a peasant under his pack. His hat had been sideways, his hair over his eyes, his face hot and sweating, his eyes puzzled. There had been some grumbling, mostly of the old familiar type, consisting of slogans that had no real meaning:

'Who called the brigadier a bastard?'

'Who called the bastard a brigadier?'

. . . but underneath the chaffing note there was genuine

resentment. The pay cuts rankled deeply with the National Servicemen and every time one of the N.C.O.s, most of whom were not National Servicemen, had chivvied them to their places, he had had the differences between them thrown in his face.

The ships, which had been slow in loading, had anchored a few miles out at sea to give the men a chance to settle down. But the day had been desperately hot, with that unrelieved stuffiness that heralded the beginning of the rains, and on the destroyer *Banff*, too recently freed from her mothball cocoon and hardly up to fighting trim, many of the radiators had rusted permanently in the 'Open' position, while most of the fans, by reason of the failure of an electrical circuit, were stuck in the 'Off' position.

The men of the 17th/105th, loaded down with weapons, rations and extra equipment, had jammed into the crowded alleyways and messdecks, searching for what little air there was, huddled in mute resentment under the stacked gear and staring bitterly at each other through an atmosphere of stale sweat and fury.

After weeks of crowded barracks, requisitioned buildings or the confusion of the tented camp, the unrest that had been apparent from the beginning, particularly among the Reservists, had grown swiftly, and morale had deteriorated just as fast. The plan had been too often changed in London and the loading had been utter confusion; and in Ginger's mind there still remained the incredible picture of a red-faced senior artillery officer shouting furiously at an equally angry sapper officer because his guns had been withdrawn in favour of the Engineer's pontoons.

Although the Marines and Guards had got themselves aboard with a minimum of disorder, among the second-line troops the loading had flagged badly as staff officers had struggled to set straight a time-table that had been altered a dozen times. Nobody aboard *Banff* had been sorry to see the ship lay alongside again, and the troops had staggered ashore, dirty, exhausted and sweating, and anxious only that the experience should never be repeated.

Ginger had half-hoped that his detention might not continue on his return, but he was no sooner back in camp than

45

he was tipped off to report to the guardroom again, and the minute he had reappeared in the doorway, the fire bucket had been pushed in his direction by Sergeant O'Mara's foot.

'Nice and red, Ginger,' O'Mara had said placidly. 'Nice bright pillar-box red.'

'I only just scraped it off,' Ginger had complained. 'Scraped it off and polished it.'

The sergeant had stared at the gleaming bucket.

'Did you?' he had said with feigned surprise. 'Who got you to do that?'

'You did.'

'Well, I never! Must have been a mistake. Better put it back on again. You'll find the pot round the back.'

Corporal Connell, the Military Policeman in charge of the guardroom, had been polishing his buttons and belt in the next room when Ginger had started work. Ginger knew him well. Until a fortnight before, he had shared Ginger's barrack room, and for old time's sake he had seen that Ginger had been supplied with a mug of tea. He had even lent Ginger his transistor radio so that he might have the pleasure of listening to it as he bent over the bucket.

'Music while you work, Ginger,' he had said gaily. 'To keep you happy.'

Now, however, much to Ginger's disgust, the music to which he had been listening contentedly had been brutally interrupted with an announcement to the effect that the Leader of the Opposition had requested the right of reply to the Prime Minister's speech of Tuesday night. The B.B.C., the announcement went on, had considered his demand carefully and had come to the conclusion that, since no emergency yet existed, he had that right and had granted him time to make his reply in the form of a party political broadcast which would not only be broadcast but, like the Prime Minister's speech, would be televised on all channels, by agreement with the Independent Television Authority.

Ginger hadn't paid much attention as the Leader of the Opposition had been introduced, and he hadn't even listened as the sombre voice outlined the gravity of the situation in Africa and the opposition to the policies of the Government

46

that was becoming apparent not only in Great Britain but in other capitals of the world.

'In the circumstances,' the slow voice went on, deliberately kept low and level so that its owner could not be accused of party political propaganda, 'Her Majesty's Opposition felt that it must demand the right of reply.

'All men,' it went on, 'have the right of reply. If we were unable to protest against injustices there would be no hope for this world. We have already observed those countries where this right has disappeared, and we are aware of what can happen when freedom of speech is impaired. The right of reply is the right of all free men. . . .'

For the first time, Ginger looked up and his hand, holding the paint brush, slowed down.

The fact that every human being had a right of reply hadn't ever occurred to him before. He—Ginger Bowen—had the right of reply, he thought. He had had the right of reply when he was ordered to paint and scrape and polish fire buckets. He had almost started to his feet in protest when he realised that he had already exercised his right. When he'd been sentenced, he'd been asked if he'd anything to say. He'd said plenty but not much notice had been taken of it. So much for his right of reply, he thought disgustedly. His hand started moving again as he began once more to apply the red paint.

'. . . the Prime Minister denied in his broadcast,' the Leader of the Opposition was saying now, 'that there is a danger of fighting breaking out. He has also stated that there is nothing he wishes more than to see the need for force disperse. On that we agree with him entirely. But we do not—we cannot—agree with the building up of a British force on the West African coast, which can only be regarded as a threat to another nation, and a danger to world peace.'

Ginger was listening again, aware for the first time, perhaps, of why he was painting and scraping fire buckets in Pepul instead of in Aldershot or Salisbury or Pontefract. He had always vaguely known of the crisis over the base to the south but, in his disgust at the effect it had on him personally, he hadn't bothered to think about it much. Now, however, his interest caught, he began to listen more carefully.

'The country is not behind the Prime Minister,' the Leader

47

of the Opposition continued. 'If the country were behind the Prime Minister there would not have been demonstrations in Whitehall last night. There would not be a sit-down strike in Piccadilly. Students would not have clashed with police in places as far afield as Manchester, London, Canterbury, Brighton and Cambridge. Workers in Portsmouth dockyard would not have refused to place aboard the freighter *Lucia* arms destined for the forces in West Africa. Engineers in Sheffield and Birmingham would not have downed tools rather than turn out more arms which might be used against the Khanzians. These people have insisted on their inalienable right to say they disagree. They are not concerned with the legal rights and wrongs of the dispute between Britain and Khanzi. They are concerned only with every man's right to decide against aggression. And they have decided that the Prime Minister is wrong in contemplating the use of force. They are, by their actions, demonstrating they have an opinion and have a right to express it and if necessary to protest, even to the point of refusing to support the actions of the Prime Minister. . . .'

Abruptly, Ginger put down the brush across the top of the paint tin, switched off the transistor, and wiped the sweat from his face.

He was not a quick thinker and the speech was interrupting the way his mind was working.

For a long time Ginger sat on his box, then, after a while, he heard the click of heels and the clash of rifles outside, and he realised that it was the guard seeing the general safely off the premises. The broadcast was over.

There was the clump of feet as they returned, hot and sweating, and the clatter of rifles as they were replaced in the rack. The Military Policemen who had also taken the pre- caution of lining up outside for the departure returned to their quarters and, having eased their belts and hats, inevitably set about making themselves a mug of tea.

Corporal Connell came in to make sure that Ginger had not absconded during his absence and leaned on the doorpost, regarding him with amused affection.

'We'll have to see if we can't have you presented with that

bucket, Ginger, when you're demobbed,' he said. 'You could have it framed and hang it over the mantelpiece at home.'

'Drop dead,' Ginger said.

Connell grinned. 'Corporal,' he reminded.

'Sorry,' Ginger said cheerfully. 'Drop dead—*corporal*.'

He poked disinterestedly at the bucket for a moment with his brush, then he indicated the transistor Connell had lent him.

'I've been listening to that,' he said. 'The Leader of the Opposition or somebody was making a speech.'

Connell nodded. 'I heard some of it. On the sergeant's set.'

'He said'— Ginger looked up—'he said that people had the right to object. He said people back in Blighty *were* objecting. It seems to me that if they could, so could *we*.'

Connell grinned. 'So you could get out of painting fire buckets?'

'It's nothing to do with that,' Ginger said, though in fact it had a great deal to do with it. 'It's this use of force. It might start a war, and that war might lead to a world war. That's what he said. He said that people objected to us being here. He said they were refusing to help.'

'It's different with us,' Connell pointed out cheerfully. 'We don't belong to a trade union.'

'Look,' Ginger said. 'I don't like being here. I don't fancy setting about some country I've never heard of. I don't fancy starting another world war, and I don't fancy getting killed because some bloody politician back 'ome's got a big 'ead. If they can object in England, I can object here, too.'

He gestured as the idea caught at his imagination. 'Especially as they expect us to do it on reduced pay,' he ended.

Connell's expression changed at once. He was a pale young man, long and thin in the manner of many youthful Military Policemen, and like Ginger, he hadn't particularly wished to find himself in Pepul. Unlike Ginger, however, he was a married man and the new rates of pay had hit him hard. Only that morning he had received a letter from his wife, threatening—with more histrionics than truth—that, to keep a roof over her family's head, she was going to have to go on the streets.

49

Connell eyed Ginger without speaking, and Ginger took his silence for agreement.

'If a bloke safe home in England can object,' he insisted, 'why can't the bloke who's going to be at the front when the shooting starts?'

'*You* needn't worry,' Connell said sharply, suddenly irritated with Ginger. 'If I know you, you'll not be at the front. You'll be in the guardroom.' All the same, he thought uneasily, Ginger had a point. If the country *were* so divided that people at home were refusing to support *Operation Stabledoor*—even though, so far, it had not been finalised and no one would even mention it either in print or by word of mouth—it was a bit hard that the men who were going to do the dirty work *couldn't*. He'd never known many Cabinet Ministers rush into uniform at times of crisis.

'If *they* can object,' Ginger was saying, 'if the Leader of the Opposition can object, then why can't *we*?'

'Because we're in the Army,' Connell said doggedly, though it was beginning to seem unfair to him, too, by this time.

'I think we're a lot of nits,' Ginger said, sensing that he had the initiative. 'We don't want to fight those bloody Khanzians any more than the Leader of the Opposition does, so if it's good enough for him it's good enough for me, too.'

Warming to his theme, he began to outline his ideas until, in the end, Connell uneasily told him to put a sock in it.

'You can get yourself into trouble, talking like that,' he pointed out. 'You can get me into trouble, too, for listening.' He jerked his thumb uneasily. 'Shove off,' he said. 'Put your paint away and hop it. We've had enough of you for one night.'

When Ginger had gone, Corporal Connell went back into the guardroom and sat on the corner of the desk. There were two or three other Military Policemen there, wiping their moist faces, and one of them, Lance-Corporal Clark, pushed a mug of tea towards him.

Clark was offering it as his opinion that the general's visit was going to make work for everybody. He'd been to stir up the officers—the rumour had already reached the guardroom—and the officers would stir up the sergeants, and the sergeants would stir up the men, and it would be the duty of the Military Police to see that they were *kept* stirred up.

'As usual,' Clark was saying, 'the general thinks up an idea in his bath and tells his colonels. They sit back in their chairs and tell their majors and captains to see to it, and the majors and captains sit back in *their* chairs and tell the sergeants to see to it. And the sergeants click their blooming heels and chuck up their salutes and tell everybody else to get on with it. The result? The general's still sitting in his bath. The colonels are sitting in their chairs. The majors and captains are sitting in *their* chairs. The sergeants are busy saying "Yes, sir" and "No, sir" and "Three bags full, sir," and everybody else is out getting on with it, working their guts out, getting shot and getting blamed— and all for a quid or so less money a week than they had three months ago.'

He looked up, expecting Connell to put in his threepenny-worth, too, but the corporal, to his surprise, wasn't even listening.

'Well, my Christ,' he said in disgust. 'I just made the longest speech of me life, and you weren't even switched on.'

Connell turned his pale eyes on Clark. 'You *could* object,' he said abruptly.

Clark grinned. He was a square solid young man who was never troubled for long by anything. 'Oh, yes,' he jeered. 'I *could*. Next thing I knew, I'd be in there polishing fire buckets with Ginger Bowen.'

'They're objecting back in Blighty,' Connell said slowly.

'Who are? And what about?'

'About us. About why we're here.'

'Well, go on. Why *are* we here?'

Connell gestured angrily. 'Christ, man, you know as well as I do that if those black bastards in Khanzi don't hand back King Boffa Port to us, we're going to go in and take it from 'em.'

'So?'

'Well,' Connell jerked a hand, 'you want to?'

The other men in the room had stopped what they were doing now and were listening to the argument. Clark stared round at them, suddenly feeling as though he'd been put on a spot.

'I don't give a bugger about King Boffa Port,' he said bluntly. 'Far as I'm concerned, they can stick it where the monkey stuck its nuts.'

Connell slammed his mug down angrily. 'But you're here, though, aren't you?' he said, his voice rising. 'You're here to *make* 'em give it back if they won't.'

Clark gazed at him, frowning. 'What the hell's bitten you?' he demanded.

'Look,' Connell leaned forward and began to use his fingers to tick off points, 'we're here in Malala. None of us wants to be. We'd all rather be home. I would, anyway, with my missis.'

'So would anybody else,' Clark agreed with a grin. 'Especially when orders say no "Here-we-go-round-the-Mulberry-Bush" with the black bints.'

'You got a point there,' one of the men at the other side of the room interjected.

Connell's face remained unchanged. He was a serious young man and he was suddenly swept away by his own logic. 'Right,' he said. 'First of all they reduce our pay. Not because they don't think we don't do enough, but because every other outfit whose pay they suggest reducing has a trade union and can object, and we haven't.' His voice rose as his indignation grew. 'Then they scrape a few of us together and dump us out here and say "Right, lads, get in there and do them Khanzians." '

'And while we're getting shot up the tarara to please some bloody politician back in London,' Clark said cheerfully, 'everybody back home's objecting, eh?'

Connell's eyes blazed. 'They're refusing to load arms,' he pointed out earnestly. 'They're refusing to make rifles. They're making television broadcasts about how wrong it all is. But *we're* still here, aren't we? God . . .' He thought once more about his wife and two children in South Wales, trying to manage on the reduced rates of pay the Government had introduced, and he suddenly felt nostalgic and bitter. '*They're* objecting! Why don't we?'

Clark eyed him for a moment, suddenly uneasy. What Connell was saying made sense. Like Connell, he was a National Serviceman, too, without much tie to tradition, and like Connell again, he also had had his pay reduced and wasn't particularly keen on being shot at for some principle to which everybody else in the world but him seemed to have the right to object.

'You go on like that,' he said uneasily, echoing Connell's words to Ginger Bowen a little while before, 'and you'll be in trouble.'

'It's right, though, isn't it?' Connell said doggedly.

Clark considered. 'Well, yes,' he agreed finally. 'I suppose it is. All the same, don't start talking like that when O'Mara's around. And don't go on at *me*.'

'Haven't you the guts to stand up for a principle?' Connell had forgotten by this time that he had been accused of almost the same thing by Ginger Bowen.

'I've got the guts to stand up all right,' Clark said slowly. 'But I'd like to think there were a few other people standing up with me.'

Connell stared at him. 'Perhaps there would be,' he retorted. 'Perhaps there would be, if you only knew.'

6

The Sergeants' Mess of the 17th/105th that Sergeant Frensham had to use was situated among the cotton trees, so that during the day it was in shade and after dark was made more welcoming by the background of heavy foliage.

Before Malala had become independent, Frensham had once been stationed at Pepul, though it wasn't quite the same now as it had been then. The huts had about them now the sour smell that Frensham always associated with Africans, though in actual fact it came not from human beings but from the smoke of the charcoal that everyone used for cooking, which permeated the clothes, skin, hair, furniture, houses, even, it seemed, the foliage outside. In addition, some of the buildings had a neglected look about them and the lawns and flower beds which had once been so carefully tended were now overgrown.

Trust the bastards not to bother, Frensham thought with disgust.

He had no great love for Malalans, though he had served with great pleasure and pride with a Nigerian regiment for a while. The Nigerians were different from this lot, though, he thought. Although they enjoyed bullying the civilians, Frensham still had grave doubts about Malalan troops against disciplined soldiers. For all their tommy guns and automatic pistols, there was still something about them which, to an experienced soldier like Frensham, seemed a bit too theatrical.

He lit a cigarette and downed the remnants of his beer. It was a bloody funny world, he thought, that saw the Guards and the Marines allied to a lot of fifth-rate African troops against another lot of fifth-rate African troops. He was old

54

enough to remember a time when one regiment of British soldiers could have wiped up the whole lot—both lots, in fact —in no time.

He paused and ordered another beer before he began to be borne down by the depression that everyone over the rank of corporal felt from time to time in Pepul. He'd managed to make something of his own men, though, he thought, with fierce satisfaction. Untouched by the ferocious heat, he had driven his teams hard, using all the language he had been able to muster in twenty years of Army life to emphasise what he thought, and his invective and sarcasm had been a fine spur to flagging spirits.

'Bloody politicians,' he said bitterly, and only half to himself. 'Pay cuts!'

He tried not to think of the grievances that troubled the troops, and set his mind to working out a new programme for the next day. Fire and movement techniques were something his men hadn't yet heard of and it would do 'em good to crawl round in the dust on their bellies. A bite of side-street work, too, because when it came, and if it came, Frensham knew as well as anyone that most of the work they'd be doing would be in and out of the battered houses of King Boffa Port. Although no one knew anything and security was so severe that everyone above the rank of lieutenant refused to regard the operation as anything else but an exercise, Frensham knew exactly why he was in Malala. Twenty years in the Army gave a man a built-in antenna that recorded every single move from above. Things added up.

They'd better also walk an infantry attack, he thought, and learn the lay-out of an assault battalion in action. It might be a good idea to get a bit of noise laid on, too. Most of the National Servicemen had minds that boggled at the idea of advancing through shot and shell, and it might be wise to teach them that, although it was noisy, it wasn't necessarily impossible if it were done properly.

He put down his glass, pleased with himself, and saw that Sergeant O'Mara was alongside him, placing his order. He nodded welcomingly, because although Frensham had a normal soldier's built-in dislike for military policemen, things were different when he had three stripes on his arm.

'I'll pay,' he said.

O'Mara nodded his thanks, took a gulp of beer, and leaned with his back to the counter.

'Needed that,' he pointed out.

'Don't tell me you've been sweating in the sun, Frensham said.

It was an old joke that all a service policeman had to do was stand in the shade of the guardroom door, flexing his muscles and looking important. O'Mara managed a wry smile. He knew the joke as well as Frensham.

'No,' he said. 'I've been talking. That's all.'

'Talking? I do that all the time.'

'Not this kind of talking,' O'Mara said angrily. 'Some bastard's been getting at my lads.'

'Getting at 'em?' Frensham gestured. 'What do you mean?— *getting at 'em.*'

O'Mara frowned. 'I mean just what I said,' he insisted belligerently. 'Getting at 'em. Preaching sedition. Stirring up trouble.'

'Who the hell wants to do that?'

O'Mara waved his beer. 'I dunno,' he said. 'Politicians, if you ask me. It sounds like politicians' talk.'

'Black politicians?'

'No. The bastards back home. This speech on the radio the other night if you want to know. They're all going round quoting it at me.'

Frensham took a swallow at his beer and O'Mara went on in disgust. 'They're going round saying this business here's just a lot of gunboat diplomacy,' he said. 'They're saying that, with half the world and the biggest part of the country back home objecting to it, they can't see any reason why *they* should be involved without being allowed to register a protest, too. Right of reply, they keep saying. The right to put *their* point of view.'

Frensham frowned, his blue eyes hard as he recalled certain disgruntled comments he'd heard from the men of A.C.T.5 when they'd considered he'd been driving them too hard. He hadn't regarded them as serious, because the men of A.C.T.5 were making too much progress to be dissatisfied, but he'd heard them nevertheless.

'Right of reply,' he said slowly. '*I*'ve heard that. It's going the rounds in our lot, too.'

That afternoon the weather grew noticeably hotter and Pepul became increasingly stifling as the advancing clouds of the coming rains marched over the mountains and hung on the tops of the cotton trees. Towards dark came the first of the electrical storms of the season, violent forks of purple lightning that slashed across the sky, and sudden squalls of wind that set the palm tops thrashing. The clouds of dust that were whipped up filled the nostrils and ears and grated against the teeth, and most of the men in Pepul camp decided to stay in camp and take a chance with the cinema.

Halfway through, however, with the film half-shown, the projector broke down, as service cinema projectors have a habit of doing all over the world, and as the canteen had unaccountably run out of beer and it was by that time too late to go into Pepul, most of the men were in their billets, hot, dry-throated and frustrated at the lack of entertainment and refreshment, and sufficiently annoyed at missing the denouément of the film for all the complaints that had started up like a lot of hares at Ginger Bowen's first whine of protest to be set in motion again.

Ginger had not been the only man in Hodgeforce suddenly to notice the possibilities inherent in the Leader of the Opposition's speech, but, while other people in the base at Pepul gave a lot of thought to it privately, Ginger was the first to state publicly his views on the matter. And, since it was already in the minds of others, Ginger's words were rather like a match that set a fuse alight. Smouldering dissatisfaction existed already and the possibilities laid bare in Carey's words and given tongue to for the first time by Ginger leapt out at everyone.

Here, it seemed—laid on the line by a politician of note, a man who could one day be Prime Minister—was the one thing that could clear up all their problems, and it ran through the force like a bushfire. Other objections were already undermining confidence—the certainty that *Stabledoor* was unjust and unrealistic; the knowledge that the rest of the world was against them; the worries of Reservists who had been called up weeks before and, because the Government in London were waiting on events instead of leading them by the nose, had been allowed to idle their time away, thinking of their jobs, their homes and their wives—all these had sapped at confidence. But the one thing, the major thing, that was in the minds of practically every man below the rank of sergeant was the question of pay.

And it was among these men—the young, the hotheaded and the easily influenced, the very types who back in England were already vigorously protesting in Whitehall and Trafalgar Square about what the Prime Minister was proposing to do—it was among these men that Ginger's idea, offered originally merely as an excuse to get him off the hook, spread through the camp like the gospel of some desert prophet.

His talk with Connell had started a train of thought that had spread from the police to the men of the guard and from the men of the guard back to their billets. Startled by Corporal Connell's words, Lance-Corporal Clark had discussed it with his older brother who was a corporal in the R.A.F. Regiment and was billeted in a hut at the opposite side of the dusty parade ground. Ginger had been merely chancing his arm to get out of an onerous chore, but by the time it reached Corporal Clark, of the R.A.F. Regiment, it had become something quite different.

Being a talkative man of an argumentative disposition, Corporal Clark had discussed it with his friends and, before anyone in authority had become aware of it, it had got round the R.A.F., the 4th/74th, the 71st/86th, the 19th/43rd and the 20th/62nd. An attempt to pass the idea round the Guards companies and the Marines and the Parachutists had run up against a blank wall; but, because the Guards, the Marines and the Parachutists had a habit of regarding the county regiments with their complicated chemical-formula numberings as hybrid organisations unlikely ever to be of much use to them or to anybody else in support, no one had bothered to report what was going on to anyone in authority. And, as Corporal Clark passed it on finally to an old school friend of his, the wheel turned full circle because this friend, Private Leach, served in the 17th/105th, and lived in the same hut as Ginger Bowen.

Private Leach was an ardent believer in Internationalism and the Brotherhood of Man, and in particular in the class struggle, whether it were against the company directors whom, until his call-up, he had consistently opposed as a shop steward; the Government, which had put him into uniform; or merely his superior officers and N.C.O.s. Private Leach, his sense of grievance honed fine during his years as a member of the Communist Party, had seen in Corporal Clark's words an opportunity to stir up trouble, and in its passage round the camp Ginger's moan became a firm protest, and Private Leach was beginning to make a great deal of the preferential treatment handed out to Regulars.

Indeed, Private Leach so persuaded Corporal Clark, who was hotheaded and not very clever, that he had a bitter grievance that he was actually prompted to refuse a duty. His sergeant, not knowing what was behind his refusal and thinking for a moment that he had gone off his head, instead of clapping him on a charge as he should have done, covered up for him and, being a weak man interested in Clark's sister back in England, even did the duty himself and said no more about it.

It was a stupid thing to do and prevented the sergeant's officer from discovering what was going on; and, what was worse, encouraged Clark and his friends to believe that not only was right on their side but also might; and other small refusals of duty had followed about the base. None of them was serious in itself, but, because section N.C.O.s did not wish it to be thought that they couldn't control their men, no reports were passed on to superior officers.

In the meantime, Private Leach and his friends were not idle. Like him, the biggest part of the men in the camp were National Servicemen who had no desire to be killed in an operation which was not only dividing the country at home but was setting the whole civilised world against them, and what had started as a mere flutter of complaint in Ginger Bowen's mind now came back to him so startlingly different he quite failed to recognise it as his offspring.

He looked up from the banana he was peeling as Leach thumped the table to emphasise the opinion he was offering.

'The British and Malalan governments,' he was saying, 'have already been labelled as potential aggressors, ready to go to war for outworn colonialism and jingoistic imperialism.'

Ginger paused with the banana near his mouth. The other men in the billet, their attention not so much caught as collared by Leach's oratory, stopped what they were doing to see what was coming next. Privates Snaith, Griffiths and McKechnie, busy over letters home, put down their pens; Privates Welch and Bolam, deep in the sports page of a fortnight-old newspaper, lowered the sheets to look over the top; Acting Lance-Corporal Malaki, his black skin gleaming in the glow of the light, put down the boot he was cleaning and picked up the other one, his expression unchanged; Privates Wedderburn and Spragg, playing fives-and-threes with a set of miniature dominoes which persistently refused to lie flat on the blanket they had spread on the bed, stopped their argument about the rules and turned round slowly with Private Michlam, who'd been an interested spectator.

'A lot of Old Etonians living in a Kipling's world.' Leach was a great one for clichés. 'That's what it is, and with their bloody sabre-rattling they'll do for the lot of us.'

Ginger swallowed the last of his banana and reached for another. The fact that they belonged to Acting Lance-Corporal Malaki didn't deter him very much. Malaki was an easy-going man and seemed to be able to get plenty by virtue of the fact that the native camp workers thought he was one of them.

'Nice thought,' Ginger said unenthusiastically.

'A few bloody roses,' McKechnie added. 'R.I.P. Here lies Private Ginger Bowen. He died to preserve imperialism.'

'That's it,' Leach said excitedly, feeling he'd made a conversion. 'You've got it, mate!'

Private Snaith put down his letter. He was a sturdy optimistic young man from a home that was by no means short of money but had managed to adapt himself to the change of conditions better than most. 'It'll never come to that,' he said firmly. 'They're already sorting it out at United Nations. There's a demand for police action.'

'They'll never get it going,' Leach said.

'Not in time.' Private Welch knew his facts. 'They've sent an ultimatum already. Look here.' He held up the newspaper he'd been reading, which contained one of the Prime Minister's pronouncements.

' "The first and urgent task," ' he said, his eye racing over the heavy type, ' "is to remove these aggressors from what is an international harbour. If the United Nations were then willing to take over the physical task of guaranteeing stability in the area, no one would be better pleased than we should. But police action is necessary and we have accepted that we must carry it out. . . ." '

The paper rattled as he pushed Private Bolam aside and struggled with the sheets. 'They'll use bombs,' he said with heavy foreboding. 'And they don't drop bombs on cities unless they're going to take 'em over. They'll follow 'em up with infantry.'

'Us,' Ginger pointed out. He looked round at the others, enjoying the excitement in the air and the threat to law and order that was implicit in every word that was spoken. 'Us, mates.'

'That's a fortnight old,' Snaith sneered. 'Things have changed since then.'

'It says it here!' Bolam snatched the paper from Welch and jammed it to within an inch of Snaith's nose, and there was a struggle as Snaith tried to grab it. Holding him off with one hand as he struggled, however, Bolam managed to read on.

'Look at this,' he said loudly. 'The Prime Minister of Ghana confesses to sadness—even distress, he says—at not being able to agree with the position taken up by two countries whose ties with his own are close and intimate.' He grinned. 'What you think of that, eh? Intimate. And listen to this: "I cannot ever agree with the action of a nation which, with her awareness of her own moral position in the world, can have sunk so low as to contemplate an attack on a nation that is merely asserting rights which, if not hers by treaty, are hers by racial instincts . . ." '

The reading came to an abrupt end as the newspaper was snatched away at last and Snaith and Bolam rolled on the floor, fighting for possession of it. Everyone craned to watch but the noise stopped abruptly as Griffiths looked at his watch and switched on the radio, and Snaith and Bolam sat up at once as the voice of the American Forces announcer in Germany—curiously always preferred by British troops to the B.B.C. variety—crashed into the room in the middle of the news.

'. . . Rioting has broken out in Khanzi,' he was saying. 'In the disputed area of King Boffa Port and in Sarges, the capital.

61

British and Malalan nationals have been assaulted and several Malalans have been killed. In addition, British and Malalan-owned business premises have been set on fire by mobs of students. It is suspected that Communist agitators are behind the rioting, though a Khanzian spokesman claims that in Sarges Malalans are responsible. . . .'

There followed a formidable array of quotes from foreign sources on the situation, which reflected a grave sense of disquiet that it might lead to a move by British and Malalan forces.

As the news gave way to music, Griffiths switched the radio off and the silence in the hut was heavy with the thoughts of the listeners.

'That's it then,' Leach said harshly. 'Isn't it? That'll start it, if nothing else does.'

'I don't believe it,' Snaith said slowly.

Leach rounded on him, jeering. 'You're naive, mate,' he said. 'Naive. You don't *want* to believe it. You think they're going to let a lot of Africans go around punching Englishmen up the nostrils without doing something? Not bloody likely. This is the trigger, mate, and it's been pulled. It'll escalate, this will, into something big.'

Ginger reached for another banana but he stopped and looked at Malaki as a thought occurred to him.

'How do you feel about setting about blackies, Joe?' he asked gently.

Malaki looked up, his face dignified. 'Because their skin is the same colour as mine,' he said, 'it doesn't follow that we're brothers.'

'They're Africans, same as you,' Leach pointed out.

'The Russians are Europeans, man, same as you,' Malaki replied. 'Would you call them *your* brothers?'

'Yes, mate, every time.'

'Don't you have any feeling at all about it, Joe?' Ginger asked.

'I'm paid to obey,' Malaki said. 'That's what I'll do.'

'But, Christ,' Bolam joined in eagerly, 'you come from a place only a hundred and fifty miles from King Boffa Port. These blokes are your mates.'

Malaki gestured angrily. 'I came from Asimano,' he said. 'It

62

was poor and there was no work, and Britain gave my father a job. *I* chose the Army and I'll stand by it.'

'Christ!' Leach rolled his eyes. 'These saints! It's a bloody fine cause to get killed in, I must say.'

'*You*'ll never get killed, Leach,' Snaith said quietly. 'You'll never make it.'

'I'll make it,' Leach said, with the air of a man preparing for martyrdom in a good cause.

'Then who says you'll be killed?'

'You ever taken a good hard look at your equipment?' Leach asked. 'Rifles that were used in Korea. Wireless sets that are out of date. Lorries that are falling apart. Ships that are scrap, and aircraft that are suffering from metal fatigue.'

'Metal exhaustion, more like,' Spragg grinned.

'Did you know,' Leach went on, 'that all the ships here came off the Reserve, and half the officers who're skippering 'em have been passed over for promotion? Naval rubbish heaps, mate, run by officers without hope.'

'Go it, Leach,' Private Wedderburn shouted, less concerned with making trouble than with having a little fun. 'Give it 'em, boy!'

Leach climbed on to his bed. It made him feel taller and bolder. 'Back home, brothers,' he said, 'they're downing tools over it! Why don't we?'

'That's it!' Spragg said. 'Down tools! We ought to have downed tools when they cut pay.'

'You want to watch it, Leach,' Welch said soberly. 'They can nick you for this. It's incitement to mutiny.'

'Get out of it, man,' Leach said. 'We're only standing up for our rights.'

'We've got to stick together,' Ginger agreed sententiously. 'If one makes a fuss he's a troublemaker. If we all make a fuss, it's a legitimate grievance.'

'Ginger wants to do his detention without having it interrupted by fighting,' Snaith grinned.

There was still a chance that the whole affair would descend to the farcical, but it so happened that Spragg had a brother in one of the transports lying in the harbour.

'Tell you what,' he said. 'Our kid's ship's printer on the *Aronsay Castle*. He'd make us some pamphlets.'

63

Ginger looked up. 'What'd we put on 'em?' he asked.

'Workers of the world, unite!' Snaith jeered.

'Up the Red Flag, and bring your own bombs.'

'Go Home, Yanks.'

'Kiss me while I'm conscious.'

The suggestions were rowdy, derisive and raucous, and nobody even now took them very seriously. Yet, somehow, beneath the chaffing, there was suddenly an element of seriousness and resentment. The pay cuts had been a blow to them all and, though none of them had complained particularly about being sent overseas—none, that is, except the few like Ginger —it was suddenly beginning to dawn on them that what they were being asked to do could earn them, in addition to hard work and possible injury and death, no thanks from their countrymen at home and disgust from the rest of the world.

Leach and Spragg had their heads together now, writing on the back of an envelope.

'Leave it to us, Ginger,' Spragg said, looking up. 'It's half done.'

'How are you going to pass 'em round?' McKechnie asked.

'That's easy,' Wedderburn said, collecting the dominoes. 'Give a handful to the hut orderlies. Leave a bundle in every tent.'

'Shove a few in the canteen,' Leach suggested.

'How about the cookhouse? Everybody goes there.'

'Put a few in the bogs,' came a derisive yell from the back. 'Everybody reads there. They won't be wasted, either.'

'How about the ships?' Spragg asked. 'We've got to have the Navy with us.'

'They'll be with us,' Leach reassured him. 'They've had *their* pay cut, too.'

'They're all anchored offshore.'

'What's wrong with ship's boats?'

Everybody in the hut seemed to be shouting suddenly, with Malaki and Snaith pushed into a corner and defending themselves against the arguments of their friends. Only Ginger, perhaps because of his greater familiarity with authority, seemed to be conscious of the danger. He was sitting on his bed, forgotten, gaping round him at the uproar.

'Christ,' he was saying slowly as he realised Leach and Spragg were serious. 'Christ, there'll be trouble.'

7

Such was the feeling of discontent among the men of Hodge-force that Private Leach's plan swept him along faster than he had hoped even in his wildest moments. The dissatisfaction was already there. It only needed putting into words and the words translating into action.

When Leach contacted a friend of his who was a fellow trade unionist and Party member, in the corvette *Duck*, he was amazed at the vehemence of the response there. The ship was blessed with a captain who had been passed over for promotion and, but for the emergency, might have finished his service in the naval backwater where he had been indiffer-ently carrying out duties of no great responsibility. The urgent need to commission ships from the mothball fleet had forced him into a command, however, and, instead of looking on it as a last-chance opportunity, he regarded it more in the nature of a nuisance, arriving as it did in the last few months of his career, and he gave remarkably little towards it.

Armed with a kitbag of inflammatory leaflets, printed under pressure by Spragg's brother on the old flatbed press of the *Aronsay Castle*, Leach returned to his friend twenty-four hours later and, in no time at all, the leaflets were being delivered by postmen and messengers aboard the picket boats of the escort vessels which had been assembled in the harbours and creeks of Pepul.

Another kitbagful had been dumped in the lap of Corporal Clark, of the R.A.F. Regiment, and the leaflets had found their way into the billets of the R.A.F. just across the road from the army camp. Before two days were out, practically everyone below non-commissioned rank had seen them. Even a few of the corporals and sergeants had seen them, but those few who had considered the pamphlet at all had been either sympathetic or had diagnosed it as the work of a crackpot.

Leach had learned his job well, however. Although he was no intellectual, he knew what to say and how to say it, and all the grievances, all the troubles, all the worries of the amorphous mass of men who comprised Hodgeforce were brought together by the bitter words on the yellow pamphlets printed on the *Aronsay Castle*.

Small groups began to gather over the tea and wads in the N.A.A.F.I., in the temporary workshops of the R.A.F., and over the beer in the shore canteens of the Royal Navy. And slowly but surely these small groups came together, like iron filings attracted by a magnet, and clotted into a solid movement. No longer was it a case of individual grievances. The grievances had suddenly become communal.

Meetings began to take place secretly behind the hangars and among the army vehicles and in the messdecks, and the word was passed round—quite deliberately but quite untruthfully— that the officers were aware of what was being said and sympathised to the last degree. The decision to hold a mass meeting on the football ground behind the naval canteen at Pepul was reached first of all aboard *Duck* but it was found, on enquiry, that other ship's companies had had the same idea, and once again the movements jelled and became one; and the idea that had started in the billets of the 17th/105th came back to them as a mass protest organised by the Navy, to which were invited men of the Army and Air Force.

It had been decided that, to bring home to the Government the genuine grievances of the men, small cells must be organised, all answerable to a central cell, which—now out of the hands of Leach—was being organised by cleverer men aboard *Duck*. Something had to be done. A protest had to be made that would cover all the objections of all those women back in England who had received a cut in the allotments made to them by their husbands or sons or brothers; that would set free all those Reservists who were sweating in Malala— apparently to no purpose—while their jobs were being snapped up by others at home; and would give tongue to the anger of those men who had been paying off mortgages or hire purchase debts and now found themselves in grave difficulties due to the pay cuts or through being Reservists. This protest, of course, would also inevitably cover the complaints of the troublemakers like Leach, and the whines of the awkward and stupid like Spragg who disliked being a long way from girl friends, cinemas, television and bright lights; and the half-hearted, half-cunning, half-jesting censures of the lazy and the unwilling like Ginger Bowen, who were really only chancing their arm to make life a little easier.

Unknown to General Hodges and the naval and air officers commanding, unknown to ships' captains, group, wing and squadron commanders; to regimental and company officers—and even, for the most part, to section leaders also—Hodge-force, which could never have been called an efficient fighting force, was being undermined still further.

It was symptomatic of the state the Army had lapsed into and it was not only unknown to the politicians in England but would also have been, to those who had never worn a uniform, quite incomprehensible.

While the Security Council in New York argued about the effect of the rioting on the force stationed at Pepul, the Prime Minister, back in England, was treading warily in the House of Commons through a maze of half-truths and more-than-truths to avoid announcing that he and his Cabinet, after weeks of hesitation and vacillation, had finally been forced into a decision.

The proceedings had continued along almost restrained lines all evening, dealing as they did with the making over of surplus stores to help the refugees from North Korea. The subject had seemed a safe one and no one had been thinking particularly of Khanzi. Indeed, along the back benches one or two Members were glancing surreptitiously at evening papers which seemed to be more concerned with the size of the force being assembled at Pepul than the reason for its presence there.

'What opposition could a state of the size of Colonel Scepwe's offer against a country as powerful as Britain?' the *Courier* was asking. 'Are we not trying to provide a drop-hammer to crack a walnut?'

Then somebody ventured to protest against what China was doing and immediately a discordant note was introduced by

Derek Moffat who had not been slow to spot the opportunity to bring up the subject of Khanzi.

'Our protests,' he said, 'would be more effective had we been able to make them with unsoiled hands.'

In the flurry of questions that had followed, the Prime Minister was stung to reply. He had, he said, in the interests of the whole of Africa, requested that Malala and Khanzi should settle their differences, otherwise British forces would have to intervene, in such strength as would be necessary to secure compliance.

He had risen to speak in a suddenly excited House and he now gave a brief account of the events which had led up to the present crisis.

'During the past few weeks,' he said, 'Her Majesty's Government have thought it their duty, having regard to their obligations under the treaty which gave Malala independence, to give assurances, both public and private, of their intention to honour these obligations.'

His speech was received, if not with silence from the Opposition benches, at least not with uproar and it seemed that for the time being the initiative still rested with the Government. Nothing had yet happened in Africa, despite the gathering of troops at Pepul, and the feeling was still one of hope that the prospect of war might slowly be fading; but a second statement later in the evening by the Foreign Secretary on the rioting at King Boffa Port and at Sarges led the Prime Minister to speak again.

He described the events, deplored the loss of life, expressed sympathy with the relatives of the people involved and ended with the sombre assurance that the Government was gravely exercised by the events and was watching the situation closely.

Immediately there were shouts from the Opposition benches of 'The truth, the whole truth and nothing but the truth,' and the Prime Minister was finally forced to reveal that, in spite of his desire for peace, he had been obliged to play his hand.

'I have given certain orders,' he said slowly, 'but I am not prepared at this moment, because of security, to divulge them.'

Immediately, Moffat bounced from his seat again. 'Is it war?' he demanded. 'Will British troops be engaged in action? Is it the Prime Minister's intention to become an aggressor?'

Starke hedged, not wishing to be drawn. 'Certain precautions of a military nature have been ordered,' was all he would permit himself.

Immediately, the whole of the Opposition began to yell in unison for a proper answer, and an attempt by the Speaker to restore order and return to debate brought Carey to his feet.

'Mr. Speaker,' he said coldly, 'how can we debate a crisis, if we do not know whether that crisis has, in fact, become war?'

There followed shouts of 'Resign!' and the debate proceeded sporadically through the noise in the atmosphere of a nightmare, then Carey rose once again. Both sides became silent at last, according him the respect that was his due as Leader of the Opposition.

'Mr. Speaker,' he said slowly, 'talk of war pervades European capitals, and in Machingo, President Braka is letting it be known—with the full support of this Government, let it be said—that Colonel Scepwe's day is almost over. Italy has told us bluntly: Don't count on our support in the event of trouble. France remains aloof. The United States and Russia are for once in accord in their hostility to this move, and China has promised to send not only volunteers but as much military equipment as is possible. It is also well known that rockets are being moved from the northern borders of Manchuria to Yunnan and Kwangsi. The import is obvious. China is prepared to forget her differences with Russia to direct her hostility towards Great Britain. There is a grave risk of escalation from limited to thermo-nuclear war. If the Prime Minister is prepared to accept that fact without trembling, then all I can say is God help this country that we have him now at the helm.'

In the burst of cheering and abuse that followed, the Prime Minister sat motionless in his seat, staring in front of him. His brows were down and his mouth was a tight line. There seemed, in the confusion of the moment, no reply.

8

When Ginger Bowen's period of punishment came to an end, he determined to celebrate and presented himself at the guardroom dressed with care and showing a dandy's regard for the shine of his shoes.

Sergeant O'Mara was standing behind the desk. 'Watch it, Ginger,' he warned. 'I've got the tumbril waiting.'

Ginger grinned as he gave his name, rank and number to a frowning Corporal Connell behind the desk. He had completely forgotten the talk they'd had, even if Corporal Connell hadn't.

'Sarge,' Ginger said. 'It'll be so quiet, it'll be like Remembrance Day. You've got a soldier on your hands.'

O'Mara jerked a thumb. 'I'd raffle you off as a prize any time,' he said. 'Shove off.'

Ginger grinned again and turned out of the camp, his mind busy with thoughts of Sulfika Achmet. Ahead of him the palms cut across the fused yellows and reds of a stormy sunset, and he could hear the crickets and the frogs in the heavy scented darkness, and the roaring of the naphtha lamps above the little stalls that lined the long straight road into town. The foliage glowed unnaturally green above them against the backdrop of the sky, and Ginger walked happily towards Pepul, keeping his own company because he was always a lone wolf when in search of pleasure. A few dogs shot out from the shadows, barking at him in lunatic frenzy, then a bus approached jammed to the hatracks with grinning, waving, singing Africans. Every spare seat was packed with suitcases, boxes of fruit and even one or two trussed live pigs blinking with little grey eyes from among the rolls of bedding.

As it stopped alongside Ginger to set someone down, he

hopped aboard, indifferent to Camp Standing Orders—which he never read anyway—which forbade the use of native buses. The singing stopped abruptly as he pushed between the crowded people; but Ginger, being Ginger, felt none of the subtle change of atmosphere and begged a light from the man next to him, one of General Ditro Aswana's Malalan soldiers in American battle equipment. In two minutes he was in conversation, his neighbour joining in reluctantly at first, and within five minutes the whole bus was shouting with laughter at him.

Cutting sharply across the instructions in the little book on how to behave that had been issued to him on his arrival, Ginger made not the slightest concession to the worried suggestions of welfare officers concerned with racialism. He slandered the Malalan armed forces and offered a few none-too-complimentary opinions on President Alois Braka, and called his neighbour a wog, a nigger and a blackie and, against all the predictions of the experts, he wasn't left for dead in a drainage ditch. On the contrary, before long the catcalls were coming at him from every corner of the bus and he was responding in kind, and the whole busload of them, smelling of sweat and charcoal and palm oil, were hooting with laughter.

As the bus stopped in the centre of the town, the Malalan soldier got off, and Ginger, his money burning a hole in his pocket, invited him to have a drink. When they left half an hour later, everybody in the bar followed Ginger into the street, laughing and waving. The sheer inexplicability of it might have worried the experts but it never entered Ginger's mind that anything unusual had happened.

Parting finally from his new friend, he made his way to the home of Sulfika Achmet, a clapboard house in the Mohammedan quarter at Passy Town, completely undaunted by the dark streets and the fires that threw the low palm-thatched houses and the tufted trees behind into silhouette like a fragile stage set against the threatening sky. Standing Orders stated quite categorically that the native quarter of Pepul was out of bounds and reiterated the danger to white men appearing there after dark. Ginger's behaviour would have given the Station Administration Officer something to think about, however, for, with a strange immunity to disaster, he moved among the crowds, grinning at the black faces that seemed to appear and disappear in the shadows as they passed, drinking in the spicy air, stopping occasionally to sink a warm beer at bars where no white man in his senses would have been seen dead, and, still unharmed, arrived at Sulfika Achmet's house.

Sulfika greeted him with a fluttering caress of her small thin hand on his arm, laughing in a cajoling tinkle as her family quietly withdrew. When he left, he ran his fingers along her naked shoulder and neck and against the long oval of her cheek, and told her he'd be back the next night. Then he slipped a pound note into her hand and walked back to the centre of the town.

Beyond the town and over the mountains, as he moved between the crowds, Ginger could see the sky lighting up from time to time with purple flashes and he guessed a storm was coming. The air seemed to be growing more closely packed, as though the clouds, like great felt blankets that blotted out the stars, were holding the heat in, so that the palm fronds about him seemed weighted.

The heat and the electric atmosphere seemed to have affected the crowds, and he was surprised in Victoria Square to see a great number of white soldiers and an unexpected number of sailors thronging the bars that crowded together under the heavy foliage of the cotton trees. There were a few Military Policemen about, but there didn't seem to be enough of them to be a threat, and none of them seemed anxious to get involved. Then he saw that all the men in the bars had pamphlets in their hands and, as he stopped at the Moyama Café for a beer, someone thrust a sheet of yellow paper into his hand.

'*The Right of Reply,*' it said across the top. '*All men have the right of reply. All men have the right to demand a say in the affairs of their country.*'

'That's it,' Ginger said, his enthusiasm engendered by the beer he'd drunk. 'That's the stuff.'

'*All men,*' he read on, '*are entitled to a union or society to represent their demands and if a man has no union or society then he is a deprived individual.*'

72

It was strong stuff that made Ginger's head swim, though he didn't for a moment recognise it as the gospel he himself had preached not so long before.

A group of sailors came into the bar, their hatbands bearing the legends *Ladybird* and *Hawthorn* and *Beagle* and *Duck*, and he noticed then that there also appeared to be dozens of them in the street outside, all surging from the same direction into the town with soldiers and airmen and a few of General Aswana's troops. Held incommunicado to a certain extent by his detention and pursuing his own activities out of camp, he had not been aware of Leach's activities and he had missed the meetings. And Private Leach had decided that since he had a habit of consorting—willingly or unwillingly—with the Military Police, there was always a chance that he might accidentally give the game away, and he had been told nothing of what was in the wind.

'Been a football match or something?' he asked.

The sailor he addressed stared hostilely at him.

'All right then,' Ginger said helpfully. 'A girl guide rally?'

'You want to keep your bloody ears open, mate,' the sailor said. 'Then you'd know, wouldn't you?'

Ginger shrugged and turned away. There was an atmosphere of distinct hostility in the bar. In one corner the arguments were already beginning to grow a little noisy, and a bottle was knocked over and a table up-ended with the crash of glasses. A couple of Military Policemen who were passing moved forward but they were halted at once by the barrage of catcalls and yells of derision that came in their direction.

The two policemen glanced at each other and, deciding they were in too much of a minority, contented themselves with picking up a couple of bottles and administering a warning that was greeted with more catcalls.

Ginger watched them, elated by the excitement that was obvious in everything that was happening. He was not certain what it was all about but, judging by the catcalls, there was a clear defiance of authority going on.

His eyes sparkled. He'd always been one to join in any up-heaval in the cookhouse or in the cinema when the projector came to its usual grinding halt, if for nothing else but the

73

laughter and the jeers and the excitement; and he assumed that what was going on around him now must be something of the same kind.

Someone bumped against him and he saw it was Spragg. He looked none too sober and Ginger remembered that it only required the smell of a cork to set him off.

'Good old Ginger,' Spragg was saying, indicating the pamphlet in Ginger's hand. 'We'll show 'em, eh?'

'Sure,' Ginger said unenthusiastically for he had no love for Private Spragg. 'We'll show 'em.'

'You're with us, aren't you, Ginge?'

'Sure.' Ginger's enthusiasm waned even more. He was far too much of an individualist to be happy in a herd.

'Here, Ginger!' He caught the smell of mosquito cream as a flag was thrust into his hand, and he saw Leach leaning over his shoulder. 'Shove this up.'

It was a red square emblazoned with a hammer and sickle, and he put it down as though it were red-hot.

'That's Russian,' he said sharply.

'We're all comrades together, aren't we?' Leach observed. 'Just wait for the cheering, then you'll see.'

'What cheering?'

Spragg gave him a wink and Ginger stared at him, suddenly a little worried. He jabbed a thumb at the hammer and sickle on the flag.

'I'm no bloody comrade of them buggers,' he said.

'Don't be daft, brother. This isn't a time for nationalities.'

'It ain't the time for singing *The Red Flag* either,' Ginger insisted.

'Go on, Ginger. You *started* it.'

'Me? I only just came in.'

Abruptly, as the crowd surged about them, they were pushed apart and Ginger saw to his startled amazement British soldiers laughing and skylarking as they pulled down Union Jacks and replaced them with the Hammer and Sickle. A few African soldiers were watching them, grinning, their teeth startlingly white against their black faces, and Ginger stared at the scene aghast for a while, deciding that everyone had gone mad, then he swallowed his drink and sniffed the air. There was a storm coming, he knew. The palm fronds which had been so still a

74

short while before had started to move sluggishly and he could feel the faintest stirring in the air.

He decided it was time to head for the harbour. His highly developed instinct for danger indicated that things seemed to be growing a little too hot, and he had had enough of trouble for a while.

The Pepul City Hotel was no Ritz. The drive was pitted with potholes and littered with stones. Trees on either side thrust through the matted untended vegetation, blossoming in luxurious pinks as the parasitic embrace of bougainvillaea choked the trunks.

The dining room was a large sombre hall with a vast picture on one wall of the new Pepul Hotel which had been planned for years but so far had not got off the drawing board because something strange had happened to the funds. It was lit dismally at only one end by the inadequate electricity of Pepul Town, and the tablecloths seemed none too clean. The nozzles of the salt shakers were stuffed up, most of the knives had loose handles, and the high moulded ceiling was dark with dust. The furniture looked bedraggled and, over tired-looking potted palms, slow-moving fans stirred the hot stale air. Through the open windows the bark of frogs and the cheep of crickets came in an all-enveloping chorus that was occasionally shot through with the menacing whine of a mosquito.

'I thought they'd got rid of the mosquitoes.'

Colonel Leggo looked up abruptly as his companion spoke, and realised he had been daydreaming.

'I thought they had, too,' he said briskly, as he pulled himself together.

Stella Davies leaned her elbows on the table and stared at him. Wearing make-up and with her hair neat, she looked quite different from when he'd seen her by the harbour in the heat of the afternoon. She was cool in a silk dress and some of the strain seemed to have gone from her face.

'You were miles away,' she accused him.

He nodded. 'Yes,' he admitted. 'I was.'

As a matter of fact, his mind had been resting on the strange phenomenon of the enormous numbers of sailors he'd seen in town as he'd arrived. Sailors had their own strange ways of

75

amusing themselves, he knew, and on the whole, unlike soldiers, they didn't tend to stick to the main streets. Yet, as he'd arrived from headquarters, he'd noticed what had seemed an abnormal number of them moving along Victoria Street, cheering and jeering and encouraging the Malalan troops to join them.

'Where were you?'

The words broke into his thoughts again and he realised he had wandered off once more.

He laughed and forced himself back to the present. 'Hong Kong,' he said.

She stared at him for a second, a spasm of pain flickering across her face. 'Food's rough,' she said abruptly.

He nodded. 'Very rough.'

She toyed with her glass for a moment. 'I was looking forward to tonight, Stuart,' she said after a while. 'I even thought it would be like it was in Hong Kong. But it isn't, is it?'

He shook his head.

'You're older,' she went on slowly. 'Nicer, though, I think. And I'm older and I guess I'm not so nice. I've grown as tough as an old peahen and I've been less concerned with the moon tonight than with whether the beer's cold and whether I've got enough cigarettes. I always did smoke too much.'

She began to fiddle nervously with the packet of Camels by her hand, but he moved it away.

'You could cut it down,' he suggested gently.

'I've never had any good reason to.'

'What do you consider a good reason?'

She raised her eyes. 'Having a home and kids,' she said frankly. 'Things like that.'

'You've had plenty of opportunities.'

'Sure.' She nodded. 'But we all have our standards. The only guy who came anywhere near to mine did a disappearing trick on me six years ago in Hong Kong.'

He found it hard to meet her eyes, and she shrugged.

'Still,' she said, 'it was best, I guess. I wouldn't have fitted into the society you came from.'

'I've never been a believer into fitting into a society,' he pointed out. 'The people who fit neatly into an army society would fit just as neatly into a stockbrokers' society or a big business society.'

'Stuart . . .'

He avoided her eyes. 'It's no good, Davey,' he said quickly.

She frowned and lit a cigarette. 'Why not?' she asked. 'Because a goddam big balloon's going to go up soon, and you're too much of a gentleman to involve me in it?'

'If you like.'

'And because you know damn' well that it might grow and turn out worse than anybody ever thought, and that now's not the time to be stargazing.'

He moved his hand in a swift impatient gesture. 'Davey,' he reminded her. 'We said we weren't going to talk about why I was here.'

She gazed at him for a moment, with a little frown of frustration. Then her expression softened.

'Stuart, you're not breaking any security rules with me,' she said quietly. 'You couldn't. I know most of what's going on. I know, for instance, that you've got pamphlets demanding the surrender of King Boffa Port already packed for dropping, and that currency overprinted "Occupation Khanzi" has been issued to the quartermasters.'

Leggo looked up, startled. 'Where did you learn that?' he said sharply.

She shrugged. 'There are things I can't say, too, Stu. Not even to you. So don't ask me. But it's never hard for a good newspaperwoman to find out. I also know that troops have been practicing embarking and disembarking—I saw 'em; that your air force has been flying jet bombers and fighters into Pepul for weeks; and that some of the world's largest salvage equipment's on its way here. Would you like me to give you details?'

He frowned. 'You needn't bother,' he said.

'I know also that American diplomats in London and Machingo and plenty of other places besides have been cut off from all contact with British and Malalan officials. I don't know what *you* make of all that, Stuart, but I know what *I* make of it.'

77

Leggo struggled to change the conversation, torn between a desire to know the source of her information and a wish to return to the nostalgia of five minutes before. He was desperately aware of the stifling heat and the breeze that came through the window, hot, moist and sticky.

'Not sure what you mean,' he said evasively.

She seemed determined to disturb him. 'O.K.,' she said. 'I'll spell it out for you: Braka's on his way out. This business that you're up to here's largely to hide the fact that the Malalan economy's in a mess. I didn't think much about it before, but I've been wandering round the town a bit. What I found out startled me. They're as Commie here as they can get.'

Leggo shrugged. 'It's not news that they've received loans in the past from the Russians,' he admitted.

'It's not loans—*or* equipment, Stuart. It's not what they've got or what they haven't got. It's an emotion. And it's been going on for some time. And, at the moment, it's worse than it ever was—because *your* boys are encouraging it.'

Leggo's jaw dropped. '*Our* boys?'

'Yes, *your* boys. Somebody's been at them. I've always had a quiet respect for the British soldier—for very obvious reasons—but those I've seen here aren't behaving in the normal pattern.'

'I'll look into it.'

'You don't have to look far. Just go home via Passy and the square. Just drive past the Victoria Statue. You'll get your answer.'

He nodded silently and she stubbed out her cigarette unsmoked.

'I hate this goddam world,' she said harshly. 'It's so—dirty.'

Leggo said nothing.

'Stuart, I thought when you disappeared in Hong Kong that that was the end of it, but it wasn't. And you know damn' well it wasn't. And now we're here—the both of us—and there's nothing we can do because we're on opposite sides and tied hand and foot by security.'

Leggo still said nothing.

'So what happens next, Stuart? What happens afterwards?'

When he remained silent, she spoke again. 'You're afraid there'll be no next, aren't you? That there'll be no afterwards?

Well, I'm optimist enough to think there will be. Can we take up where we left off in Hong Kong, Stuart?'

He managed a smile. 'I'd like that,' he said. 'I'd like it very much indeed.'

She gave a wry laugh. 'You goddam Englishmen! An American would probably have tried to whip me into bed. You make it sound as though we were going to a symphony concert.'

He looked agonised and she helped him. 'Stuart,' she said urgently, 'don't talk. Don't say anything. Just nod at the end when I've finished if that's the best you can manage. I know you always did have a knot in your tongue and I know you're not promising anything, because of what's in the wind. But I'm getting the hell out of here tomorrow—this is one story that *Now* won't get because I've got to opt out of it—it's too personal—and I've got to know something before I leave. I know—and I know it as surely as if you'd said it—that what happened in Hong Kong was a mistake. And I know that when this thing is over—this thing we've both promised not to talk about—we should try to put it right. O.K., nod, like I said. Nod, for God's sake!'

He grinned suddenly at her anxiety, and nodded, then he put his hand over hers. 'I'll do better than that,' he said. 'I'll promise that as soon as it's over I'll contact you. We'll meet. London. New York. Hong Kong. Somewhere. I suppose you could manage that.'

She nodded, unsmiling and grave. 'I guess I can,' she whispered.

'Then let's leave it at that. I ought to be getting back. The general's due in at midnight and I've got to be there to meet him.'

'O.K.' She paused and was about to light a cigarette again when she changed her mind and pushed it back into the packet. 'I'll start now,' she said firmly. 'I'll cut 'em down from about a million a day to five hundred thousand. Maybe even I'll eventually cut 'em out altogether.'

She managed a shaky smile and, as she finished speaking, there was a sudden stirring of the heavy leaves outside as a squall swept through the gardens. A shutter slammed and a waiter crossed the room quickly to replace the menus which had blown over. Once again Leggo was aware of the heat and the imminence of a storm. The tension in the atmosphere seemed also to have affected Stella. Her smile had vanished and her face looked strained and tired. She pushed at her coffee cup, her eyes down and hidden.

'I'm not supposed to do this,' she said quickly. 'Because this business between your country and Khanzi's no affair of mine. In fact, my country's against it. My president's hopping mad about it. But if it goes wrong, Stuart, *you*'re involved. I . . .' She paused. 'I wouldn't want you to be involved in something that goes *that* wrong.'

He stared at her for a moment. 'Suppose you tell me,' he suggested.

She nodded. 'O.K. It's none of my business, but if I can help to stop it, then here we go. I was in King Boffa Port before I came here, as you know. Stuart, they're ready for you.'

'Who said we're going to King Boffa Port?'

'Nobody, damn you, but I know you are and you know you are!' She brought out a map from her handbag and pushed it across to him. 'They're waiting, Stuart. I don't know what you're expecting, but I can tell you that the Russian experts they've had there for the last eighteen months have done wonders. They can muster eighteen brigades now, ten infantry, three armoured, one coastal defence and one ack-ack, together with three in reserve. The coastal and ack-ack are hot-shot outfits and the Border Defence Corps is good, too. The police are a para-military organisation trained by Nasser's men, and they're loyal. And, just to clinch things, the Russians have just flown in a new consul, Dhevyadov, who's hot stuff at subversion and propaganda.'

Leggo said nothing. Most of what she had told him was news to him and he tried not to show it. 'Go on,' he said numbly after a while and she glanced quickly at him and continued.

'Right,' she said. 'Hold your hat on. They've got rocket batteries round the harbour.' She jabbed her finger at the map. 'There's one there. I saw it—they're not as good at security as you are. There's another here. And they're both placed to cover the beaches and the entrance to the port. Did you know about them?'

His control slipped a little. 'No,' he said. 'We didn't.'

She studied his face for a second then she went on quickly. 'There are reserve brigades in the jungle around Chinsa,' she said. 'That's only three hours by train from King Boffa Port. They've got Congolese officers and good weapons. You know as well as I do that the Russians have been working arms into the area for years.'

Leggo was itching to ask questions but, knowing how freely the information was being given and with what heart-burning, he refrained.

'There are airfields,' she went on mercilessly. 'At Lo and Kij-Moro, I think. And there are Migs. I don't know how many but they're modern Migs, Stuart. I know they're modern because I've seen plenty of Migs in my working life. The stuff on the airfield at King Boffa's old hat to let you believe they haven't got anything else.'

Leggo was silent now and she went on urgently, not meeting his eyes. 'I can give you a breakdown on all they've got,' she went on. 'Never mind where I got it. You won't like it.'

She seemed to hesitate at the look of agony on his face, then she hurried on, almost as if what she were saying hurt her, too.

'They have around fifty tanks,' she said. 'Centurions and Soviet T34s and JS3s. And mechanised infantry in Ford wagons, armoured personnel carriers and Soviet BTZ scout cars. Their ack-ack brigades have 30-millimetre Hispanos and 40-millimetre Swedish Bofors. Their field artillery has around a hundred-fifty guns—British 25-pounders and Soviet 22-millimetres—and they have at least seventy-five Shees and more than a few 17-pounders and 57-millimetre anti-tank guns —even a few Russian SU 100 self-propelled guns. The infantry has the Russian 7.62 millimetre rifles and they're better than you think, Stuart. They've also got a few Ilyushins, two KZ-class destroyers and two Governor-class frigates—from my own beautiful country which hasn't been behind the door when it came to handing out weapons. And they have around five hundred four-wheel-drive military vehicles. Did you know they'd got all this?'

'Not all that.' Leggo could hardly keep the shock from his voice.

'Well, here's more: Tasia next door has thirty modern Migs, Akondja has thirty-five Centurions, thirty older Migs and a lot of smaller equipment. Hajaia has an unspecified number of the new Viking tank destroyers, and ten old Migs. Akondja's also got thirty M11 Whippets from the States. Hajaia, which my own sweet Congress has been lavishly equipping for years, has six Galleon transport aircraft, eighteen M52 medium tanks and eighteen M43 Howard-Terrier light tanks. And they've all been offered in case of emergency. Your own country's sold to Malala in the life of the present government military and para-military equipment amounting to twenty-seven million pounds, most of which has found its way to Khanzi. I got the figure from an unimpeachable source.'

Leggo sat silent for a moment then he spoke slowly. 'Good God,' he said.

'Don't quote me, for God's sake,' she begged. 'But I'll tell you something else, too—free, gratis and for nothing. You'll not get into King Boffa Port, Stuart. They've got blockships in position across the entrance. I saw them loading them with cement, scrap-iron and explosive. They made no bones about it. And I'll tell you why, Stuart. The Khanzians are right behind Scepwe. He's no Braka, Stuart. I've met him and he's a right guy. He's the sort of guy they want in Africa, and you could never say that of Braka. They don't want your goddam army.'

She drew her breath sharply. 'And I don't blame 'em,' she ended abruptly. 'And I wish to God I'd never come here and that I'd never seen you again because I'm not sure I can handle it.'

The sky had a strange glow in it through the darkness as Leggo headed for Pepul Camp, and the lightning, which seemed to be increasing, lit up the tin roofs of the town with a violet glow. As he moved along the waterfront, the sea was poppling and bubbling among the rocks and the air was like the inside of a laundry. On the outskirts of the town the streets were full of figures shooing goats and pigs and chickens before them into the wooden houses.

A scattering of rain fell, nothing much, but with heavy drops that burst like bombs on the broad leaves of the banana plants; and Leggo increased speed, using his horn to part the crowds. The black-faced white-shirted figures that crowded the streets, the shrieking mammies, the ancient, lop-sided buses thronged with people that laboured up the hill from the harbour to Hastings Hill, seemed to be all stubbornly headed in the wrong direction.

The centre of the town was a sea of bicycles and the smell of frying coconut oil was strong around a market in the main square. The jam of humanity slowed Leggo almost to a stop and he had time to see little wooden stalls selling second-hand clothing and cigarettes which were said to be made up locally from fag-ends, among the sunglasses and cycle accessories and the rolls of purple and yellow cloth.

Here and there he saw British soldiers, some of them none too sober, and young airmen in a riotous mood. Near a beggar's tame baboon crouching beside a wall, clumsily attempting to peel a banana, one or two Malalan soldiers in ill-fitting uniforms grinned at a couple of spindle-shanked girls whose feet were encased in split-sided high-heeled shoes. The night was noisy with the sound of voices and the bleating of goats penned near the harbour, for driving aboard a ship to Machingo the following morning; and the local inhabitants, sensing the storm, pushed through the white men urgently, anxious to be home before the rain came.

What he had learned had worried Leggo. It had worried him so much, in fact, he had stopped the Landrover at the bottom of the drive from the Pepul City Hotel and jotted down for Hodges a list of figures in his notebook before he forgot them.

As he struggled out at the other side of the market he saw more groups of British soldiers, sailors and airmen, and he was surprised to see them so much intermingled, not only with one another but with the steel-helmeted Malalans. The Services had never regarded each other with brotherly affection as comrades-in-arms—let alone allied troops of other nations—but he thought nothing of it until, by the light of naphtha flares from the market behind him, he noticed something odd about the towering statue of Queen Victoria and he remembered what Stella had said.

The sandstone plinth separated the crowd like the bow of a

ship driving through a tide race, and across it in large white letters he saw the words, PAY NOT OKAY. WE WANT TO GO HOME. He frowned, then with a shock he realised that what worried him about Queen Victoria was not so much the slogan as the fact that she was painted bright red.

The statue had been erected as a cheapjack job during the Diamond Jubilee by a sculptor who had specialised in making royal likenesses for places around the Empire with more loyalty than money to spare, and the features had been those of a rather superior monkey. The cheap soft stone had been worn down by the weather until they had become blurred, and managed after eighty years to convey an impression of amiable drunkenness; and now it seemed as though someone had up-ended a large pot of red paint over the crown, and the scarlet streaks had rolled over the face and ample bosom and run down the voluminous robes like so much blood.

Leggo was so startled he stopped instinctively to see better, not noticing that it had started to rain again and that the drops were tapping heavily on the hood of the Landrover.

A lot of people, many of them sailors, were staring up at the statue and laughing at it, and he noticed that a large number of British and Malalan flags which had hung outside the bars had been replaced by red banners carrying hammer-and-sickle devices, and that a group of men in uniform were singing *The Red Flag*.

'Good God,' he said aloud. 'It's like a damned revolution!'

Then, as he stared, the rain began. It came abruptly, the drops changing to a deluge in a second, as though something had burst in the heavens above them. It came in torrents that roared majestically on the tin roofs, against the foliage of the trees, each leaf tilting its cascade to the ground, and on the awnings of the bars and the hood of Leggo's Landrover, filling the monsoon ditches in seconds and scattering petals in blood-red swathes from the bushes across the road. At once the figures round the statue scattered, white- and khaki-clad figures bolting for the bars and houses, black and white men alike huddling in the doorways and staring out at the down-pour and the dripping hibiscus and banana plants.

Leggo still sat staring at the statue as though transfixed, then he became aware that the fine mist the downpour had raised was drifting through the open sides of the Landrover, chilling his bare skin, and he jerked to life abruptly and, pulling his cap lower over his eyes, took off the brake and jammed his foot hard on the accelerator.

9

The following day there was a lunch-time cocktail party aboard *Banff*. Not only was she to carry troops but she was there as an escort to Hodgeforce, though no one had any illusions that she was not as much in need of assistance as anyone else. It was quite a gay affair, however, and Captain White enjoyed it, though a damper was placed on the affair by the fact that the ship's captain was missing.

He and White were old friends and White had been looking forward to seeing him again, but the ship's Executive Officer sought him out over the pink gins with a rueful smile on his face.

'Captain's compliments,' he said. 'Had to leave. Conference somewhere. Couldn't even stay long enough to leave a message, except that he was sorry he couldn't make it.'

White thought very little more of it until he returned to camp. He was feeling vaguely disappointed, however, and doubly conscious of the abrupt change in the weather that made him realise how long he had now been in Pepul.

Although the storm which had cleared Victoria Square the night before had passed beyond the town by this time, the clouds hung on the hills grey against the wet green, and the sunshine was pale and watery. The roadways were scattered with twigs and small branches and there was a mist hanging like damp gauze curtains among the trees.

At the guardroom, Sergeant O'Mara came out to meet him. 'Colonel Drucquer wants to see you, sir,' he pointed out. 'I think there's something on. Something about an exercise.'

White stared at him, frowning. Drucquer wasn't the sort of man to get worked up about an exercise for which everybody had been ready for days.

86

Then he remembered that the day before the officers of the 17th/105th had themselves thrown a party to repay a little of the hospitality they'd received from other messes. General Hodges had been invited but had gracefully declined, but they had firmly expected Colonel Leggo, his Chief-of-Staff, and the commanding officers of the other regiments, to say nothing of at least one of the two infantry brigadiers.

They had all arrived late in a body, with the excuse that Hodges was engaged in planning a big four-day exercise and had called them for an unexpected briefing, and now, with the call from Drucquer and the absence of the *Banff*'s captain, it wasn't hard for White to put two and two together. Following a policy that had obviously been decided on in London, no one was telling anyone anything, but no naval captain would be absent from his own party unless there was good reason. It was no four-day exercise they were starting. It was the real thing. After so many weeks of waiting, it came as a bit of a shock.

Using the guardroom telephone, White rang the A.C.T.5 office and asked for Sergeant Frensham.

'I'm coming round to pick you up, Sergeant,' he said. 'There are a few things I'd like to talk to you about. Drop what you're doing. It's urgent.'

There was a momentary silence at the other end of the line, and he knew that Sergeant Frensham was also sufficiently experienced to guess what his words meant.

'I'll be ready at once, sir,' he said.

At the base, everybody was busy preparing kit, loading vehicles and waterproofing trailers. Sergeant Frensham had just finished fixing a free-running reel of cable to the back of a one-tonner so that, instead of having to have it manhandled, it would be paid out quite simply as the vehicle moved forward.

'Seemed a good idea, sir,' he said, as White appeared.

There was none of the usual backchat going on, and White noticed immediately that the men of Lieutenant Jinkinson's section weren't at ease with him. Their looks were veiled and their replies to his questions were brisk but entirely uncommunicative.

'What the hell's the matter with them, Sergeant?' he asked quietly.

'I dunno, sir,' Frensham said. 'There's a bit of monkey business going on somewhere, I suspect. Normally at a time like this you can't hold 'em down.'

'What we were discussing the other day, perhaps, do you think?'

'Should think so, sir,' Frensham agreed. 'But, on the other hand, perhaps not. This is different. They're all in it. O'Mara had a word with me about it the other day, and I'm told the C.O. of the 4th/74th has threatened his lot with bloody murder. They ain't pulling their weight, and I don't like it, sir.'

When they'd finished talking in White's office, Frensham ran White over to headquarters in the Landrover, neither of them saying much. There seemed to be a lot of Malalan troops on the move past the camp, tramping stolidly towards the north where their harbour was situated at Korno. They waved and shouted as the Landrover roared past, and pointed to the brightly-coloured banners they carried, an odd mediaeval habit that seemed strange in the twentieth century.

'Wogs are restless,' Frensham commented succinctly.

'Africans,' White corrected him, but without much enthusiasm.

Frensham nodded but made no attempt to put the matter right.

At the battalion office, clerks were typing loading lists and complaining about the amount of work involved, and one of them, standing by the fresh-water jar, was just wiping his brow as they arrived.

'Pity they can't arrange a bloody exercise without all this bumph,' he was saying.

Asking for the C.O. at the Chief Clerk's office, White noticed the quick movement as the warrant officer pushed a map across the top of his desk.

'The Colonel's in his office,' he was told. 'He's expecting you.'

White nodded, not saying anything. Underneath the corner of the map, he'd seen a pile of pay books. The Chief Clerk was extracting the names of next-of-kin, and it didn't require much intelligence to guess from it that in a very short time they would very probably be going into battle.

The two men's eyes met as White turned away and it was quite clear that they had both understood the message in the other's gaze.

Colonel Drucquer was sitting at his desk, surrounded by all his officers of the rank of captain and above. They looked round as White entered.

'Sorry I'm late, Colonel.'

'That's all right. Well in time, but as you're the last we can make a start.'

Colonel Drucquer was a Guernseyman and a deceptively mild character. Slightly built and colourless, he had a narrow head and pale hair and eyes, and in the African sun suffered agonies from a peeling nose. He had a languid and old-fashioned manner that somehow reminded White of something out of P. G. Wodehouse, but it required only a glance at the ribbons he wore to realise there was more to him than met the eye.

His news wasn't good. What he still insisted on calling an exercise was, he said, liable to be chaotic. The navy, in their trial runs, had found it difficult to co-ordinate the speeds of the old ships in such a manner as to keep steerage way, and as the 'exercise' had been moved forward unexpectedly there was likely to be a certain amount of confusion. Old and faulty equipment wouldn't help to make it easier.

'We just have to face it, gentlemen,' he said. 'You will have to be prepared for every emergency. This exercise isn't going to be an easy affair—I'm as well aware of that as you are but—we've got our orders and it's up to us to do the best we can. There's been a riot and we're being sent in to rescue British Nationals. That's the idea behind the—er—exercise.'

A few of the officers glanced at each other but no one spoke. Drucquer had paused, glancing at a sheet of notes in his hand, almost as though he were allowing them time to absorb what he was saying and to relate it to international events and form their own opinions.

'Troops will embark in khaki drill,' he went on finally, 'but they will carry long trousers, mosquito boots and groundsheets with them. Battle dress and heavier clothing will be packed in kitbags and delivered to the Quartermaster for carriage to the exercise area.'

He tapped the ash from his cigarette. 'You must accept,' he continued slowly, 'that, as things stand, all essential equipment, particularly wireless equipment, will be of the man-pack type as I can't guarantee that our vehicles will travel in the same ship as we do. I've hardly been here long enough to make my presence felt and there seems to have been some confusion in the loading.'

He ran over a few other instructions and then smiled and took a deep breath. 'Officially,' he said, 'this is an exercise, as I've told you, and orders are still a little confused. I understand, in fact, that supporting naval ships will fire only their light equipment at the shore, though even at this late stage no one seems quite certain even about *that*. There seems to be a little uncertainty still in London about whether we're going to war or for a waltz round the daisies. As far as I'm personally concerned, however,' his smile vanished abruptly, 'where men are likely to be shot at—*my men*—I'm prepared to stick my neck out. My instructions, gentlemen, are that if anyone shoots at you, you shoot back. Because all this talk we've heard lately about what will happen if the Khanzians refuse to come to heel has become largely academic. I might as well be frank. Following the rioting in King Boffa Port, a final ultimatum was sent by Her Majesty's Government and Colonel Scepwe has intimated that he intends to reject it.'

There were a few more sidelong glances among the seated officers, then Drucquer rose and turned to a blackboard behind him which was covered with a dust-sheet.

'Now,' he said, 'perhaps you'll direct your attention this way for a moment while I give you chapter and verse.'

He pulled aside the dust-sheet, and on the blackboard beneath was pinned a map. It was clearly a plan of a seaport and White could see the harbour marked on it, together with such obvious installations as the electricity, gas and water works; the Customs House, Pump House and the Cable and Wireless Station. Although the name of the place had been covered with a piece of pasted brown paper, White recognised it at once as King Boffa Port.

Drucquer smiled and borrowed a walking stick from one of the officers.

'Gentlemen,' he said, jabbing at the map, 'the—er—exercise area.'

Part Two

1

Near the Customs House, three ancient L.S.T.s had nosed in to the concrete ramp that ran down to the water's edge, and Military and R.A.F. Police, among them Sergeant O'Mara, were doing their best to keep order among the stream of vehicles that was inching down towards the sea.

Standing by the Harbourmaster's telephone, Ginger Bowen watched the scene with as much pleasure as the hundreds of Malalans who, in between selling limes, bananas and oranges to the sweating troops, laughed and cheered and turned somersaults every time the traffic stream became snarled up.

As the vehicles came to a stop for the fiftieth time that morning, he felt glad he wasn't part of it. From the goodness of his heart and, determined to get Ginger aboard without him finding more trouble, Sergeant O'Mara had managed to have him detailed to his party as a runner. It didn't involve Ginger in much beyond remaining always under the eye of the police and saved him the frustration of lining up to go aboard the old destroyer, *Banff*, that lay alongside the mole. Ginger would walk aboard calmly and in comfort later in the day, safely escorted, true, by Sergeant O'Mara or one of his corporals, but at least spared the misery of exhaustion at that moment being endured by the rest of Lieutenant Jinkinson's section.

'You'd have thought they'd have given us something a bit better to travel in,' Private Wedderburn said, staring up at *Banff*.

'You ain't a first-class fare, brother,' Leach commented. 'You're a fifth-rate individual. Sergeants, corporals and regulars are fourth-rate—they haven't had their pay stopped. Officers is third-rate. Majors and above is second-rate, and the General's first-rate. He travels on a cruiser,' he glanced towards the bay where the old radar and helicopter cruiser, *Leopard*, lay, her anti-radiation paint dazzling in the sun, her awnings down and stripped for action, 'if you can call *that* bloody thing first-rate.'

'They're shoving blokes on a harbour installation job over there,' one of the sailors standing by the gang-plank intervened. '*You* should complain. Packing 'em in among the buoys and chain cable.'

Wedderburn, sweating under his rifle and pack, turned aggrieved eyes up to the deck of the destroyer, where a few listless men waited. 'What's the matter with this bloody navy of ours?' he demanded. 'Haven't they got any decent ships these days? Why do we have to travel in old scows like these?'

The sailor by the gang-plank frowned, unwilling to let the insult pass. 'Take a look at some of your own bloody equipment,' he suggested.

'This ship was built thirty years ago,' Wedderburn pointed out indignantly. 'I know. My old man worked on it on Clydeside.'

'And them bloody lorries of yours was probably built about the same time,' the sailor retorted. 'Judging by the way they keep breaking down.' He indicated a traffic jam on the concrete ramp near the landing-craft, *Thruster*. 'Look, there's another. And it's one of yours.'

Alongside the halted lorry, Lieutenant Jinkinson was bawling out the driver, Private Spragg, who was standing wooden-faced and unco-operative beside the open bonnet with his mate, Private McKechnie.

'Can't you get the bloody thing moving?' Jinkinson was saying.

'No, sir.' Spragg's moist face was blank and uncommunicative. 'Starter's gone, I think.'

'Didn't you check it?'

'Yes, sir. It should have been changed. Workshops said so. There was no spares.'

'Couldn't you fix it?'

'I thought I had, sir.'

There was a stubborn, unwilling look on Spragg's face, and Jinkinson stared hard at him.

'You're a National Serviceman, aren't you?' he said.

'Yes, sir.'

'You up to something?'

'Up to something, sir?'

'Pulling a fast one, because the Government cut your pay?'

Spragg stared back at Jinkinson unblinkingly. 'Stopping a lorry wouldn't make much difference to that, sir, would it?' he said. 'I'm a National Serviceman. I'm the lowest form of animal life. I can't change that.'

'Cut that out,' Jinkinson snarled. 'We're all in this together.'

'Yes, sir. Only you're getting a lot more pay for it than I am.'

It was while Jinkinson was still staring, baffled, at Spragg and McKechnie that White appeared with Frensham.

'We're behind schedule,' he pointed out.

'The bloody thing's conked,' Jinkinson said in despair.

White indicated his own vehicles. 'If we don't get our people on board,' he warned, 'you'll miss us like hell when it comes to hitting the beaches.'

'Oh, come off it,' Jinkinson said. 'It's only an exercise.'

White frowned, cursing the instructions that had allowed Drucquer to inform only his senior officers and had obliged them to leave the subalterns in the dark.

'We'll still do it properly,' White snapped. 'Since A.C.T.5's working with your section, I'm insisting.'

'Oh, very well!' Jinkinson looked desperate and indicated Spragg. 'I think that bastard's pulling a fast one, though,' he said. 'But I can't prove it.'

'You're jamming up the works,' White pointed out angrily. 'You shouldn't be ahead of us, anyway. You've got out of turn.'

'Well, what can I do?'

'Off-load the blasted thing, man! Get the gear out and *shove* it on board. They'll have time to fix the engine while we're at sea.'

Jinkinson gave him a look which was compounded of sourness at the reprimand and relief at the suggestion.

'O.K.,' he said. He turned to McKechnie and Spragg. 'Let' have some of the chaps up here. Chuck all that equipment out.

In the admiral's quarters on board *Leopard*, General Hodges was frowning over the proposed bombardment task-table and the recommendations of the Support Committee on opportunity targets. Alongside him, Leggo leaned over the table with Fraschetti and Lyall, Hodges' senior staff officers, who were arguing over a course with the ship's captain and the Fleet Navigation Officer. The Naval Officer in Command, Rear-Admiral Dennis Downes, was by the door, poring over maps and charts and carrying on a disjointed conversation with Hodges over his shoulder.

The Senior Naval Officer had that spotless look of efficiency that seemed peculiar to so many seafaring men, but he looked irritated and frustrated at that moment, as though things were not going to his liking. He was small and slight, with an impressive row of ribbons and probably more sea time than any other officer in the shrunken Royal Navy, and he had a reputation for being the sort of man who stood no nonsense from anyone, not even the First Sea Lord.

'The aircraft are due to go in at 0500,' Hodges was saying. 'That's half an hour before the opening of the naval barrage, which is the same time as the parachutists start to drop on the outskirts and one hour before we start putting our chaps ashore.'

Downes looked round. 'Is that the last alteration to the plan?'

'London says so.'

'That's what they said last time.' Downes frowned. 'And what's all this damn' nonsense about the R.A.F. carrying only 14-pound bombs?'

'Westminster.' Hodges looked over his glasses. 'Politicians never fail to imagine that zeal can replace lack of weapons, and ardour make up for lack of weight. They've always felt that the force of an idea—a country re-born, that sort of slot-machine claptrap they talk in the House—can make up for deficiencies in *matériel*. They think our enthusiasm's sufficient, Dennis, and I suspect they're afraid of world opinion.'

Downes frowned. 'Fourteen-pound bombs can kill as well as blockbusters,' he pointed out in a growl, 'but they're not so bloody good, Horace, at softening a place up for an invasion. It's a pity that blasted rioting at King Boffa Port didn't start a few weeks later.' He glared at the chart for a second, then glanced at Hodges again. 'Who was responsible for that little bunfight, anyway, Horace? Us?'

Hodges smiled. 'Shouldn't think so,' he said. 'Wouldn't put it past Braka though—to nudge us into a bit of action. Aswana came round to put *his* spoke in afterwards. The usual load of blood and guts. He seemed to think it the duty of a Deputy C.-in-C.'

Downes scowled. He had no love for the Malalan Commander-in-Chief either.

'Horace,' he went on. 'What's wrong with 'em at home? Those bloody landing-craft they allotted us first were almost useless and some of the wooden-hulled sweepers were rotten. I'm told the R.A.F.'s worried sick about unserviceability, too —because it's not all due to spare-part shortage.'

'I heard that,' Hodges said shortly. 'I'm worried, too.'

Downes' heavy brows knitted again. 'It's also come to my knowledge,' he said, 'that naval liberty men have been holding meetings. In Pepul Town somewhere. I've not been able to find out why yet, but I'd hazard a guess.'

Hodges faced him, his eyes steady. 'So would I, Dennis,' he said.

Downes' frown became ferocious. 'It might have been bearable,' he said bitterly, 'if we had the backing of the rest of the world.'

Hodges nodded. 'It would have helped,' he commented shortly.

'Chap I know in town here,' Downes waved a hand. 'Radio expert. American. Saw him two days ago. Showed me some reports he'd picked up from the American stations. Seemed to think they might make me change my mind. As if I could.'

'Reports?' Hodges' mind was not entirely on what Downes was saying.

'He'd taped 'em and had 'em typed out for me.'

'What sort of reports were they?'

'One of 'em mentioned that a British R5 had been shot down over King Boffa Port by the new Migs. The report suggests the pilots weren't Malalans and that they had a damn' good radar system working.'

'That's a nice thought.'

'I wish that were all,' Downes admitted. 'There was another one about a serious division within the Commonwealth and the deplorable divergence of opinion between the U.K. and the States. They're saying in New York that we're making a major error and that if we go any further what's left of the Commonwealth will break up.' He looked up. 'It nearly did over Suez, you know.'

'Go on, Dennis,' Hodges said.

Downes stared at him for a second, then he drew a deep breath. 'They're saying that the last vestige of European influence in Africa will disappear,' he went on, 'and the Chinese will move in. They said . . .' He stopped and, unlocking a drawer, took out a buff envelope. 'Oh, hell, see them for yourself, Horace! They make sorry reading. I was going to destroy 'em, but these things have a fatal fascination, don't they?'

'Yes,' Hodges said. 'They do.'

He paused, then he looked at Downes again. 'It might interest you,' he said, 'to know that I've had a few reports of my own. In fact, I've had the Mayor of Pepul to see me, and a visit from the Police Chief. About this statue of Queen Victoria that's been defaced.'

Downes' grave face softened into a grin. 'Wouldn't have thought the old dear meant all *that* much to 'em these days,' he said.

'I don't suppose she does,' Hodges agreed. 'But even if you don't like the shape of your own gatepost, you're still going to object if the kids of a chap down the street daub paint all over it.'

Downes nodded. 'What happened?'

'I said I'd try to find the culprit. Don't suppose I shall, of course, but the offer seemed to satisfy them. They promised not to pass it on to Machingo. They will, of course—unofficially.'

'I shouldn't think Braka's very concerned about Queen Victoria,' Downes observed.

'*I'm* concerned, Dennis. It's symptomatic of what's going on all round us, isn't it?'

Downes rubbed his nose uneasily. 'Some bloody fool on

Duck,' he said, 'painted a hammer and sickle on one of the gun turrets.'

Hodges' eyebrows raised. He found he wasn't surprised.

'I've demanded an enquiry,' Downes growled, his blue eyes glinting. 'I expect there'll be a report along.'

'I expect there will,' Hodges said dryly. 'We go in for reports in a big way. I've got another on an incident in the 4th/74th. Some fool of an officer got drunk and, after urinating on one of the boats at the small boat jetty, he offered the harbourmaster corporal a couple of bottles of beer to keep him quiet. His colonel's seen him and docked him six months' seniority and I've sent both men home. It's not much, and there are always a certain number of fools in any force, but the corporal would normally have made nothing of it. This time he reported it. Why?'

Downes lit a cigarette and stared fiercely at it as Hodges went on.

'Even here in Pepul,' he said, 'there hasn't been whole-hearted support. The Provost people tell me that in Saba Town a chap who was working for us has been murdered, and another chap has had his shop burned down for selling to the troops. I don't like it, Dennis. All these reports of yours and all these of mine, together with a few others I got from Stuart Leggo last night but which I won't go into just now, they all add up to something I don't care for.'

Hodges gazed at Downes and held out his hand for the naval man's envelope. 'Mind if I keep 'em?' he asked. 'I might need 'em.'

Downes shrugged. 'Of course,' he said. 'That was the idea.'

Hodges took the papers and placed them on the maps on the table. Leggo and the others were deep in their discussion and didn't seem to notice his concern.

For a moment he stared at the envelope, thinking. The newspaper correspondents who'd been assigned to what they still fondly imagined was an exercise had begun to arrive in Pepul and he had to face them in a short time. He'd held them off as long as possible but he still had to brief them.

God knows what I'm going to say, he thought. They'd ask too many questions as usual and, for once, he hadn't got all the answers. He wondered for a moment if he could push the job

99

on to Leggo, but he decided that would be unfair and cowardly. It was his job and he had to do it, much as he hated evasion and half-truths.

He glanced at Downes with a wry smile. 'If it's any help, Dennis,' he said, 'remember you're only the driver. I'm the passenger you're carrying to do the job.'

Downes stared back at him for a second, realising how much greater was the burden on Hodges.

He nodded. 'That's right, of course,' he said. 'Wish I could have done my bit better, Horace. But the base facilities here have been so bloody awful. All ships over five thousand tons have to remain outside, and at Korno the Malalans are having to load from lighters. I wish someone in Westminster had made their minds up a bit more quickly. The whole operation's been plagued with uncertainty. For instance, we put bunks in the only helicopter carrier we had, so it could be used as a trooper, then we had to burn 'em all out again. *All of 'em*— because it was decided to use extra choppers instead.'

He paused. 'There's one other thing,' he ended. 'It may interest you to know I've had a signal from the Director of Naval Intelligence. There are reports of Russian submarines at Point Z—' he jabbed at the map—'in the area between Pepul and King Boffa Port.'

Hodges' face showed no emotion, not even surprise. 'What are they doing there?' he asked.

'We don't know,' Downes admitted. 'And neither does the D.N.I. It's none of our business. They're not in anybody's territorial waters, of course, but if we take this lot to sea, they'll probably be smack in our path.'

Hodges lit his pipe and began to blow out blue smoke. 'There's nothing we can do,' he said. 'They'll sort out that one at UNO.'

At least, he thought, he *hoped* they'd sort it out at UNO. Personally, he had an idea it was going to take some sorting out.

The load that was on General Hodges' shoulders seemed at that moment no heavier than the load that rested on the shoulders of Lieutenant Jinkinson.

There had been another downpour but, although it hadn't

lasted long and the roar of the rain had changed quickly to the hurried patter of drips as the sun came out and the steam rose in twisting wraiths where the greedy heat sucked up the moisture, it had been enough to make the hold-up alongside *Thruster* even greater.

Space was crowded because the L.S.T.s, *Driver*, *Holness* and *Harker*, were all being loaded from the same ramp as *Thruster*, and the string of lorries was increasing all the time. Even Colonel Drucquer had been along to see what was causing the delay, and he had left Jinkinson red-faced and humiliated, to work it all off on his sergeant who had taken it out of his section. His section had not retaliated, however, and there had been no muttering, but everybody had seemed suddenly to be all fingers and thumbs and a case had been dropped on McKechnie's foot. McKechnie had immediately announced that bones were broken and the delay had brought White back again with Frensham.

'What in God's name's holding you up?' he demanded.

'Every bloody thing possible,' Jinkinson said bitterly. 'These bastards are up to something and I don't know what.'

White's eyes narrowed. He, too, had been aware of sulky looks around him and, though there had been nothing definite to put his finger on, even in his own section there had been a strange new stolidity that worried him. It seemed to be time to do something about it. Sullenness could change rapidly to open disobedience, and he'd heard rumours about acts of defiance about the camp.

He glanced at Frensham. 'Right,' he said to Jinkinson, making his mind up quickly. 'Let's spike their guns. March 'em off. I'll get my chaps to unload it. You can pick it up when we've finished.'

Ten minutes later the gear from the lorry was being stacked at the side of the road, and the men of A.C.T.5, annoyed at having to do someone else's work, were throwing out private gear with a great deal of sang-froid.

White moved away and allowed Frensham to take control of the proceedings. Uneasy suspicions were forming in his mind, suspicions that he wouldn't have believed possible in his earlier service. He swung round and stared at his own men, frowning. They were obviously displeased, and a kitbag bounced on to the road, followed by a suitcase. Frensham pounced on them at once.

'The bastards were told no private gear,' he snorted, giving the suitcase a shove with his foot.

'It's split, Sarge,' one of his men observed.

'Good,' Frensham said unfeelingly. He glanced at the suitcase, then his frown turned to one of bewilderment as he saw stacked sheets of paper through the jagged opening at its corner.

Still frowning, he bent over the case then, staring more closely at it, he knelt down alongside it.

'Surely to God they aren't taking their H.Q. documents with 'em,' he said.

He tugged at a yellow sheet that was sticking through the split, a small square sheet of cheap paper, and held it up in front of him, squinting at it. For a second his eyebrows worked up and down, then he swung round to one of his men.

' 'Ere! You! Get Captain White! Quick!'

Two minutes later White was alongside Frensham, staring at the sheet of paper.

'Get Jinkinson,' he snapped. 'Better go yourself, Sergeant. We don't want this spreading around.'

It took considerably longer to find Jinkinson who seemed to have given up in despair. His men stood in a group, sullen and angry, while Jinkinson, his hat in his hand, his long fair hair damp with sweat, paced up and down near the water's edge, sucking at a cigarette as though his life depended on it.

They saw Frensham approaching the moment he appeared round the dockside crane, heading towards them in a purposeful manner than spelled danger.

'They've found out,' Spragg said nervously.

Leach glanced at Frensham. 'Just stick together, brothers,' he growled. 'They can't do a thing.'

Malaki gestured sadly. 'It's wrong,' he said unhappily. 'It's all wrong, man.'

Leach swung round on him angrily. 'Are you with us?' he demanded.

Malaki said nothing and Leach persisted. 'Don't you agree with it?'

Malaki lifted his eyes as though they were weighted. 'No, man,' he said. 'I don't.'

'Going to tell?'

'No.'

'Why not, if you disagree?'

Malaki didn't know why not. It had something to do with the feeling he'd always had that he was never quite part of the section. They accepted him, they included him, they even obeyed him, yet he'd always felt that until he'd endured with them he was still not one of them. He'd hoped that *Stabledoor* would be the testing point, but he'd never expected to be tested in a way that tore at his loyalties. It never occurred to him that, in permitting him to know what they'd planned, they had *already* accepted him.

His reply was still in his throat as he endeavoured to frame it into words, when Frensham halted in front of Jinkinson and slammed to a salute.

'Sir! Captain White's compliments. Will you see him immediate?'

Jinkinson looked puzzled, then he threw away his cigarette. Two minutes later he, too, was staring at the yellow sheet of paper.

White waited until he had read it before he spoke.

'We found what seems to be a whole suitcase of 'em,' he said. 'Hundreds of 'em. It belongs to one of your people. Know anything about it?'

Jinkinson glanced up at him nervously. 'Christ, no,' he said.

White turned. 'Sergeant Frensham! March those men back here. At the double.'

Three minutes later, Jinkinson's party came to a panting stop alongside White, who swung round on them as they stood at ease, hitching at their belts and wiping their sweating faces.

'Right,' he snapped. 'Whose is this suitcase?'

His hand jerked and there were a few glances among the squad of men.

'Come on,' White said. 'It belongs to one of you. Step forward. And damn' quick.'

Spragg stepped forward hesitantly, his eyes flickering at Leach.

'Name?'

'Spragg, sir.'

'Got the keys?'

Spragg hesitated, glancing desperately at the others for the support he expected. No one moved.

'Come on, have you or haven't you?'

'Yes.'

'*Sir*,' roared Frensham.

'Sir.'

'Open it up,' White snapped.

'That's my private case,' Spragg said aggressively.

'I don't give a damn if it's your mother's coffin. I suspect you've got something in there that you shouldn't have. Open it up!'

Spragg hesitated a moment longer, then he fished in his pocket and, producing a key, stooped over the case.

White stepped forward as he raised the lid. The case was jammed with yellow leaflets and White picked up a handful and shoved them at Jinkinson.

'Right,' he said. 'Shove him under arrest. I'll let you know what to charge him with later. There'll be a cell on board. See the Military Police.'

Jinkinson stared back at him for a second, then he glanced with fury at Spragg and slammed to a salute.

A quarter of an hour later White was standing in the Harbourmaster's Office that was doing temporary duty as police office and guardroom. Jinkinson was alongside him, hot, nervous and ill-at-ease, while in the background the slim Malalan policeman waited quietly, his eyes moving from one to the other.

White indicated the suitcase full of pamphlets that stood open on the table, and his eyes bored into Jinkinson.

'You seen any of those before?' he asked.

Jinkinson nodded. 'One or two,' he admitted. 'I found one on my desk.'

'What did you do about it?'

'Made enquiries. Didn't find anything out, though. I heard that the 4th/74th's seen one or two.'

'What else did you do?'

'Well—nothing. I thought somebody was acting the goat.'

White stared at the youngster, a pitying look in his eyes.

'Next time,' he said, 'for Christ's sake assume that they're not.'

The telephone clicked and he turned his attention to it.

'Colonel? This is Dick White. I've got something here that I think you ought to see.'

2

In the big cabin they'd set aside in *Leopard* for his personal quarters, General Hodges looked across at Colonel Drucquer with sombre eyes. Leggo had poured them all a drink and they stood now, enjoying the cool clink of the ice as they squinted at the grey light that came through the porthole.

In the early evening before dark, a storm of particular intensity had broken over Pepul. For an hour or more there had been violent electrical disturbances, with purple flashes and great squalls of wind, then the rain had come down in straight glassy splinters that shattered as they struck, and drenched in seconds the deck parties and the exhausted troops still struggling aboard the transports and landing craft. It came in a devastating downpour that rattled on the steel like stones and gurgled noisily in the scuppers. The sound of it had been a steady roar, threaded through by the hollow plop-plop as it had dripped off gun mountings, searchlights and radar gear, then it had stopped as abruptly as it had come, leaving only the weeping aerials and an atmosphere that was heavy, humid and depressing, and seemed to rest like a load on Hodges' shoulders as he stared at Colonel Drucquer.

The briefing of the correspondents had gone off better than he'd ever hoped—largely thanks to a few well-timed interruptions by Leggo which had deflected the worst of the questions. It had been noisy, because the newspapermen were excited, and there had been one or two tricky questions, chiefly about equipment and morale, but they had skated skilfully round them, and Hodges had thought that for the day his worries might be over.

Then Drucquer had phoned, requesting an interview, and the feeling of achievement had dispersed at once.

He and Drucquer were old friends. They'd served together several times, more often of late as the Army had diminished and the same old members of the fire brigade had been called out every time there'd been a minor outbreak. They'd served in the same theatre in World War II as subalterns and then in Burma and Korea and Kenya, and finally in Borneo and Aden. They were both experienced soldiers who knew each other well, and it was only the need for sound regimental officers that had prevented Hodges from asking for Drucquer for his staff.

He listened to Drucquer's statement gravely, not interrupting with questions, then he turned to Leggo who was standing by the table where the maps were spread.

'Shut the door, Stuart,' he suggested. 'And lean on it.'

Leggo did as he suggested, and Hodges studied with interest the pamphlet that Drucquer had brought, as the Colonel continued with his story.

'I've got them all in my cabin at the moment,' he was saying. 'They're locked up. They were found under the gear in a lorry. One of mine, I'm afraid, but I've made a few enquiries and I gather a few others have been seen in other units.'

'Any special sign of disaffection in your people?' Hodges asked. 'You can speak freely.'

'I've hardly got to know 'em yet, sir,' Drucquer admitted. 'I've only been here seven days. There's certainly nothing you can put your finger on, though I know it's there.'

'Is it pay?'

Drucquer shrugged. 'Perhaps, sir,' he said. 'Not sure. It was in a section I'd told Captain White to keep an eye on, though he's not one of my officers. He's a good man and the section officer's only a youngster. Needs stiffening with a good sergeant as soon as I can find him one.' He paused and sipped his drink. 'I had a word with one or two other commanding officers,' he went on gravely. 'Naturally, sir. I was worried and I was anxious to know whether I was alone in this. It seems I'm not. Greatorex's got the same trouble in the 20th/62nd and so has Berkeley in the 19th/43rd. In the 4th/74th, I think it's reached the proportions of danger. They've had them in the parachute regiments and even in the Guards. There, though, they didn't catch on. One would expect that, of course.'

When Drucquer had left, Hodges stood for a moment, frowning, then he turned to Leggo. 'Pass me that file, Stuart,' he said, and Leggo crossed to the table and picked up a blue file, tied very securely with white tape.

Hodges opened it and spread it out on the desk. On the top of the papers it contained, there was a yellow pamphlet exactly like the one Drucquer had brought, and there were others underneath, attached to report forms.

Hodges spread them out, fan-shaped like a hand of cards.

'See that, Stuart?' he said. 'Half the units under my command and almost every vessel. They've been turning up all over *Duck* and *Beagle*, according to Downes, and Neville tells me there's a pocket in 677 Squadron of the R.A.F. And they've all come in, in the last twenty-four hours. It's clearly some sort of movement, even though they vary a bit—as though several people have had a hand in it. They've all picked the same theme. The Right of Reply. They've all picked up that damned speech.' He looked at Leggo. 'Thank God the newspapermen hadn't got hold of this.'

He paused for a moment. 'Stuart,' he said slowly. 'Make a signal to commanders of all units. For their eyes only. Mark it secret. I want a report from every commanding officer, no matter how small his unit, and no matter whom he's attached to. I want them all to investigate this—*at once*. I want all replies before we sail. Mark it top priority and pass copies to the Navy and the R.A.F.'

He indicated the pamphlet. 'Where was it printed, by the way?' he asked. 'Any ideas, Stuart?'

Leggo studied the pamphlet for a moment. 'Not ashore, I'd say, sir,' he said slowly.

'Thank God for that,' Hodges said. 'I thought it might be, and we know there's an element in Pepul who're against us being here, even though we're going to try to get King Boffa Port back for them. What makes you think that?'

Leggo gestured with the pamphlet. 'You can recognise the local printing anywhere, sir,' he said. 'The type face's always badly worn. I believe they buy it second-hand from England.

And they make mistakes that European printers would never make—phrases we wouldn't use, old-fashioned words and stilted sentences, that sort of thing. I'd say it was run off aboard ship by a ship's printer. All the passenger ships carry them for bulletins, menus and so on. They make quite a bit of money when the ship's in use as an army transport, producing smutty books.'

'Let's find him, Stuart,' Hodges said shortly. 'It shouldn't be difficult. We haven't all that many transports. Get the Provost people to do a little detective work on the paper and the print and the ships' captains before we sail.'

By the time night had fallen, most of the ships had been loaded, naval vessels, ancient transports and troop carriers, and a great many over-age landing craft.

It had not been possible to make *Stabledoor* an air invasion because there were too many things against such an operation. For one thing there wasn't the elbow room at King Boffa Port for an air landing, and what was more important, an air operation would have been too incisive. It would have been too easy to become committed, and all the time and even now, the brains behind the operation in London had hoped that the Khanzians still might retreat from King Boffa Port and evacuate the great base alongside; and a seaborne operation had been chosen deliberately to give them time to do so.

The problems had been incredibly involved, nevertheless, for there weren't many signposts for an invasion of what was still considered to be a friendly nation who were expected to welcome the troops with open arms—*but might not*. How did one behave? How much was needed? The build-up had been slow. There had not been sufficient troops. The new National Service Act had not had time to provide sufficient trained reserves, and the responsibility had been given to the same old firemen who had been to every other bush fire for the last twenty years.

And, until Hodges' arrival from Germany, not enough had been done at Pepul. The different types of fighting vehicles that had been scraped together had created tremendous difficulties for the·staff with their multitude of spare parts. On the air base next door, several machines were grounded now for nothing else but missing screws or cotter pins, or because mechanics had arrived from England without the necessary conversion courses on to unfamiliar engines and airframes. The tank regiments were suffering from the same diversification of equipment, and even the radios varied in age and range and design.

But the miracle had been achieved. They were all aboard at last. The aircraft were waiting with their parachutists who were to seize the harbour intallations, and the ships were getting under way. Above Hodges' head feet scurried as restlessly as rats, as *Leopard* stirred. There was a grinding and clanking of heavy machinery and a series of dull thuds, then the ship shuddered and the little chintz curtains over the porthole began to quiver. The humming of turbines became a muted throb of power and the great ship swung round and headed towards the open sea.

Slowly, as darkness increased, the ships began to take station, attack transports, slow, rust-scarred cargo boats, small liners, a hospital ship, weather-beaten tankers, and groups of fussing tugs. To starboard were the columns of shallow-draught landing ships containing the first wave of the assault troops, and behind them the troopers with the Malalan soldiers who were to be used in reserve. Ahead of the convoy were the minesweepers, harbour installation vessels, buoy layers, motor launches and the escort vessels—the British ships astern, ahead and to port, the old carrier, *Liverpool*, now converted for helicopters, in the lead; and the Malalan naval vessels, an over-age frigate, a corvette and two wooden motor launches, moving erratically to starboard where the Malalan troops were.

It was an impressive-looking gathering of equipment, and the newspapermen were busy in *Leopard*'s wardroom preparing reports on the show of strength. Hodges, who knew the defects, was not so happy as they were.

They had arrived at a point he'd hoped and prayed would never be reached. The code word 'Dash' had arrived that morning, as he'd been expecting from the moment they'd received the preparatory warning following the news on the radio of the rioting in King Boffa Port. The panic button had now been pressed, and he hoped to God it wouldn't be the first in a series of escalatory movements that would trigger off something too big to be stopped.

He stood by the table in his headquarters cabin with Leggo, staring across the piles of maps and papers towards Fraschetti and Lyall, who were busy with a new series of opportunity targets that had just come in. On the large table in front of him were charts of the beaches round King Boffa Port and the more inland objectives of the base they were to capture, together with a time-table of events in chronological order, prepared by Leggo. In the centre, on the top of the maps, was the blue file tied with white tape.

On the bulkheads of the cabin next door there were batteries of radio receivers and transmitters, connecting them with London and the radio link set up at Pepul, as well as with the troops who were to land on the beaches. Across the corridor was the cabin of the Gunfire Support Committee and Downes' quarters, containing his staff and the fleet navigators and gunnery officers, and the R.A.F. liaison team.

Behind the bridge was the dark cabin where the radar scanners sent their sweeps revolving across the screens with a cold phosphorescent fire that lit the faces of their operators and the air was filled with the faint pinging of the sonar; and next to it the communications centre, with its clicking tele-printers, where the radio operators bent over their sets, expertly plucking information from the cacophony of morse signals in their headphones.

Hodges stood for a moment, watching the officers grouped over the chart table. Outside, he could hear the sound of voices and the engine noises vibrating as the speed increased. Then the door opened and a naval petty officer appeared, holding out a slip of paper for Hodges.

'Message from the Commander-in-Chief, Malalan Forces, sir,' he said.

Hodges took the sheet and glanced at it. 'COMEMFO to COMHOJ. We stride together towards victory. Full speed ahead and damn the torpedoes.'

Hodges' mouth twisted as he passed it to Leggo. 'General Aswana always did like drama,' he said. 'He's heard of the Navy's penchant for clever signals.'

He turned to the petty officer who was waiting with his

signal pad. 'Reply,' he said. 'COMHOJ to COMEMFO. Thank you. Good luck.'

The petty officer raised his eyes as Hodges turned away. 'That all, sir?'

Hodges nodded. 'That's all,' he said firmly.

He waited until the door had closed again, then he turned to Leggo.

'For what it's worth, Stuart,' he said, 'and unless someone at home changes their mind, we're committed.'

Hodges lit his pipe slowly, deliberately, in a manner that told Leggo he was far more worried than he showed. When it was glowing to his satisfaction and the air of the cabin was blue with smoke, he moved away from the table and indicated to Leggo to follow him to one side.

'Right, Stuart,' he said. 'Let's hear what you found out.'

Leggo turned and picked up the blue file. Opening it, he removed a yellow pamphlet which he passed to Hodges, following it with another sheet of yellow paper unmarked by ink.

'We've found the printer, sir,' he said. 'The captain of the *Aronsay Castle* identified the paper at once. The Provost people had the chap up and, though he's admitting nothing, of course, I don't think there's much doubt. He had stocks of it and it's exactly like the stuff the pamphlet's printed on. Not that that means anything, but his type face seems to check, too.' He passed across a menu card and a notice for a carnival dance, relics of the *Aronsay Castle*'s days as a cruise liner. 'You'll notice that there are flaws in the "t's" and the "w's" on the pamphlet that show in these, too. There's also one other coincidence that seems to clinch it. The chap's name was Spragg.'

Hodges looked up from his study of the menu card. 'Should that mean something to us?' he asked.

'I think so, sir. The suitcase Drucquer's pamphlets were found in belonged to a Private Spragg.'

Hodges sucked at his pipe, waiting, and Leggo continued.

'The Provost people talked to this chap, Spragg, sir. He won't say anything and his address is different from Private Spragg's, so it's hard at the moment to pin him down, but I dare bet we'll find they're related. Drucquer's Spragg isn't married and this one is, and that, of course, would explain the difference in addresses. I think the coincidence's too big to be ignored.'

Hodges thought for a moment, sucking at his pipe, then he looked at Leggo.

'Thank you, Stuart,' he said. 'We'll let it lie for the moment. Signal the captain of the *Aronsay Castle* to keep a sharp eye on this Spragg, though. He's not to go ashore—*anywhere*—without our permission. There may be a case here for the civil police, but as we have no civil police with us, there isn't much we can do until we get back—*if* we get back.'

He blew out smoke for a while, then he stared at the blue file in Leggo's hands, his eyes glittering as though he regarded it as something poisonous and dangerous.

'Every unit under my command,' he said slowly. 'Every single one. Apart from the Guards, the Tank regiments and the Marines, there isn't one which hasn't shown some sign of disaffection. In the 20th/62nd it's a sit-down strike over food. In the 19th/43rd tyres are deflated as the trucks are moving aboard. In the 4th/74th, ammunition's mislaid—deliberately, the commanding officer thinks. *Duck*'s suddenly dropped out of the operation with faulty engines and the captain reports that he suspects sabotage. Good God, Stuart, what's happened to the Army?'

He sighed. It was a very different army from the one he'd joined as a young man. Nobody then had imagined for a minute that with nothing in the way of tanks and mechanisation, that they had much of a chance against Hitler's panzers. But the country then had been fighting for its life under a Prime Minister who had everyone's confidence, and they'd all firmly believed in what they'd been fighting for.

Now it seemed that in an attempt to see that there was to be no more scuttle, the Prime Minister was risking not only his country's military reputation but also its honour. Not many people were behind him, and it was clear the troops didn't have much faith in what they were doing. The country wasn't fighting for its life. It was merely standing, somewhat dogmatically, for a very small principle which could easily have been thrown overboard.

'I wish,' Hodges continued, 'that I were even happy about the support troops. But I'm not. Whatever Braka says and whatever General Aswana insists, the fact remains that they're entirely inexperienced.' He sighed. 'Still,' his words came slowly and as though with difficulty, 'inexperienced troops are better than unwilling troops.'

As he finished speaking, the door opened and Admiral Downes appeared. His mouth was tight and there were two deep lines between his brows.

'Nasty bit of information for you, Horace,' he said quietly.

Hodges said nothing, but he seemed to brace himself for the worst.

'Radar's picked up two or three pips,' Downes continued. 'Bearing two-two-five and about twenty-five miles away from here. One large one and two—probably three—smaller ones. They look like submarines and a mother ship.'

Hodges frowned. 'Whose? Not ours?'

' 'Fraid not. I suspect Russian. You know we received a signal saying they were around. But I didn't think they were so close.'

'What are they up to?'

'I'd like to know. We've been watching them for some time. Decided not to worry you until we could confirm them. They appear to be waiting for us.'

Hodges frowned and Downes went on.

'It may be normal practice, of course. It's been common to report sightings and radar pick-ups of Russian submarines near exercises of NATO and Western Alliance fleets and this may be the same. On the other hand . . .'

'. . . it may be something else.'

'Exactly!'

Hodges was silent, considering this new hazard, and Downes gestured.

'I've arranged for the chopper boys to fly off as soon as it's light, for a look-see,' he said. 'We'll have their report for your breakfast reading.' He managed a grin. 'I hope it won't spoil your appetite,' he ended.

3

From a point high above the sea, it was possible to penetrate into its very depths. Sometimes, in shallow waters on a clear day when the sun pierced the unexplored fathoms, you could even see the very bottom and the sad wreckage of ships, and sometimes, with the sun rising or sinking, and a sheen of gold across the water, ships and the big single-sailed fruit boats heading through the islands for Machingo stood out sharply like silhouettes against the glow. But, with the water stirred as it was now into low slow swells, the pale rain-washed light diffused by the uneven surface, it became harder to pick up floating objects and searching became a chore.

The dawn had provided a soggy beginning to the day, with weeping grey skies and an oily lift to the sea, but the rain had stopped as the light grew stronger and, though the clouds still obscured the sun, they were thin and the light was surprisingly bright.

Hodgeforce was clear of Malalan waters by midnight, though the departure from Pepul had not gone unaccompanied by mistakes, and now, with the first of the daylight, they were heading on a course of a hundred and seventy-eight degrees in the direction of King Boffa Port.

Ten miles to the south, near a small convoy of fruit boats bound for Machingo, a naval helicopter, startlingly bright against the drabness of the sea, chattered low over the sweeping water, the blue-green waves, diminished and oddly solidified by the height, stretching as far as the pilot could see.

Lieutenant Charles Childers, the pilot, peered downwards, his eyes squinting a little behind the sunglasses that the perspex cabin made it necessary to wear, particularly with the sun pushing through the cloud cover. Just below him, the little convoy slid away behind, the bright triangular sails stiff in the breeze, the black faces of the crews and passengers turned upwards, gaudy strips of cloth fluttering as black arms waved at them.

They weren't looking for fruit boats but it was necessary to investigate everything, and it was an old dodge for hostile submarines to hide beneath friendly fishing vessels and small coastal craft to frustrate radar. The helicopter had therefore circled the heavy wooden boats with their lateen sails for several minutes, watching for the lurking shadow in the water. But there was nothing, only the heaps of bananas and limes and oranges and paw paws, and the mammies in their gay printed lappas lounging on the high afterdeck where the helmsman leaned on his heavy oar.

Childers glanced backwards briefly, then he noticed that Petty-Officer Rubens, crouching near the radio, was flapping a hand at him, his heavy Jewish face rapt as he listened to the sound of a voice overlayed by the crackling of interference.

'They've changed course.' Rubens looked up and jabbed a finger to starboard. '*Leopard* reports they're moving away. We need course two-three-oh.'

'Course two-three-oh. Right.'

The helicopter's blades tilted and the aircraft lifted, its tail lurching round as she headed, nose down, further towards the west. The chopping noise of the engine came through the fuselage like a pulse, and they could hear the wind scratching at the fuselage like a horde of small animals trying to get inside.

Listening to it, his eyes never leaving the sea, Childers found himself wondering what he was involved in. Nobody had explained his mission to him, but someone had whispered that he was there to search out a Russian ship which was supposed to be shadowing the convoy.

Even to Childers, who normally never worried very much with politics, the implications were obvious, and he found himself wondering what a Russian ship was doing moving on roughly the same course as the great armed convoy he'd just left. Not long before, he's seen a squadron of navy fighters scream over his head, the sun gleaming on their polished fuselages, their needle-shaped snouts picking out the light.

They had swept above him with a majestic indifference, as though investigating him, then they had turned north with the curious lurching swing of high speed, one of them swinging wide and losing its position in the formation as they headed back towards Pepul.

Doubtless they'd just come back from the area of King Boffa Port. Childers knew the convoy's course and he knew that the fighters were keeping a sharp watch ahead near their destination, and while he was never the man to question what he was told to do, he was conscious nevertheless of an unnamed and even hardly shaped worry at the back of his mind.

Childers was an orphanage boy who had never known a home and having only recently got himself married and set up house after courting the same girl for years, he had an unholy fear that what had suddenly seemed like paradise was soon to be cut short by some major holocaust before he'd even got used to it.

The helicopter was now heading on to its new course and the watery sun was glinting off the perspex directly into Childers' eyes; and it was because of this that he didn't see the vessel to his left until a hand banged his shoulder and he saw Leading Seaman Phillips, the winchman, pointing.

'Over to port, Skipper,' he was saying. 'Looks like a big tug or something.'

Childers moved the steering column without speaking, and, as the tail of the helicopter swung round, he felt a sense of relief as the sun ceased to leap from the perspex at his eyes.

Almost immediately, he saw the vessel in the distance, just edging into view beyond the edge of the fuselage, a chunky little ship, pushing along with a white bone beneath her forefoot. She had a jutting prow and a short stack, from which small smudges of diesel smoke burst in puffs.

'Faster than she looks,' Childers observed at once. 'Raked bow. Cutaway stern. She's no tug.'

He caught the bright red band on the funnel and, pressing closer, he swept round the stern of the strange vessel until he saw the gold hammer and sickle design against the red.

'Towing something,' Phillips said, staring down.

'Trawl of some sort.' Rubens lifted his head from the radio for a moment. 'Biological or hydrographic. You can see the cable streaming out. There, from that gallows on the forrard well.'

'Probably just a phoney,' Childers pointed out. 'To make her look innocent.'

While they watched, two men just aft of the ship's funnel began to struggle with a meteorological balloon which beat against them as it whipped backwards and forwards in the wind caused by the ship's passage. The men grabbed and clawed at the swinging bag, trying to hold it steady, while a third man fought to clear the coils of nylon cord which appeared to support instrument boxes.

'Radiosonde and radar target,' Phillips said.

Childers shook his head. 'The way they're handling that bloody balloon,' he commented, 'I'll bet they're not in the habit of doing it very often. There isn't much wind.'

The balloon had broken free now, bouncing its way along the deck, and the nylon cord snaked out and snapped taut as it jerked upwards, then the big orange ball hung in the air, a bright blob astern, rising swiftly.

'They shoved it up pretty damn' quickly,' Childers observed. 'Funny they should do it just when we were watching.'

'Think they did it for our benefit, Skipper?' Phillips asked.

'Let's have a picture of her just in case. Watch that cord for me.'

While they swung round in a wide arc ahead of the strange ship, they continued to discuss her, as Rubens radioed her position and course to Hodgeforce.

'Bigger than she seems,' Childers went on, staring down. 'Plenty of room for extra bunkers. Big fuel valves on deck. Big booms and winches. Radar and wireless antennae. She looks East German to me. Seen plenty like that in the Baltic—from Rostock or Pomerania or even Riga.'

A group of men on the Russian's bridge were staring up at them now as Rubens lifted his camera, and from among the superstructure and fittings they could see other faces. They looked brown, as though they'd been in tropical waters a long time, and the ship looked too clean and well-found to be anything but a naval vessel.

'That chap on the end of the bridge looks like you, Rube,' Phillips said. 'Same sort of black hair and blank look.'

'Drop dead,' Rubens said.

As they swung east they caught the full reflection of the light on the sea and were temporarily blinded, but they could see the bedspring wireless aerial moving above the bridge of the ship.

'Reporting us for "buzzing" 'em,' Childers said. 'There'll be a lot of diplomatic activity in Whitehall tomorrow when the protest arrives.'

'Something to keep the politicians busy.'

As they swept close once more, one of the men on the stern of the vessel, bare-chested in the sunshine, waved, then he made a gesture which, started during the Second World War by Winston Churchill, had long since been adapted by Servicemen the world over into an obscene gesture.

'Up you, too, mate,' Phillips said.

'He deserves a bomb on him for that,' Childers grinned.

He glanced back at the Russian sliding away beneath them, and moved his hand in a circular gesture.

'Let's have another look round,' he suggested. 'There must be some reason to explain what he's doing in these waters because, by God, I'll bet he's not fishing.'

Childers' report reached Hodges' desk via Admiral Downes whose face contained a trace of sly humour, so that Hodges wasn't certain whether to be annoyed with him for his cynicism or cheered up by the fact that there was one among them who could still see a funny side to what he personally was beginning to consider an approaching tragedy. Downes seemed to regard them all as puppets in the hands of the politicians, and the politicians as utterly beyond the pale.

'We think it's the *Chorniye Kazach*,' he told Hodges. 'If it is, she's a submarine mother ship.'

'What's that? A depot ship?'

' "Mother" 's a better description. Fuels them and supplies them. But if she's here, it stands to reason there are submarines here, too.'

'Did the helicopter see any?'

'No. But radar's getting blips now—quite distinct ones. Even sonar's picking them up now, so they can't be too far away. Probably below surface just over the horizon, following us by radar. They're on the same course.'

Downes' smile died and his face became grave. 'If they get the word "Go", Horace,' he said, 'there never *was* an invasion so badly placed for its jump-off as this one. Huff-Duff's been reporting foreign-language transmissions from them for some time, so I think we can safely assume that our estimate's a sound one.'

Hodges sucked at his empty pipe for a moment. 'Any idea what they're saying?' he asked.

Downes' grave face broke into a grin again. 'Data regarding the weather,' he said. 'They seem to be subjecting the atmosphere round here to a hell of a lot of tests. They don't normally wear out the ether with this sort of activity and they certainly don't send information of this kind by radio. It's simply logged and evaluated at the end of the trip. What's more, from what we know about this area, it's all a bit suspect because it doesn't match. So—assuming that everybody aboard her isn't a bloody fool—I'd guess they're using anything they can set their minds to, to hide information of a different kind.'

'Such as?'

'Us. I suspect they're discussing us in some sort of code.'

Hodges nodded. 'As if we haven't enough worries,' he said, 'with what Leggo turned up the other night and what Drucquer produced yesterday.'

He glanced quickly at Downes. 'This trouble among your people,' he said. 'The hammer and sickle on the gun turret. *Duck* turning back. Anything else? More serious, I mean.'

Downes grimaced. 'There's been no disrespect to officers,' he said. 'But I've been aware that things have been far from normal.'

'How?'

'No direct insubordination, but there've been a few refusals of duty.'

'Could you itemise these things?'

'Given an hour or two.'

'I'd like you to. I think also, in the circumstances, I'd like to speak to commanding officers of brigades. That includes you, of course, and Group Captain Neville. Can you arrange it?'

Downes smiled. 'Of course. Easy enough by helicopter.

Always frightens *me* to death but I expect *they* won't mind too much.'

As he left the cabin, Hodges turned to Leggo who was working at the desk.

'Can you arrange a conference for this morning, Stuart?' he asked.

'Of course, sir.'

'Nothing big. Just the brigadiers and the Navy and Air Force people. I feel, with things as they are, we *ought* to talk.'

'I'll arrange it, sir.'

Hodges stared through the porthole for a moment. The rain had continued most of the night in a steady and sickening descent, the water bubbling in the scuppers, while every over-hang had dripped its weight of water to the deck. In the deck parties, tempers had grown frayed and nerves had become on edge, the men looking pinched and cold in spite of the tem-perature and the fact that they were sweating and drained of energy under their oilskins.

A swell had got up now, too, and the seas were big and ugly so that the masthead lifted to the sky. The few soldiers who were visible looked seasick and unhappy, and even the sailors looked frayed and nervous.

An albatross had joined the ship and was trailing it, clinging like foam to the waves to knock off the spray with its wide wing-tips before sliding down the far side, inches from the surface of the water, slow and dignified and divorced in its magnificence from all the folly of the humanity in the great grey ships.

Staring at the convoy heaving in slow curtseys, Hodges felt faintly depressed. One of the Malalan launches had dis-appeared during the night after signalling that its engines were giving trouble and, as it had turned to follow *Duck* back to Pepul, the Malalan force had closed up to fill the empty space.

As he watched, a string of bunting fluttered at the masthead of *Leopard*. The British ships responded immediately, but there was a noticeable pause before the Malalan vessels ran the signal up.

'Not finding communication easy,' Hodges observed, as the flags came down again.

He swung round, suddenly angry. 'Do you know,' he said, 'there's been a war going on almost all my life and all the politicians do is tell us we ought to stop it. As though we enjoy it! We do the dirty work and all they do is sit on committees and make sure they're not personally involved.'

'Bit strong that, isn't it, sir?' Leggo protested.

Hodges took a deep breath. 'Yes, I suppose it is,' he admitted. 'But there *is* something in war, in spite of all that these mass peace movements say. There *is* some mystique in courage, self-sacrifice and unselfishness, Stuart, though, of course, it never makes up for the rest of it. But it's something *we* know about and something *they*'ll never know about and never understand.'

He seemed to refer to the politicians and the committee men—the unnamed 'they'—as though they were his personal enemies. He felt and sounded faintly rebellious and he knew it, and he decided it was time to change the subject.

'What do you make of it all, Stuart?' he asked. 'Not just the pamphlets—everything. World opinion. Our equipment. These divided loyalties. We're set on a collision course and God knows what could happen, and I'd like to hear someone else's views in case they're different from mine.'

Leggo frowned, aware how lonely Hodges felt but unable to help him.

'General,' he said, 'I don't know what to think. I hate the idea of being involved in precipitating a third world war, but it still makes me squirm to see my country being pushed around. I wish I could be more helpful. I wish I knew the answer, sir, but I don't.'

'No,' Hodges growled. 'And neither do I, Stuart, apart from just going ahead as we are doing and hoping for the best.'

4

The senior officers of Hodgeforce entered Hodges' cabin warily. They knew why they'd been called to *Leopard* and they'd brought with them whatever hasty notes they'd been able to make on the subject. It was a gloomy gathering, not improved by the grey filtered light. It had been raining again for an hour now, and as they gathered round the table, their eyes on the maps, they could hear the gurglings and tricklings of water in the scuppers, while the air, stifling in spite of the fans, gagged in their throats in the humid heat of the afternoon.

Hodges arrived a few minutes later with Leggo, Admiral Downes and Group Captain Neville, the head of the R.A.F. liaison group. He waved a hand and the others sat down. Reading, the tank brigadier, and Rattray, the Marine, two solid-looking men with rock-like faces who, together with Ricketts, the Parachute commander, another man of the same mould, had become known throughout Hodgeforce as the Three Rs—Reading, 'Riting and 'Rithmetic—sat separately at the back of the cabin, curiously alike in their toughness and confidence. Downes lounged on the chintz-covered settee under the porthole, one hand draped languidly across the back, casual and apparently indifferent. Brigadier Calhoun, a short sturdy man with bandy legs and a florid complexion above his thick neck, sat in the armchair, and Brigadier Dixon, a tall thin bespectacled man, sat neatly on a stiff chair at the end of the table. Neville, the R.A.F. officer, sat with his legs astride his chair, his elbows on the back, a small man with a sharp-featured face who reminded Hodges vaguely of a terrier at a rat hole.

As the conference started, Hodges allowed Leggo to open the ball, and he gave a short report on the subject of the pamphlets and on what he'd seen in Victoria Square before the convoy sailed. When he'd finished, Hodges leaned back in his chair.

'Right, gentlemen,' he said briskly. 'I've been making enquiries about all this, as you know, and I've found out that this attitude of objection seems to run right through every unit in this command. In some I'm sure it's nothing more than a dissatisfaction with pay. In others, it's a problem of Reservists who've been kept waiting around too long, while their jobs are in danger back home. Nevertheless, because you're nearer to it than I am, I'd like to hear what you have to say.'

Reading and Rattray dismissed the suggestions of disaffection briefly. There'd been nothing among their own units, although they'd seen pamphlets, and Hodges turned to Calhoun.

'Cal,' he said. 'How about you? You must have had some thoughts on this. The report from your brigade isn't a very rosy one.'

Brigadier Calhoun considered for a moment. He was newly promoted and very troubled by all the signs of unreliability in his command.

'I don't like it, General,' he admitted. 'I'd like to tell you I had no worries, but that wouldn't be true. I have. There's been a lot of sullenness and I'm afraid I don't trust a lot of my people. In fact, I have grave fears that radio links will fail. I don't feel the men who're due in first are going to refuse—there are too many Guardsmen and we've got Rattray's Marines, and I think they'll carry the others with them—but I don't like the idea of them being out on a limb all the same, with a lot of bloody fools letting them down from behind.'

'What about the officers?'

Calhoun shrugged. 'Nothing much,' he said. 'There's one officer under arrest in the 4th/74th. He says he's prepared to resign his commission rather than be involved in an operation he doesn't believe in.'

'Background?'

Calhoun pulled a face. 'Not army,' he said. 'But the boy's good. Radio specialist. Just the sort of man we want. Brainy, perhaps a little too sensitive, perhaps a little too conscious of the rights of other people and the other side of every question. But that's rather infectious everywhere these days, and most young people have it in their minds.'

'They shouldn't in the Army,' Hodges commented.

Calhoun shrugged again and Hodges frowned. 'Do you expect any more?'

Calhoun looked worried. 'Greatorex of the 20th/62nd says he suspects there's a movement of some sort in his mess. He's heard rumours and there's been a certain amount of cliquishness among the younger members. Pike says he's had reports from his R.S.M. of trouble among the sergeants. I understand you know all there is to know about the 17th/105th.'

Hodges rubbed his nose and turned to his other brigadier. Dixon, in command of the reserves, was one of the brains that Calhoun admired so much.

'Same sort of problems as Cal, sir,' he said in a casual manner. 'To paraphrase the Duke, nothing among the top people but we might pick up a private or two.'

'Can you be more precise?' Hodges said sharply. He wasn't sure that he liked Dixon very much and he tried very hard to force down the feeling that it was envy for Dixon's brain. Dixon had come into the Army from Cambridge, and he had an honours degree in science. His promotion, in an army of technology, had been rapid, but Hodges sometimes wondered if the Army didn't demand more of a man than merely brains, and he had a feeling that while Dixon believed firmly in his scientific instruments, he didn't take enough trouble with his men.

Dixon was shrugging. 'A little worrying from the 71st/86th,' he said. 'One or two men under arrest. A few of the Reservists in the 19th/43rd presented a petition. Several——

'What was the petition?' Hodges demanded sharply.

Dixon waved a hand. 'On there, sir,' he said, indicating a pile of documents he'd brought in with him. 'Said they were tired of hanging about. Wanted to go home. There was a bit of trouble from the National Servicemen, too.'

'About pay?'

'About pay. Refused to take orders from the N.C.O.s until they were on the same rates. They were both squashed pretty quickly.'

125

'What's your opinion in the event of action? How will they support the Guards?'

'They'll support them, sir.'

'To the limit?'

'Of course, sir.'

Hodges stared at Dixon. He wasn't sure that he didn't prefer Calhoun's anxiety to Dixon's almighty confidence. His own view was somewhat different, because there appeared from the pile of documents in front of him to be more cases of disloyalty in Dixon's brigade than there were in Calhoun's. He turned to Downes.

'Admiral?'

Downes' report was brisk, incisive and direct. 'The ships have been infected for a long time,' he said. 'Since the alliance with Russia, they've been regularly into Baltic ports and they've picked it up there, and it's spread. There've been cases in every ship under my command. The pamphlets were obviously delivered in Pepul by liberty boats and boats carrying non-urgent signals and mail. There's obviously been a great deal of dissatisfaction over the pay cuts and the methods taken to explain them to the men. I think also there've been a lot of agitators—as I think there must have been in the Army and Air Force units—who've been forced into the Service by unemployment at home, the National Service Act and the calling up of Reservists. These last are men who've had the opportunity to become thoroughly versed in trade union activities, and they're trying to apply the same methods in the Services. A few members of the Party even, by God, even a few Ban-the-Bomb-ers.' Downes looked a little sick. 'There've been incidents in several ships—small refusals of duty, that sort of thing—but the worst trouble's been in *Duck*. The starboard watch failed to obey an order to fall in to clean ship and locked themselves in their messdecks, and intimidated the men who disagreed. I replaced the commanding officer and arrested four men, but as you know she's dropped out with suspected sabotage. I don't think it's finished, and it could spread. It's not very difficult to include subversive messages in fleet signals. I also found out about the meetings in Pepul. I understand some sort of code signal's been arranged.'

'What sort of code?' Hodges asked.

'I don't know. Perhaps a group of letters sent by signallers between ships. As I say, it's the easiest thing in the world for operators to insert them in messages and to have them picked up by other operators who don't include them in the message when they receive it. Maybe by word of mouth, by ship's boats, or even a cheering code between ships, though that's probably a bit old-fashioned now.'

'What would it be used for?'

Downes shrugged. 'I don't know. They've been remarkably tight-lipped and we've been able to find out surprisingly little. Might be anything. For instance, it might be used to indicate they were to hold back in the event of an assault. Something like that.'

Hodges nodded, grateful for the clarity of Downes' report.

'Thank you.' He turned to the only airman present, Neville, who thought for a while before replying. He had a red weal on his face caused by burns received in a crash after being hit by anti-aircraft fire at the time of Korea, and his hands were bright red, his fingers twisted by shrunken flesh into claws, the nails more like an animal's talons than anything human. His injuries had in no way destroyed his spirit, however, and he had fought against doctors and Service psychiatrists to be allowed back into flying, and had led a wing at Suez, and was now one of the leading exponents of orthodox methods.

'There's been a bloody high incidence of mechanical failure,' he said slowly. 'God knows though, sir, with the mixed bag we've got, I'm not surprised. They dug up some of these blasted aircraft from all over the shop, and some of 'em are pretty ancient. But what's worse, there are hardly a dozen alike. Presented no end of problems with spares.' He paused. 'That's not all. Some of these spares have gone adrift. Can't be accounted for. Don't like it. Looks bloody fishy to me, sir. And we lost an aircraft due to a stupid accident when they were bombing up. Nine men and an aircraft due to indifferent training. The Air Force Reserve Act was valueless. Everybody who'd served could get a pension if he was available for call-up and they all put their names down to get the money. They never expected to serve, of course, and I saw one bloke walking about with a stick. They were bloody useless, sir, and all had to be slung out again.'

He paused in his tirade, his face angry, the scar-tissue crimson.

'How about the flying crews?' Hodges asked.

'Think we can count on 'em to a man,' Neville said. 'We did have a bit of trouble, but the A.O.C. stamped on that a bit sharpish, and there's nothing wrong with what's left. The A.O.C.'s worried about the ground staff, though. It's come to our notice there's been a case of a corporal in one of the ground defence units refusing duty and his sergeant trying to cover up for him. The corporal's since been placed under arrest and the sergeant demoted. It's a symptom and we daren't let it go any farther, because there are too many problems over servicing already.'

'Deliberate, do you think?'

Neville nodded. 'Yes, I do,' he said. 'Mutiny can mean anything from the hasty decision of a group of men to remain in their hut until they're promised better porridge for breakfast to an uprising against and the overthrow of their officers. *This* certainly comes between these two extremes.'

'Can you supply any explanation?'

'Yes, by God, I can, sir. I think some bastards have been getting at the chaps. I know there's a lot of dissatisfaction over pay and about what we're doing, but I still think somebody's up to no good. I've heard this Right of Reply thing too often for it to be an accident.'

Hodges sat for a moment silently, then he put his finger-tips together in the form of a steeple and looked at the other officers.

'Leggo here,' he said, indicating his Chief-of-Staff, 'has a friend ashore. From—er,' he hesitated, deciding it might be wiser not to indicate the sex of Leggo's informant, 'from this source, he's discovered a few things that might be of interest. I would normally have passed this on to you immediately, but owing to the fact that the word "Go" came almost on top of it and we were more concerned at the time with getting ourselves aboard and under way, I've had to postpone it until now. Carry on, Stuart.'

Leggo crossed to a blackboard that had been erected behind Hodges' chair and lifted a dust sheet. On the blackboard were maps of Khanzi and King Boffa Port and the harbour installations.

'*Operation Stabledoor*, gentlemen,' he said briskly, and there was a shuffling among the seated officers.

'You all have maps like this,' Leggo went on. 'Perhaps you'd like to make notes. I've prepared typed lists of what I'm going to tell you, too, though. You can pick them up off the table.'

He jabbed at the map of the harbour installations. 'Here,' he said, 'my—er—information is that hidden among the trees facing the harbour is a rocket battery, equivalent to our 4-inch. There's another one here.' He jabbed at the map again. 'And both are placed so as to cover the beaches and the entrance to the port.'

Dixon glanced at Calhoun, but no one said anything.

'I'm also well informed,' Leggo went on, 'that here and here and here— 'he made several jabs at the green-shaded portion of the map of Khanzi—'there are reserve brigades. There are white officers, in some cases mercenaries from the Congo, and I'm told these troops are very good. They're there to back up the local units and they've got a lot of experience of this sort of fighting. And they've got good weapons. You know as well as I do, gentlemen, that the Russians have been working weapons into the area for years.'

'What about airfields?' Neville asked abruptly.

'Here and here.' Leggo indicated points on the map of King Boffa Port.

'My information,' Neville said slowly, 'is that most of what's on those fields is old stuff that we gave them. I understand there are no Migs on those fields at all, but we know for certain they've received a great number of the latest Mig 41s.'

Leggo nodded. 'That's my information, too,' he agreed. 'But I'm afraid we haven't yet established where these Migs are, though we think they're at Lo and Kij-Moro.' He jabbed at the map of Khanzi again. 'There are certainly open areas here and there, and it could well be that they are there.'

Neville frowned. 'The R5s have seen nothing of them,' he said. 'Mind, they're surrounded by jungle. Easiest thing in the world to hide 'em and camouflage them.'

'Easiest thing in the world to camouflage installations in jungle areas, too,' Hodges added.

'What about runways?' Neville asked.

'The ground's stony and well-drained. So long as it's good and flat, there's no problem there.'

'If they're there,' Neville said, 'they've been damn' careful with their vehicles. Nobody's spotted any tracks.'

'Go on, Stuart,' Hodges said bleakly.

Leggo glanced at him and went on mercilessly. 'There's a blockship loaded with cement, scrap-iron and high explosives already in place,' he said. 'It only needs winching across the entrance to the harbour and triggering off.'

'Is there, by God?' Downes said. 'Well, I suppose it was to be expected.'

Leggo nodded and went on in cold, precise terms to list the Khanzian army units and describe the morale and equipment of the various brigades.

'Eighteen brigades?' It was Dixon's turn to pull a face. 'They told us *nine*.'

Leggo ignored him and began to read from a typed sheet the figures he'd written down after his meeting with Stella Davies. He saw the faces in front of him fall.

'Those aren't the figures I've got,' Dixon said sharply. He sounded irritated.

'Nor me,' Neville agreed.

'I think I can vouch for them,' Leggo said.

Calhoun stared at his notes. 'Seems to make a bit of difference,' he said, his voice edgy as though he were a little shaken. He reached across to the table. 'Let's have that break-down a moment.' He picked up a sheet of paper and began to read it, his lips moving, his brows coming down as he worked through it.

'Fifty Centurions, T34s and JS3s. Seventy-five Shees.' He muttered the words half to himself. 'A hundred and fifty guns, BTZ scout cars . . .' He looked up. 'According to your report they've got about a third more of everything than we bargained for.' He glanced at the sheet again. 'SU 100 self-propelled guns, 22-millimetre guns, 57-millimetre anti-tank weapons.' He looked up again. 'My God,' he said. 'Not much ground work was done in London before they took the decision to send us in. Where did all this come from?'

'At least one Communist vessel a week's being unloaded at King Boffa Port,' Leggo pointed out. 'I gather the total purchases are around two hundred and fifty million dollars, to say nothing of twenty-seven million pounds' worth in neighbouring states who've offered it in the event of an emergency.'

Calhoun looked shaken. 'It's a pity Intelligence didn't let us have this appreciation before,' he said. 'It might have helped in the planning. Anything more?'

'Several things,' Leggo said. 'It's all listed. And there's a new Soviet consul just been appointed—Dhevyadov, one of Tchikov's pupils and an expert at organising subversion, defence and propaganda.'

There was a muttered discussion for a while, and Hodges caught a note of alarm in it. He broke it up before it got going.

'Right, gentlemen,' he said sharply. 'What we've just been discussing makes a vast difference to *Stabledoor*, I think.'

Nobody spoke and he went on slowly. 'You know how far disaffection's gone in your own commands. You know what you have to face. You know your orders. Now—as far as I'm concerned I've received my instructions but I'm not entirely happy about them and, while I'm prepared to carry out whatever I'm told to do, it seems only fair to me that the people at home should know just what we're facing. Quite apart from Leggo's figures, we're now pretty certain there are Mig fighters within easy reach of King Boffa Port and we suspect there are at least two—if not more—Russian submarines within striking distance of this convoy. How much of this is known at home, I'm not sure. They seem to know precious little, and I'm proposing to tell them, not because I'm afraid of what might happen to us but because I feel they should still have the opportunity to withdraw from this adventure if they feel they ought. I want to know what your views are on this operation. I should point out that any final decision will be mine. Cal, what do you feel?'

Calhoun glanced at the others. He was obviously very unhappy at being the first to speak. It was an invidious position he was in, especially if all the others were to disagree with him.

He swallowed, lit a cigarette and drew a long puff at it.

'I'm a bit worried about it,' he said at length.

The others glanced up quickly at him and Hodges leaned forward.

'Would you like to enlarge on that, Cal?' he prompted.

'Yes.' Calhoun blew out a cloud of smoke. 'I've thought for some time that *Stabledoor* wasn't properly equipped for what it's expected to do. Our gear's not even as good as the Malalans' and it's not interchangeable. It seems now that not enough thought was put into it at home. I think the whole plan was rushed at the beginning, and it's been stop-go ever since, with nobody in London willing to go the whole hog.'

He paused and went on cautiously, choosing his words with care. 'Because the Reservists were restless, we dismantled bridges and re-wired the camp,' he said, 'but it was collective training they needed, not that. As for the vehicles, half of 'em are over-age and a lot of their fittings were missing and never did turn up, and all the changes of plan have caused considerable confusion in the loading. The force had to be tactically embarked and it's a fundamental principle that what the men need first must be embarked last. But after all the changes we've had from London, we'll probably find that when we arrive the equipment'll bear little relation to what we need. Some of the stuff, I'm told, belongs to units which aren't even taking part any longer, and I know for a fact that half my gear's in one ship and half in another. With what's been happening in individual units, I think it sounds very tricky, but I'd like to reserve my final opinion until I've heard the others.'

'That's fair enough. Dixon?'

Dixon took off his spectacles and polished them. Without them, he looked more myopic and somehow less sure of himself. He replaced the spectacles on his nose and cleared his throat.

'I think we should go in,' he said firmly. 'I know we've heard a lot about what we're likely to face, but I think we can discount some of it. I think it's been exaggerated by people with the wind-up.'

'Who, for instance?' Neville asked aggressively.

Dixon waved a hand. 'Oh, nobody in particular,' he said. 'Intelligence, generally. I think also we're over-estimating how much these people are supporting Scepwe.'

Leggo interrupted. 'My information, sir, is that they're solidly behind him. They don't wish to be part of Malala and, in fact, originally they never were. They were an independent kingdom but got swept in when Macmillan's "wind of change" began to alter the face of Africa. They never settled down and they've taken the first opportunity to opt out. And it so happens that our treaty was with the Malalans and not with the Khanzians, and they don't want a British base there.'

'International base,' Dixon put in. 'That was the agreement.'

'That's a lot of old rope,' Neville rapped out. 'That was just to cover the politicians. It's a British base and always was.'

'A treaty's a treaty!'

'Only so long as both sides agree on it. When they don't, the whole bloody thing falls to pieces.'

'Gentlemen!' Hodges stopped the argument in its tracks. 'Shall we try not to stray?'

Dixon looked vaguely sulky, as though he were defending his views simply for the sake of it and in the teeth of the facts. 'We mustn't ever forget that the Khanzian troops were never of the best,' he said. 'They're not like the Nigerians.'

'They've been trained by Ghanaian officers,' Neville growled. He didn't seem to like Dixon very much.

'That doesn't make them good troops.'

Hodges cut them short before the discussion became acrimonious again, and turned to Reading.

The Marine looked puzzled. 'Well,' he said, 'the landing ships we've got are mostly obsolete and my chaps haven't had much chance to practice amphibious work. They've been doing internal security duties in Malta. And if the Khanzians have got the latest Soviet tanks then we haven't got the anti-tank guns to knock 'em out. Our signals equipment's indifferent and the radio links on the whole have been bad.' He gave a short humourless laugh. 'I'd say it'll be easier to get our information from the B.B.C. news than from Pepul. Still,' he paused, 'it'd be disastrous to call it off now, especially if it had to be put on again later. I say go.'

'Thank you. Rattray?'

Rattray glanced at Reading uncomfortably, as though he disagreed with him and didn't fancy saying so. His hands moved over a book he was holding and Hodges saw the title—*Das Vollständig Panzerbuch*. Rattray was obviously a man who took his job seriously and did a lot of homework.

' "A" Squadron of the 7th/9th Tanks,' he said slowly, 'spent the last two years detached for demonstration duties at the Infantry School. The men of "B" Squadron were without their vehicles and attached to the Territorials. The rest were on garrison duty at their base at Bilworth. There was no chance to get the men together, and shooting practice's been out of the question. They've got old vehicles and they're damn' short of stores and training. It's the same with the 4th/6th, and these Soviet tanks the Khanzians have got are outstanding. Speed, manœuvrability, fire power and armour leave nothing to be desired, and their turret designs reduce vulnerability to a direct hit to nil. If I'm told to go, I'll go and do the best I can, but I'd be dishonest if I said I thought it'd be easy.'

Hodges swung in his chair towards Downes, whose languor disappeared as he sat up. 'I'm of the same mind as Calhoun,' he said sharply. 'Not enough's been put into this from London, and there's no sense of certainty at home—even now. My orders are that we're not to fire on shore installations except with secondary armament, and that we're not to touch civilian areas. What sort of order's that? If anyone lobs anything at my ships, I shall give orders to flatten it with anything we've got. If men's lives are involved, then I'll take the responsibility. Concerning morale, I'm not happy about the crews. There are too many Reserve officers, who've a lot to lose and nothing to gain, and too many Reservist seamen who think now like trade unionists. I'm not happy about *Stabledoor* and if the people at home were to signal that it was all off, then I'd be the first man to cheer.'

'I think that would be my attitude exactly,' Calhoun said.

Hodges tried hard to avoid showing any kind of feeling, and turned to Neville.

'How about the R.A.F.?'

Neville's attitude was uncompromising. 'With respect, sir,' he snapped, 'I think the whole bloody operation was dreamed up by a half-witted deaf-mute in between visits to the heads. According to Leggo's information, we can expect our jets to be outflown by Scepwe's Migs and we've known all along that side-loading transports for the parachutists are out of date. What's more, we'll be flying into the sun in the early morning, but the sun-vizors we asked for never arrived and that won't help to make the pilots more accurate with their sticks. The helicopter planning at home was bad, too. I think our people have let their prickly pride get them into this one and they're anxious now not to back down in case they lose face. I expect it's politics they're worried about, if the truth were known, and I suppose they're busy counting votes. It may not have escaped your notice that there's an election due in a year's time and this seems to me a good time for a bit of poker playing. It's all or nothing. If they fail to pull this one off, they'll lose nothing, because public opinion polls seem to indicate they'll be out on their ears, anyway. But, by God, sir, if they *do* pull it off, they're in again. We all know that. I think the P.M.'s gambling again, sir. He gambled at Singapore, and by the grace of God, it came off, and like all gamblers he thinks the circumstances are the same and it'll come off again. I think the whole thing stinks, sir. I've got a job to do and I'll do as I'm told to the best of my ability because I can't afford to resign, but by God, I don't take much pride in it.'

Hodges warmed to Neville's abrupt forthrightness, thoroughly agreeing with everything he said. Nevertheless, he was surprised that it was the R.A.F. man, with his bang-on reputation, who'd shown the most shrewdness.

'Leggo,' he went on. 'I think you should let us have your views.'

Leggo frowned. 'With respect, General,' he said, 'I think not. My information was unofficial and I hold no command.'

Hodges managed a wry smile. He wasn't sure how much Leggo's refusal stemmed from honesty and how much from a desire to avoid responsibility. If a wrong decision were taken and he weren't associated with it, his chances of promotion wouldn't be damaged.

'Very well,' he said. 'My own opinion's somewhere around centre, I must admit.' He stood up. 'Gentlemen, I'm seriously considering sending a signal home to the effect that I have the gravest doubts about *Stabledoor*. I have an uneasy feeling that we have another Dieppe in the making, and I've no desire to be responsible for it.'

He turned away. 'And now, let's all have a drink.'

They began to rise and Leggo offered drinks round. Hodges was just about to raise his glass to his lips when he caught sight of Neville standing with his head on one side.

'Listen,' the airman said. 'What's that?'

They were all silent for a second. Above the hum of the ship's turbines and the muffled sounds of movement from outside, they could hear voices.

'Shouting,' Leggo said.

The sound was disjointed and disconnected, but as they listened it seemed to clot and congeal and the shouts became one.

'That's not shouting,' Neville snapped. 'That's cheering.'

5

It had been raining in London and the streets were wet and shining and, across the open spaces of Westminster where people hurried close to the walls out of the rain, the taxis turned the corners with whining tyres and a thin spray of water from their wheels.

There was a break in the clouds over towards Tower Bridge and the Prime Minister, catching sight of it from his official car as it turned into Whitehall, wondered if it were symbolic of some similar ray of light in the political scene.

It had been a rowdy session of Parliament. When the House had met, the news of the result of the General Assembly debate in New York was still coming in; and the Leader of the Opposition had at once asked the Prime Minister if the Government were prepared to accept the decision of the United Nations for a halt in whatever operations were contemplated in Africa.

Taking advantage of the fact that one or two of the new African nations, still very conscious of British financial help, had voted against the resolution and that there had been one or two abstentions from Commonwealth countries not involved, the Prime Minister had replied that he needed time to study the resolution and the speeches. The Leader of the Opposition had expressed his dismay and a long bitter wrangle had followed. The General Assembly had been described as a majority which the Government in all honour had to accept, and there had been one or two speeches from the Africa Group of Government back-benchers who claimed they were sick and tired of the Opposition's ability to side with the enemies of the country. But the Prime Minister had noticed that the speeches had been surprisingly half-hearted, and that at least one Member behind him had spoken out firmly against *Stable-door*, considering that the Prime Minister's attitude was intolerable at a time when the prestige and good name of the country had already reached the very bottom.

While a lot of the Opposition's reaction had not been sincere, and the Prime Minister knew it was not sincere but an attempt to make party capital out of his difficulties, he was well aware that underlying it all there was also a great deal of distaste and unhappiness at the names that were being thrown at England.

'Bombs will be dropped,' the Leader of the Opposition had said bitterly. 'Men will be killed and buildings will be destroyed. No matter what the Prime Minister might call it—and he can describe the operation as a police operation as much as he likes—what will happen in Africa cannot to my mind be called anything else but war. All the words in the dictionary can't alter that fact, and if we are not careful we shall not only be at war, but will also have been labelled the aggressors.'

The Prime Minister moved restlessly inside his overcoat. Carey's speech had seemed a little holier-than-thou, and he didn't quite see it that way. To him, the operation was proof that Britain, like anyone else, had the prerogative to stand up for her rights. Everyone else had been standing up for their rights ever since World War II and, as a result, Great Britain had lost her empire and the Commonwealth no longer had much meaning, and he had determined when the crisis had first blown up that this time Britain should stand up for herself. It had therefore come as a surprise that the rest of the world had not seen it that way. What was standing up for rights in smaller countries was apparently aggression in big ones, especially where they had a record of imperialism behind them.

The Prime Minister frowned. It seemed these days, after years of being in favour, that the current was running against him. The meeting at Rudkin and Hale had been a disaster and the lunch and dinner addresses had quite failed to draw sympathy. It was, in fact, the first time he had ever heard of a Prime Minister being booed by members of an august chamber of commerce. He had tried to have things explained to the lobby correspondents later but somehow that had not come off, either, as the results in the newspapers showed.

As the car stopped outside Number Ten, the policeman on duty saluted. The Prime Minister caught a glimpse of a crowd, thinned down by rain, cold and boredom, and a few faces that obviously belonged to students. Miraculously banners appeared.

'JAW NOT WAR', he saw at once. And 'WAIT, DON'T HATE', and the usual lunatic 'THE END OF THE WORLD IS NIGH' as some crackpot tried to muscle in on the scene.

He flinched at the storm of booing as he headed for the open door of his official residence. He had always had a reputation of not being able to handle hecklers and, like Carey, he'd never had the 'Constituency Smile', so that, in spite of his long experience of politics, he knew he had never conquered his dislike of being unpopular.

As he crossed the black and white tiled floor, passing the second policeman without a glance, the door shut behind him and the storm of protest outside was abruptly muted. His Principal Private Secretary appeared as the manservant helped him off with his coat.

'They're all here, Prime Minister,' he said briskly. 'With the exception of the Chief of Defence Staff. His office rang and said he'd been delayed but that he was on his way.'

The Prime Minister nodded and, moving along the red-carpeted corridor with its busts of Pitt, Melbourne and Disraeli and the photographs of past Cabinets and Imperial Conferences, he opened the door of the Cabinet Room. It seemed to be full of people. Some of them were sitting at the long green-baize-covered table and others were standing in groups talking. The Foreign Minister stood beneath the drab portrait of Walpole, who had always been one of the Prime Minister's heroes. For a long time he had liked to see himself as the man who had also kept England great without foreign adventures, building up her economy rather than her army, and as he stopped in the doorway he felt bitter that, having run down the Services like Walpole, he now found himself in a position when he was having to call on them to rescue him from a situation which was not of his making.

As the doors closed behind him, the other men turned to face him. The Home Secretary, a tall lean man with cold grey eyes behind his rimless spectacles, straightened up alongside the table where all the newspapers were kept. He didn't join in the greetings of the others but moved silently to his place among the mahogany and black chairs. Someone had switched the lights on against the grey light of the day and the old panelling gleamed faintly in the glow.

The Prime Minister sat down in silence before the green scrambler telephone and the panel of buzzers. As though it were a signal, the others also began to take their seats, and red leather document boxes were opened.

'I've called you here today,' the Prime Minister began, 'because I've had rather a disturbing signal from Hodgeforce. It's one I feel you should know about and one on which I feel I need your advice.'

His Parliamentary Private Secretary placed a file in front of him labelled *Stabledoor* and he opened it quickly. On top of a series of decoded telegrams that the Foreign Office had sent across, Hodges' signal lay in front of him, to the Prime Minister as dangerous as a bomb.

'The Commander-in-Chief of Hodgeforce,' he went on, 'has originated this signal and its implications are so serious I felt I needed to know more about it. General Hodges is now at sea with the rest of Hodgeforce heading for King Boffa Port. Together with one or two members of the Inner Cabinet, I took the decision that set the ships in motion after the rioting that ended the lives of a number of British nationals at Boffa and Sarges. For the most part, you were not involved. Now, however, you *have* become involved. I need your help.'

He picked up the flimsies on which Hodges' signal was printed and read them slowly.

'General Hodges' message is a long one and he makes it quite clear that he's in no way questioning his instructions. He's only concerned with the ability of the force under his command to do what it's set out to do. This, he feels, would not have been easy at the best of times but, now, he feels he's faced with a new problem. It seems there's been disaffection among the troops.'

There was a startled murmur from among the men round the long table. The Service chiefs tried to avoid the eyes that were directed towards them, and the Prime Minister coughed to gather their attention once more.

'Now, gentlemen,' he went on, 'you'll all know what's happening. The Khanzian radio has already started a loud outcry blaming us for the deaths in the rioting. This is all incorrect and specific orders were issued to Hodgeforce that civilians were to be protected; and these riots are not of our doing.'

'It's never easy to particularise,' the Foreign Secretary said. He was a short plump man with a reputation for being difficult to pin down, but he was one of the abler members of the Cabinet whose reputation had largely sprung from his detestation of the newspaper and television interviewers who tried to get him to speak without a prepared statement. He had long since been accepted as the man most likely to step into the Prime Minister's shoes.

He gestured as the Prime Minister looked at him. 'It's one of the things we have to accept,' he said quietly.

The Prime Minister frowned. 'Undoubtedly,' he said. 'Although the orders are that civilians are not to be harmed, it's still obviously going to be difficult to direct a bomb exactly. And bombs will have to be dropped and guns will have to be fired. Perhaps we can do something about that, but this is not why we're here. General Hodges reports that there's a great deal of dissatisfaction over this operation among the men, and that most units are affected. The chief problem seems to be that the troops consider they have the right to object to what's taking place and they're acting accordingly.'

He glanced at the paper in his hand. 'There's a high incidence of unserviceability in the R.A.F., and at least one of the British escort vessels taking part has dropped out of the convoy with engine trouble due to suspected sabotage. There have also been cases among the military units of lost and even damaged equipment. General Hodges also reports meetings in canteens—meetings in protest against *Stabledoor*.

'Now, gentlemen, you have the facts as I have them. The fleet is due off King Boffa Port three days from now and the R.A.F. will go in when it arrives to soften up the place. It was my belief when this project was authorised that a landing would be virtually unopposed, and even welcome, and it was with this is mind that we took the decision to launch *Stabledoor*. It was my belief also that this country was behind us.'

The Foreign Secretary coughed. 'The country may be,

Prime Minister,' he said, 'though, with respect, I have begun to doubt it, but we have certainly made many enemies abroad. Ambassadors' reports show a grave disquiet in European countries and, further east, our embassies have actually been stoned. In Jakarta, our embassy has been burned down and totally destroyed by a mob of students. There's also mounting American anger—I might even say fury—because many of our ships and troops carry American equipment. They're objecting very strongly to this on the grounds that it was provided against Russian aggression in Europe or Chinese aggression in the Pacific, and that it was never intended to be used for British aggression in Africa.'

He stopped, looking like a man who had had an unpleasant task to perform and was glad it was over and done with. The Prime Minister stared angrily at him, fully aware that the interruption would swing the talk away from the point he wished to debate.

'One can't rush to put out a fire without treading on someone's toes,' he snapped.

'Or without a great deal of cost to the taxpayer,' the Chancellor of the Exchequer commented gloomily, diverting exactly as the Prime Minister had feared. 'There's not the slightest doubt, Prime Minister, this is going to involve us in a vast expense which is bound to have an effect on the next Budget. And that,' he reminded, 'is at a time when we're expecting to go to the country within a matter of months. It's usual to be more optimistic at that time.'

The Prime Minister was about to reply when the Foreign Secretary interposed again, his manner determined as though he had decided that he must have his facts known before the Prime Minister could sweep them aside.

'There's one more thing,' he said, 'that you ought to know. The Russian leaders haven't been seen for forty-eight hours and, while this in itself is unusual, it's also been noticed that Marshal Yostopov didn't turn up at the Bolshoi Theatre last night when he was expected, and Marshals Younich and Bastroi failed to put in an appearance at an embassy party.' He paused and gestured. 'Yostopov, Prime Minister, is the man they expect to head the Army in case of any involvement, and Younich and Bastroi, as I'm sure you know, are the heads of the Navy and the Air Force. I have to confess I find this very worrying, particularly as I'm now pretty certain that both the Americans and the African states have been getting at President Braka of Malala.'

The Prime Minister's eyes narrowed, his own attention diverted now. 'Getting at him?' he said. 'How?'

The Foreign Secretary shrugged. 'It's my information,' he said, 'that the African Group of States are threatening him with an economic boycott if he persists in supporting us, and that the Americans are offering him a thumping big loan if he doesn't. Two hundred million dollars is the figure I've heard.'

The Prime Minister sat back in his chair, stunned, his train of thought broken, but, as though to pile on the agony, the Home Secretary, two seats down the table, now looked up and began to speak. He was a dynamic man who had served in a number of governments and not only was he experienced in office, but he was also considered to be something of an expert in war. As War Minister in Starke's previous government, he had been sent to the Ministry of Defence to integrate and re-organise the Services after years of neglect. He hadn't been over-successful because the unexpected need for economies had thwarted him, and the Prime Minister always felt it was held against him that the Home Secretary's ideas in those days had never been carried through.

'There have been refusals to load arms at the docks,' he was saying, and the Prime Minister got the impression that the members of his Cabinet were growing alarmed at the trend of events started up by *Stabledoor*.

'I thought we'd decided to use Reservists in that eventuality,' he said coldly.

'They'd been in touch with the dockers and had to be called off,' the Home Secretary pointed out. 'There were also riots in Oxford yesterday. And the Strand, Haymarket and the Mall had to be closed to traffic for three hours owing to student demonstrations.'

'Spontaneous combustion,' the Prime Minister snapped.

'I think not,' the Home Secretary retorted. 'There were far too many students involved and I don't think they were all from London. I intend to find out.'

'What if they weren't?'

'Students' Unions these days have become politically conscious and very militant and, ever since 1967, they've been prepared to throw their weight behind any cause they consider worthwhile. I think this could be dangerous.' The Home Secretary paused. 'There were several casualties, which are always a bad thing, and one child—a girl of eighteen from the London School of Economics—has died in St. Luke's Hospital.'

The Prime Minister looked grave. 'I'd like a report on this, please, Home Secretary,' he said quickly. 'I don't think we should be unduly alarmed yet, but if someone was to blame for the child's death we must do something about it. It can't be laid at the door of the Government.'

The Home Secretary nodded and made a note on a sheet of paper in front of him.

'I'm not so interested at the moment in reactions at home, however,' the Prime Minister went on before anyone else could interrupt. 'I'm more concerned at the moment with *Operation Stabledoor*. Can we please return to it? General Hodges has been making enquiries about the incidence of disaffection among his troops, and he's summarised these for me. He reports cheering between ships which is clearly organised, and he suspects, though he can't find out exactly, that it's between troops who have no other means of direct communication, to indicate their solidarity. He believes this solidarity is against the operation they're now engaged upon, and he reports thirty per cent mechanical failure in R.A.F. machines.' He glanced at the R.A.F. officer down the table. 'What would you say is the limit to which we can go, Air Marshal, before such failure could endanger the operation?'

'Twenty-five per cent, sir,' the R.A.F. man said immediately.

The Prime Minister was clearly startled. 'He reports ten per cent in the Navy.' He glanced at the sharp-featured admiral slumped over his papers.

'Ten per cent is the limit, sir,' the naval man said.

'And fifteen per cent among army vehicles.'

'We can go up to twenty per cent, Prime Minister.'

The Prime Minister frowned. He was just going to speak again when the door opened and the Chief of Defence Staff appeared.

General Viscount Burnaston was a tall man, with a hawk-like face. He was related by marriage to the Royal Family, but had managed, by his ability, to overcome all political opposition to him on this score.

'Prime Minister,' he nodded.

'I'm glad you've managed to arrive,' the Prime Minister said coldly. 'You've just come in time. I'm anxious to hear more about *Stabledoor*. This signal of Hodges has me worried.'

'Has me worried, too, Prime Minister,' Burnaston said briskly.

'You've seen Hodges' signal and you'll know what Service chiefs consider the limit we can go to in unreliability?'

'I know that, Prime Minister.'

'It seems we're on the wrong side, doesn't it?'

'It does indeed. But a good general can overcome that if he has to. It's been done before and it can be done again.'

The Prime Minister felt vaguely relieved. It seemed that the Chief of Defence Staff was prepared, in the teeth of opposition, to throw his weight behind *Stabledoor*.

'Hodges claims that there's disaffection in his command,' he said. 'Is he an able commander?'

'The best. He's been one of our chief fire-fighters for years. He knows the ropes.'

'Then why is he so worried?'

The Chief of Defence Staff's brows came down over glittering eyes and the Prime Minister saw at once that he'd been mistaken. Burnaston was not on his side.

'If Hodges is worried,' Burnaston said sharply, 'then he has good cause to worry. I've known him a long time and I've never known him bleat unnecessarily.'

'What's your view?' the Prime Minister asked more slowly.

'That he's probably dead right. I can't tell at this distance, but there've been quite a few demonstrations against *Stabledoor* at home, and I see no reason to be surprised if there are some abroad, or in our own force. Not these days.'

The Prime Minister frowned. 'I thought we could rely on our troops,' he snapped.

'Prime Minister,' Burnaston turned his icy glance down the table, 'if I may speak without appearing to be disrespectful, you can't expect men to have their heart on risking their lives when the pay they get for it's just been cut.'

'Are you suggesting it was a mistake?'

'The Services were against it from the start. But, as we were told it was an economic necessity, we accepted it. We didn't like the way the Government announced it—on television when it ought to have been a more personal affair which the troops should have heard before the general public—but we went along with that, too. However, we mustn't be surprised if we find it's now causing trouble when we have to use these same troops in a fire-fighting operation.'

The Prime Minister glanced hopefully at the Chancellor of the Exchequer who shook his head emphatically.

'There's little opportunity of an increase just now.

Starke frowned. 'We must *make* an opportunity,' he said.

'Prime Minister,' the Chief of Defence Staff leaned forward, 'with respect, *not* now. It'd seem too much as though we were giving way to pressure. Next month, when all this is over, yes. Next year, yes. But not now, though, of course, there could be no objection to a promise.'

The Prime Minister frowned. 'Very well,' he said. 'I must confess, I'm very worried about Hodges' signal. Disaffection's a thing which isn't normal in British troops.'

'It was in the Thirties,' Burnaston pointed out quietly. 'And for the same reason—pay.'

'But surely,' the Prime Minister gestured angrily, 'since it's occurred, the commander on the spot ought to be able to deal with it.'

The Chief of Defence Staff heaved his bulk round in his chair, almost as though he were turning his back on the Prime Minister, even as though he'd lost patience.

'It would have been easier,' he said, 'if they could have announced a month ago that the pay cuts were being restored —even if only partially.'

'We couldn't do it,' the Chancellor of the Exchequer snapped. 'We'd just had to borrow one thousand million dollars from the United States and similar sums from the International and Swiss Banks. They were insisting that we make some effort to cut our expenses. We were trying to.'

'We could have cut a few other services,' the Chief of Defence Staff rapped back. 'It never seems to me to make much sense to subsidise houses for people earning fifty pounds a week, or to give golf and ski-ing lessons at after-educational establishments. This could save us a great deal more than Service cuts.'

'It wasn't possible,' the Prime Minister said gruffly.

'It never is,' the Chief of Defence Staff said bluntly. 'It might lose votes.' He was a very wealthy man and he was not afraid to speak his mind. 'The Services are also conscious that when it was proposed to cut Civil Service pay, their unions protested vigorously. It must have seemed to Servicemen that, since they don't have unions, it was easier to cut *their* pay.'

The Prime Minister was about to speak but Burnaston continued steadily. 'I realise I'm being harsh,' he said. 'But I have to say it. I wasn't in this country and therefore wasn't asked my opinion when the cuts were decided on and I have to make my protest now. However . . .'

There was a silence as they waited for his next comment. There was a vague feeling of discomfort in the room—as though, the Foreign Secretary said later, someone had turned up a severed hand in the green salad at a city banquet.

'. . . however, the trouble in Pepul and with the force now at sea is not *entirely* due to cuts in pay. There are too many of the wrong sort of men in this operation. Due to the running down over the years of Service establishments, we had no alternative but to call for men wherever we could get them. Inevitably, we got the wrong ones. It would be better—and I've always advocated this—to have less regiments and make them good ones. A large number of regiments looks re-assuring on paper but it's meaningless if they're not up to strength and if the quality of the men serving in them isn't what we want.'

The Prime Minister was frowning heavily now. He had always disliked the Chief of Defence Staff's habit of using every opportunity he could to air his grievances, and he wished now, as he had often wished, that Burnaston either wasn't so brilliant as to be indispensable or less wealthy so that he couldn't afford to be so forthright.

'It could be'—the Chief of Defence Staff moved his papers restlessly—'that the trouble with Hodgeforce is caused by the knowledge of what's ahead. I've had a very disturbing signal from Hodges about what opposition to expect at King Boffa

Port. It seems his Chief-of-Staff picked up certain figures—
and *they don't match ours.*'

'I suppose we have to thank Intelligence for letting us down
over that,' the Prime Minister said tartly.

The Chief of Defence Staff smiled grimly. 'Yes, Prime
Minister,' he said. 'Military Intelligence can't ever hope to
function effectively as a civilian civil service department.'

The Prime Minister kept his eyes down as Burnaston
trumped his ace with the reminder that he personally had removed Intelligence from the sphere of the military three years
before on the grounds that it had become *too* secretive.

'Nevertheless'—the Chief of Defence Staff gestured—'it isn't
in my opinion the opposition to be expected that has caused
the trouble with General Hodges' force. I had my own ideas
about that and I sent him a signal. His signal in reply confirms
what I thought.'

All eyes in the room turned towards him and, for a moment,
there was silence.

'The slogan of the disaffected men,' Burnaston went on
quietly, 'seems to be "Right of Reply", and that phrase, Prime
Minister, was used only a few days ago in a party television
and radio broadcast made by the Leader of the Opposition.'

The Prime Minister frowned. He'd fought hard to prevent
Carey going on the air, but it had been difficult to claim the
country was at war when all the time he was trying to say in
Parliament that she wasn't. And so long as she wasn't at war,
any political party had the right of reply to the Government in
the form of a party political broadcast. It seemed now that the
troops felt that right was theirs, too.

'What do you suggest, then?' the Prime Minister asked
angrily. 'That we should ask the Leader of the Opposition to
retract what he said in that broadcast?'

The Chief of Defence Staff nodded immediately. 'Yes, sir,'
he said bluntly. 'I do.'

The Prime Minister stared. 'I can't do that,' he snapped.

The Chief of Defence Staff laid his hands on the table in
front of him, palms down, as though he had come to the end
of the argument. 'I'm afraid,' he said, 'if you don't want a
disaster on your hands, you'll have to.'

6

The Leader of the Opposition had had a house near Brighton for years. Originally, it had been his parents' home, but on his marriage and their retirement, they had exchanged dwellings and his family had grown up in it. On his election to Parliament, he had considered selling it, although it had always been a useful retreat when London became too much for him, and he had so quickly made his mark in his party that he had soon found the need for something big enough to be used to meet his colleagues and the foreign diplomats who had done him the courtesy of meeting him.

It was a Georgian house, as gracious as only Georgian houses can be, set a little back off the main road from London, and sufficiently hidden by trees to be out of sight of snoopers. Its interior was graced by family portraits dating back through several generations and its exterior by a garden that had lasted almost as long.

It was to this house that George Greenaway, a member of the party in office, discreetly rang with a request to see the Leader of the Opposition.

Greenaway was one of the elders of the party in power. He had held office, but not for some years, and he was now on the verge of retirement from politics altogether. The Prime Minister had chosen him to contact the Opposition because he was a respected Member of the House and his name had never at any time been linked with anything even remotely underhand. Indeed, at the time of the trouble over Aden, he had resigned his office rather than lend his support to something of which he couldn't approve. He had the respect, not only of his own party, but also of the Opposition; and Carey always got on well with him, despite their differing views.

As he put down the telephone, he turned to Moffat who was sitting in the deep armchair opposite him, waiting for him to finish.

'Greenaway,' Carey explained. 'He wants to see me. I wonder if it's anything to do with *that.*'

That was the highly secret arrival of another message—from certain back-benchers of the party in office, who had expressed themselves as being so concerned with the trend of events that they were prepared if necessary to cross the floor and vote with the Opposition.

Moffat gestured. He didn't place much reliance on the back-benchers' message, and was even inclined to doubt its good faith.

'It *could*,' he said. 'But so what, Spencer? Greenaway makes only one more and we've known for years that he didn't entirely agree. As for the others, they won't make much difference to the situation. Starke's got a sound majority and there aren't enough of them to affect it much.'

Carey considered for a moment before speaking. 'It's a sign, all the same,' he said. 'Think they could gather a few more into the fold?'

'I don't give them much of a chance.'

'Neither do I, quite honestly,' Carey agreed. 'There aren't many M.P.s these days who're prepared to risk withdrawal of Party support on a matter of principle. Nevertheless, it's there, Derek, and it's a trend in our direction. You know what set it off, of course?'

'Yes.' Moffat smiled. 'Marchmant and Harding. I don't suppose they ever expected when they were demobbed that they'd ever be called up again. It was unfortunate for Starke that when they were, they were involved in *Stabledoor* and able to give tongue about all the inadequacies.'

'To *me*, Derek,' Carey said in a quiet voice.

'To *you?*' Moffat's jaw dropped.

'To me. They came to me *first*. That's where I got all my information and that's why I believe this little rebellion might be more than it seems. They insisted that I mustn't quote them, but it was quite clear they didn't expect to get any change out of Starke.'

Moffat leaned forward. 'Does Starke know about it?' he asked.

'I don't know.'

'It'd spoil his meals for a day or two if he did.'

'That, and the by-election at Rudkin and Hale. I gather our people are delighted with the way it's going.' Carey jabbed a finger abruptly at the newspaper that lay open on his desk. 'I just hope,' he said, 'that the Chinese in Korea don't save him. They *could* just turn everybody's attention away from him if they did something outrageous. That's why he keeps trying to make so much of it, of course.'

'What's our move then?'

'There are a few,' Carey said slowly, 'who still feel the situation can be saved with a coalition. Obviously no one wants an election just now, and they feel that with a few ex-Ministers from our side in with him, it might suit the country's mood. I know Starke's considered it, too, as a way out of his problems.'

'Would you agree?'

'Not under Starke. There *are* men I could accept—for a limited period, until the crisis is over.'

'Do you think that's why Greenaway's coming?'

'Let's wait and see, shall we?'

Carey met Greenaway as he came through the door, appearing down the long curving staircase at the back of the hall rather like an actor making an entrance. Greenaway smiled at him as he handed over his hat and coat, and looked round at the hall with its white-painted balustrade and the sombre old pictures.

'I always did like this place,' he commented as they moved towards the study.

'It's a pity we don't agree more,' Carey said. 'You could then come here more often.'

In the study, they sat at opposite sides of the fireplace.

'You know why I'm here, Spencer, of course?' Greenaway asked.

Carey inclined his head. 'I've made a guess,' he said.

Greenaway nodded. 'It had to be done,' he pointed out. 'They chose me, because I'm the safest. If what I've come to do doesn't come off and the story leaks out, they can disclaim me and say I acted without instructions. On the other hand, if it *does* come off, then they can claim all the credit. I'm too old to care much either way now, and they know it.'

The Leader of the Opposition made no comment. He knew as well as Greenaway that what had been said was true.

'It's a very worrying situation,' Greenaway went on.

'More for your side than mine,' Carey said. 'Much as I deplore it, I have to admit to myself that my party can do nothing but profit by it. It's a long time since we were in office.'

Greenaway sipped his drink and didn't reply, and Carey went on quietly.

'I feel the country's ready for a change,' he said, as Greenaway raised his eyebrows. 'Rudkin and Hale's going against you, George.'

Greenaway's mouth twisted. 'Can you be certain?' he asked.

'As certain as I can be of anything.'

'It was always *our* seat.'

'It won't be this time.'

Greenaway drew a deep breath. 'I hope that won't make it any harder for me to say what I have to say,' he observed.

Carey smiled. 'Try it,' he suggested, 'and see.'

Greenaway gestured. 'It all seems a bit pointless when you know why I've come,' he said.

Carey smiled again. 'We have to do it properly,' he pointed out. 'We have to follow protocol—even in this—and it has to be said, so that it's on the record for the future.'

'In fact,' Greenaway said quietly, 'this is *off* the record.'

The Leader of the Opposition nodded. 'I thought it might be,' he said.

'The Prime Minister's worried.'

'So he should be.'

'You don't like him very much, do you, Spencer?'

'I'm afraid I don't really trust him.'

Greenaway tried a new tack. 'If this thing against King Boffa Port fails,' he said, 'not only would we stand condemned in the eyes of the rest of the world, we'd also be humiliated, too.'

'That's Starke's fault,' Carey said. 'His alone.'

Greenaway's gesture was suddenly faintly irritable. 'We accepted the role of aggressors,' he said quickly. 'Having done so, we shouldn't be asked to renounce the essential benefits we could derive from that aggression. If this thing succeeded, Scepwe'd be finished and his regime would collapse. It'd be a capital political error not to go ahead with it now. We're within two or three days of pulling it off.'

The Leader of the Opposition's eyebrows rose. 'Are we?' he asked. 'My information's rather different. I understand we have a very high incidence of mechanical failure in all three Services, so high, in fact, that there's a danger that the thing will fall apart when it has to take the strain.'

Greenaway nodded. 'I've heard that, too,' he admitted. 'But it's not the mechanical failure that's worrying the Prime Minister and the Chief of Defence Staff. It's something else. It seems the operation's more likely to fall apart through disaffection among the troops.'

Carey's face changed subtly and he eyed Greenaway warily. 'Perhaps I *don't* know why you've come, George,' he said. 'I'd heard it was to make an appeal for us to support him. I can't do that, George.'

Greenaway brushed aside the suggestion. 'That's not why I've come,' he said. 'It's suspected that this disaffection among the troops sprang from that speech you made the other day.'

Carey was looking puzzled now and Greenaway pressed on.

'You said you'd claimed from the B.B.C. the right of reply, and you said that every man had this right. That's the crux of the matter.'

Carey leaned forward. 'Go on,' he encouraged.

'Someone in Hodgeforce,' Greenaway continued, '—and we don't know who, perhaps several people—seized on this point and it spread like wildfire. No one seems to know where it started, but the phrase seems to have become some sort of rallying call. There are a great many men with Hodges who don't agree with this operation . . .'

'There are a great many at home, too,' Carey snapped.

'This is war,' Greenaway said quickly. 'They can't disagree.'

Carey jerked a hand. 'The Prime Minister insists it *isn't* war,' he pointed out.

Greenaway shrugged. 'That's politics,' he said.

Carey frowned. 'So's my speech,' he said quickly.

Greenaway looked at him, his eyes challenging. 'Were you after office?' he asked. 'Was that why you made it?'

Carey's hesitation was only momentary but Greenaway noticed it.

'Whether it was or not,' Carey said, 'I still believed every word I said. With the world in two great camps, and the threat of the Bomb over us, no one has a right to go to war over a piffling little base. Good God, we can get another base. There are enough African states who're sufficiently short of money to be prepared to turn over some of their territory to us in return for financial help.'

Greenaway realised he was getting into the deep water of a political argument, and that he wasn't doing the job he'd come to do. He drew a deep breath and took the plunge.

'He wants you to withdraw,' he said abruptly.

The Leader of the Opposition had sat back, faintly shocked. 'Withdraw?'

'That's what he wants. Your speech couldn't have come at a worse time and, unfortunately, it's given the impression that you're being meddlesome, awkward and dangerous.'

Carey was staring at him, annoyed. He'd been fully aware how dangerous politically his speech could seem, but he'd put his doubts aside, and the thought that crossed his mind now was how much damage it might have done—not only to Hodgeforce, as Greenaway suggested, but also to himself and his party.

Greenaway interrupted his uneasy musings. 'He wants you to speak again,' he said. 'If you can't go that far, he wants you at least to withdraw your remarks.'

The Leader of the Opposition sat for a moment in silence, then he got to his feet and moved to the window.

'He says England's committed,' Greenaway went on, 'and that at this stage it's impossible to call Hodgeforce off.'

'It's never impossible!' Carey swung round and snapped the words.

'From the information he has,' Greenaway insisted, 'together with what *you* said, there could be failure.'

'Then let him call it off!'

Greenaway turned in his chair. 'He's not prepared to,' he said. 'He claims—and I think he believes it—that we've too much to lose, and that our prestige would be lower if we called it off than if we took a chance and succeeded.'

'He's quite right, of course,' Carey agreed calmly. 'Politically, he's quite right, but ethically and morally, he's dead wrong. If he's in any doubt, he should never have started it.'

'You hadn't made your speech then,' Greenaway pointed out. 'You know as well as anyone that there's a great deal of guesswork to any military operation, and what wasn't allowed for is the effect that speech of yours has had. The ball's in your court, Spencer, whether you like it or not.'

Carey sat down again, motionless for a moment.

'George,' he said in a harsh voice, 'I can't go back on what I said.'

'The Cabinet feels you ought.'

Carey was on his feet again, moving restlessly about the room. 'This operation's come to the ears of other powers,' he said. 'They're angry about it because they feel we're prepared to go to war over something which more properly ought to have been taken to the International Court or to UNO. He should call it off and use negotiation, as he should have done from the very beginning.'

Greenaway tried to placate him. 'He's aware of all this,' he said. 'But it's too late now. They took a calculated risk on it being settled before anyone could argue about it. And if it had been settled—to our advantage—there'd have been sufficient pleasure in the country for the Government to have survived, no matter what the rest of the world thought. Let's face it, UNO these days couldn't have done much, particularly if it had been carried through with small loss of life. There'd have been a lot of protest, of course, but it'd have died out. You know as well as I do that politics, international, national or local, isn't the prettiest of games.'

Greenaway paused. 'But things didn't work out that way,' he went on after a while. 'When they began to get down to it, it was found we weren't prepared for such a swift operation. Your party are as much to blame as anyone for that, Spencer.'

Carey frowned. 'I admit that much.'

'The absence of *matériel* and men delayed it and allowed everybody else to get wind of it. There are reports now of "volunteers" and Russian equipment, and this doesn't help General Hodges, especially now that he feels he can't rely on his own people. He's signalled to that effect.'

'Good God!'

'Burnaston took up his message and Hodges confirmed what he thought. It was your speech that started it, and it was because of this that the P.M. felt justified in asking you to withdraw it.'

The Leader of the Opposition looked haggard. 'George, I can't withdraw,' he said. 'It wasn't political word-spinning.' Carey paused, wondering if he had been, because he'd not only been trying to state the objections of a great mass of protesting people without voices, but he'd also instinctively been trying to talk his party back into office.

He shook his head. 'I believe,' he insisted, 'that these men *do* have the right of reply. I know that at Suez, when it was stopped, most of the men in the Forces and, indeed, many people at home thought they'd been let down by the politicians just when they were going to pull the thing off. But this isn't 1956. Things have changed and I think we should never be prepared to risk a world war for a base that isn't even as important as Suez was. And *that*'s what I believe the average man in the Forces and in the street thinks, too.'

Greenaway sat in silence as Carey pressed on, aware of his disapproval, even disbelief.

'George,' he said, trying to explain himself but conscious in the face of the older man's silence of moralising, 'you know as well as I do that decisions aren't made by Parliament. That stuff about democracy's a load of rubbish. The decisions are made by a caucus of half a dozen men—and if those men are wrongly advised or wrongly directed, even if they're simply wrong, then they should be told so. What the Prime Minister decides these days is only rubber-stamped by Parliament and, in this case, when the decision had to be made quickly, he didn't even have *that* problem. It can only be protested afterwards and, by God, George, I'm protesting. *That's* what I meant.'

'If this thing went wrong,' Greenaway said, 'it could mean the loss of many lives—British lives. It could mean a great deal of humiliation and perhaps even a new period of economic distress.'

'I fully understand that.'

'He insists our allies are still with us.'

156

Carey frowned. 'Alliances are useless under the Bomb,' he pointed out. 'De Gaulle spotted that profound truth years ago. While we're prepared to stand by each other in the case of aggression, no one's prepared to be dragged into a nuclear war simply because someone's pride is hurt or because they're growing greedy. Our allies in Europe would never support us, if it came to the crunch.'

Greenaway was looking uncomfortable and it seemed to Carey to be time to make a decision.

He still hesitated, however, because while the decision was easy enough to make, it wasn't so easy to find the words that would make the decision acceptable to the country at large.

'George,' he said at last, 'it would be the easiest thing in the world to turn you down because I saw all this as a stepping stone to putting myself in Downing Street. It would be just as easy to play the saint and to withdraw my opposition so that Starke could get up in the House and praise me for my support.'

Greenaway looked up. He'd been in politics long enough to know what was coming, and he suddenly felt a little weary of the half-truths and the more-than-truths that made up the system.

Carey was standing by the fireplace now, erect and distinguished—almost, Greenaway thought cynically, as if *that* were for the record, too.

'Either of those,' Carey concluded slowly, 'would be easy. But I think what is being done is wrong, and whether men die or not, whether it helps me to power or sends me into the political wilderness—and believe me, *some* of my party want to go through with this, like you do—whatever it does, I'm not withdrawing. I'm standing by what I said.'

7

The rain had come down steadily all morning in a shining curtain that made the ships grey metallic shapes, until at noon the clouds parted once more and the sun began to drink the moisture from the pools on the deck. It had now held off for some time, but General Hodges was under no delusion that they had left it behind.

'No wonder no one believes us,' he said slowly. 'Nobody in his senses would start an exercise at the beginning of the rainy season.'

He turned at a knock at the door. Leggo looked up from his desk and spoke to the naval officer who arrived with new R5 photographs of King Boffa Port.

'Been waiting for those,' he said. 'The gunners are wanting the bombardment task-table. Do we have copies?'

'Processing at the moment,' the naval man said. 'These are the first ones for the general and the Support Committee.'

'Fine. Ask the chopper boys to stand by to deliver them round the fleet.'

Hodges crossed to the table as Leggo spread the photographs out. He was growing increasingly worried now. *Stabledoor* was drawing nearer its destination with every hour that went by and there had still been no answer to his signal from London. He was still committed to an operation of which he didn't approve, and in which he had no faith. And, with equipment as short as it was, *Stabledoor* was poised on a razor-edge of doubt.

From the early photographs they had of King Boffa Port, it was possible to tell how many floors there were to each building near the harbour installations, and even how many rooms on each floor, and from this they had been able to decide how many men would be required to comb them out in a given time. Everything had been considered and allowed for in greater detail than usual—bearing in mind the importance politically of success—and there was plenty of time to brief the men for battle. Unfortunately, by this time, and in view of the revelations of Leggo and Drucquer, Hodges had begun to entertain grave doubts about the quality of comradeship in his command. While the officers were largely on the side of *Stabledoor*, it seemed that the men were not.

Leggo was leaning over his charts now, tracing with a slender forefinger the white-ringed points shown in the pictures and glancing at the appreciation that accompanied them.

'New gun position in the old Governor's Garden, sir,' he was saying. 'Another defended area at Sesapont Beach. And what's this?' He peered closer. 'Anti-tank guns by the jetty, and what looks like dug-in tanks near the old Europeans' Club.' He turned to Hodges. 'Those are new, sir.'

'I hope they're all that *are* new,' Hodges said bleakly, running his eye down the appreciation.

Leggo jerked his hand at the desk and the lists he was preparing.

'Can we organise the task-table now, sir? Support Committee's getting worried.'

Hodges nodded. 'We'd better,' he said. 'We can't delay any longer. The gunners'll have to know the targets and Downes' people will want them for positioning their ships. If we get any amendments they'll have to be passed out later and marked in by individual officers.' He turned away, then paused, and swung back to Leggo. 'And, Stuart, ask the gunners to try to make a better job of those co-ordinates than they did on the dummy run back to Pepul. Some of their targets then were out at sea.'

Leggo managed a twisted smile which Hodges didn't return. Filling his pipe, he went out on deck, feeling the need to be alone and think a little.

The air was like the inside of a velvet bag, hot, stuffy and stifling, with the constant mutter of thunder over the horizon; and the long grey swells from the north-west swept in endless succession beneath the convoy. As each one arrived the ships bowed their obeisance to it—sterns up, bows down, sterns down, bows up—so that they looked like a lot of rocking-horses on a fairground roundabout, and he remembered then that another Malalan launch had pulled out of the convoy during the night and had followed its predecessor and the British corvette *Duck* back to Pepul. He wasn't really sur-prised. They hadn't anticipated the most expert support from the Malalan forces, and mechanical failure had been anticipated. He'd inspected the Malalan ships in Pepul harbour, escorted by General Aswana and a whole string of high-ranking black officers, and while everything was done in the fashion of the Royal Navy, where most of the Malalans had been trained, he had even then detected the subtle shortcomings of a nation whose Europeanisation had been too swift.

Immediately ahead of them and to the flanks were *Liverpool* and the escort screen. Deliberately, the planners had insisted that all nuclear submarines should be withdrawn to home bases, and they were now all moored at Holy Loch, their presence well reported in the newspapers in a trumped-up story of a need for modifications, because Westminster was anxious that the world, whatever else it might think, should not for a moment imagine they were trying to start a nuclear war.

Hodges was still staring at the ships, sucking at his unlit pipe, his eyes following the albatross that was still accompany-ing the convoy, sweeping low over the swells, its wings never moving, graceful, dignified and curiously menacing, when a voice in his ear made him turn.

'Makes you think of the *Chorniye Kazach*, doesn't it?'

It was Downes, more hawk-like than ever with the lines of strain beginning to show on his face.

'Is she still there?' Hodges asked.

'She's still there,' Downes said. 'Still on the same course as us. The submarines are there, too, also still on the same course.'

'Does anybody else know?' Hodges asked.

'Officially, no. But every ship's got radar and they'll all be wondering what those blips are. They'll be making guesses.'

Hodges thought for a moment. 'I've always hated trooping,'

he said slowly. 'There's always far too much time for the men to sit and wonder what's happening.'

'And get up to all sorts of bloody nonsense like cheering,' Downes added.

Hodges nodded. The cheering had gone unexplained, though he had immediately set off enquiries into it. The officers had been met only by blank faces, however, and the suggestion that it was nothing but an indication of the high morale of the men involved.

The explanation hadn't carried much weight because Hodges knew that morale was about as low as it could be, and curiously there had been little explanation from the non-commissioned officers whom he might have expected to know what was going on. He suspected unhappily that the petty officers and sergeants knew perfectly well what had prompted the unexpected bursts of cheering which had passed from ship's crew to ship's crew but that they secretly sympathised with the men's complaints and preferred to stand aside, taking neither the men's part nor the officers'. Most of them were long-serving sailors and soldiers with a lot to lose, and their position was a tricky one, viewed either upwards from the messdecks or downwards from the wardroom.

'I'd have liked to have found out what it was all about,' Hodges said, his voice stubborn as he spoke over his shoulder to Downes.

'So would I.'

'I'm not pretending that because it's stopped whatever was behind it's stopped too. There are too many men in close proximity to each other.'

Downes smiled. 'How about letting us try the guns?' he suggested. 'It's rather a good show and it might take their minds off things a bit. It makes a bit of noise and I always did say there was nothing worse for the nerves than the tension of waiting without the culmination of the kill for relief. It used to be hell during the war when you were after a submarine.' He shrugged. 'It won't do the gun crews any harm to have a bit of practice either,' he ended grimly. 'I'll make a signal round the fleet and have everybody make an announcement. Otherwise your chaps'll all think we're being attacked.'

Hodges' unease was reflected in the mind of Colonel Drucquer aboard the destroyer, *Banff*, out on the port wing of the convoy under the broad lifting stern of *Liverpool*. He was standing in the shadows with Captain White while Lieutenant Jinkinson spoke to his section of the 17th/105th. Now that they were approaching King Boffa Port, the men had been informed of their destination, and each troop, squadron and company had commandeered its own portion of deck and gone into a close huddle round its officers while the news was given.

Unseen by the men, Drucquer was free to watch their faces as they listened to what was being said. They didn't seem surprised and there were none of the expectant smiles Drucquer had seen before on similar occasions. Well-trained confident soldiers, as he well knew, never jibbed at an operation and rarely questioned it, and normally even expressed a certain amount of pleasure at what they were about to do, but this time Drucquer was not surprised to see resentment in the faces of the men before him. Most of them were National Servicemen, and most of them were young enough to have been affected by the wave of pacifism which had swept the world since Vietnam. In another age and under different circumstances, they would have been spoiling for a fight and, like good housewives objecting to being done out of what they felt they deserved, would have been delighted to set about the Khanzians to take back what they considered belonged to them. Not this time, however. They were far from being wholeheartedly behind the politicians who claimed that King Boffa Port was the property of the British man in the street and that they were in duty bound to recover it.

Jinkinson's briefing was not a success. There were no questions, no queries as to how things should be done. There weren't even any protests—only complete indifference and a strange sort of expectancy that worried Drucquer.

As Jinkinson put away his notebook, Drucquer saw he had a puzzled frown on his face and, turning away, he saw the same look on Captain White's face.

'Watch the concert last night?' he asked abruptly, the question coming unexpectedly across White's thoughts on the way the briefing had gone.

He looked startled. 'Yes, Colonel,' he said. 'I did.'

Drucquer nodded thoughtfully. The ship had been blacked out and overpoweringly hot and the men had listlessly amused themselves with impromptu turns at the stern of the ship, the stage a single layer of ammunition boxes, the audience sitting cross-legged on the deck or clinging to the gun mountings.

The opening number had been a close-harmony group of Marines with a guitar, but their song had been one of the protest numbers made popular by the folk singers of the Sixties. The other turns had been of a lower standard, some of them descending not unexpectedly into smut, and the inevitable act of two privates who had aped their officers in exaggerated accents had for once not been funny. It had seemed to have a more sinister import, and instead of laughter there had been jeers.

'What did you think of it?' Drucquer asked.

White glanced at him, wondering what was in his mind. 'Usual low standard, sir,' he said. 'In every sense of the word.'

'It didn't seem like the usual concert to me,' Drucquer commented. 'Not very spontaneous. Not very funny.'

'They never are, Colonel.'

'No. But everybody always laughs. They didn't last night.'

White kept his eyes averted and Drucquer knew he was deliberately refraining from meeting his gaze.

'Much seasickness?' the Colonel went on mildly, as though he were enquiring after the health of the battalion.

White smiled. 'Just the usuals, who'd be sick on the Serpentine.'

'Have they got anything for it?'

'Yes, sir. Avomine.'

Drucquer gave a bark of laughter. 'They give that for early morning sickness in pregnancy, don't they?' he said.

He paused for a moment, then he turned again to White, speaking quietly, his mildness gone, his eyes sharp and his manner alert.

'What's going on, Dick?' he asked.

White deliberately avoided looking at him, and fell back on Sergeant Frensham's habit of repeating the question until he could sort out the answer. 'What's going on, sir?'

Drucquer smiled. 'You know as well as I do,' he said, 'that

163

something's going on. You found those pamphlets at Pepul. You put Private Spragg under arrest. It might interest you to know that General Hodges wasn't the slightest bit startled. The pamphlets had turned up in other units.'

'I'm not surprised, sir.'

'I don't suppose you are. Well, you saw the concert last night and you've watched Jinkinson's briefing just now. Even allowing for the fact that Jinkinson's a bit of an ass, it wasn't exactly a success, was it? There's a mood I can't explain. It's a mood I've not come across before. Have you noticed it?'

White considered. 'Yes, sir,' he admitted. 'I have.'

'In your own unit?'

'Not really, sir. Mine's small and more technical. They've probably not had time to think about it. But I've seen it elsewhere.'

Drucquer paused. 'Something's in the wind, Dick. I think it's something serious and concerted, too; though, of course, there's nothing I can be sure about. You might keep your eyes open. You probably spent longer in the ranks than most of my officers and you know how the chaps think. Just let your beady eye flicker about a bit, will you?'

Back in his cabin, Drucquer picked up a small radio he'd brought with him from Hong Kong. It was a battery set, Japanese made and extraordinarily powerful. Marvelling at the strides that had been made in technology in the last twenty years, he switched it on to the B.B.C., which was giving what was obviously a carefully censured bulletin on what it chose to call 'the Combined Forces manœuvres off the West African coast'. There was no mention of King Boffa Port and, dissatisfied, Drucquer moved the dials in an attempt to get an unbiased view.

The American Forces Programme from Wiesbaden appeared to be full of condemnation of *Stabledoor*, and the American sense of outrage showed clearly in the violent speeches being made in Congress and the cold fury and indignation of a Presidential statement. The concerted disapproval sounded the chilling note of a bell buoy on a lee shore, though Drucquer was sufficiently man of the world to suspect that a great deal of it sprang from the fact that the Presidential elections were due and that no candidate wished to be accused of supporting warmongers. Nevertheless, the air seemed to be alarmingly full of demands that Hodgeforce should remain away from the coast of Khanzi, and so far there had been no response from London, and Drucquer doubted now if there would be.

He felt sad as he switched back to the B.B.C., and he found little comfort as he caught the latter end of the British bulletin. The House of Commons, never an institution that Drucquer admired much, had descended, it seemed, to the nadir of bad behaviour over *Stabledoor*, with shouting and Opposition insults and gross and abusive insinuations about Ministers' actions and integrity. It was a sickening thing to hear, even second-hand, and Drucquer had the feeling that the people at home were shocked and ashamed by what was being done in their name.

The news terminated with a flash to the effect that the British Battle Class destroyer, *Alamein*, had run across the path of the Khanzian frigate, *Pijehun*, fifteen miles outside Khanzian territorial waters. While nothing had happened, for a while it had seemed, as the two vessels had watched each other closely, radar aerials moving like the antennae of fighting beetles, as if nothing on earth could have stopped an engagement.

The report troubled Drucquer. Without doubt, *Pijehun* would have radioed base, and base would have informed the Khanzian Government at Sarges. Without question, by now, messages were rushing across the ether full of accusations and propaganda. Everyone in the world would be aware now of what they were up to, and the Khanzians would know they were on their way—if they hadn't known already, because even in Pepul and Korno and Machingo it was clear there wasn't a great deal of support for Alois Braka, and that there were plenty of people who believed in Africa for the Africans and would have preferred the Khanzians having King Boffa Port to the British having it.

It was an unsatisfying news bulletin, without newspapers to amplify it and no knowledge of what was going on at home.

As Drucquer switched off the set, the ship's loudspeaker system crackled and he looked up, expecting to hear instructions of some sort to the troops on board.

But it was only a simple warning announcement.

'This is the Commanding Officer.' The iron voice crashed into the cabin. 'Naval escort ships are about to fire their guns. There should be no alarm. We are not being engaged. This is only a practice shoot. . . .'

8

Wango, wango, wango.

The shock of the naval guns, like a set of doors being slammed one after another along a corridor, seemed to jerk the Starboard Cross Passage aboard *Banff* with vibration, and the men crowded in there looked up quickly as the swift tonk-tonk-tonk of the quickfirers followed on its heels.

'Sounds nice and reassuring,' Ginger Bowen said cheerfully.

'From *this* end of the gun,' Private Snaith commented laconically from among the tangle of packs, weapons, hammocks, clothing and equipment that filled the alleyway. 'How about from the other end?'

That thought had never occurred to Ginger and he subsided, frowning and suddenly disturbed.

He seemed to have been penned up in the area round the Starboard Cross Passage and the fragment of deck that had been assigned to them to enable them to draw rations and get to the heads, for what seemed weeks now. They had been herded in there by the ship's First Lieutenant, had hammock rolls thrown at them by a disgusted petty officer, and told to make themselves comfortable, because, in an attempt to overcome the shortage of transports, *Banff*—like the other naval vessels in the convoy—was jammed with troops. They were in messdecks, alleyways, store-rooms—even in the petty-officers' recreation room—much to the disgust of the petty officers and those sailors who had had to double up or, at the very least, by-pass in their movement about the ship, the corridors like the Starboard Cross Passage which were now in use as living quarters.

Meals were difficult sitting on the crowded deck, and ablutions worse as they scrambled round the few wash-basins inadequately supplied with water only at limited periods of the day, and the men of Lieutenant Jinkinson's section—and Ginger Bowen especially—were cramped, bored and tired with insufficient sleep because the hard deck didn't make a good bed, while the air in the Starboard Cross Passage was foul with the odour of sweating bodies.

There had been a few jeers as Ginger had arrived, escorted to the watertight doors at the end of the alleyway by Sergeant O'Mara himself, but while he had enjoyed the notoriety, it had left him with a vague feeling of being out of things. Private Leach had had a feeling, not without foundation, that, notwithstanding his capacity for getting into trouble, Ginger would have disapproved of everything that had been planned and, with Snaith and Malaki unwilling already and Ginger in a position to tip the scales, he had threatened to knock the block off anybody who might be tempted to split to him.

The result was that, cut off from the rest of his section by an invisible barrier, Ginger had been thrown on his own company for too long. No one had avoided him but he had been very conscious of the strained relations between them, and he had put it down to the fact that his absence in detention had caused the others extra work and that they were therefore naturally a little anti towards him.

To amuse himself, he had struggled through two letters, quite an achievement for Ginger who was never normally inclined to put pen to paper. He had written to his family at home—the usual 'Hoping this finds you as it leaves me at present' and a somewhat tedious missive that contained little affection, because Ginger didn't feel a great deal of affection for his family; and a more torrid epistle addressed to Miss Sulfika Achmet, care of the Moyama Bar, Passy, Pepul, Malala, West Africa. Into this one, in disjointed phrases full of mis-spelt words, he had poured all his feelings. It was prompted not so much by loneliness or by love as by the heat and the memories and the incandescent dreams that persisted in coming every time he fell asleep. It had relieved his feelings a little but he still hadn't posted it and he wasn't sure now that he would.

Most of the men in *Operation Stabledoor* had spent the

voyage writing letters during the long hours of waiting. They had been penned up for so long now that the task gave them some sort of emotional release.

They were huddled all over the ships; on the decks; in, on top of, and underneath their vehicles. They smoked, played cards and talked longingly about women. They were nervous and a little scared, and in the high, clumsy landing ships they were exhausted by the lurching motion and were fighting against the continuous nausea of sea-sickness that came from the swell and the motion of the waves and the smell of diesel oil, vomit and blocked-up latrines. They were abominably crowded and, where they could, they glumly lined the rails and stared at the other ships in the convoy, which came rank after rank, to port and starboard, ahead and astern.

Most of them by this time had grown introspective from boredom, and the concerts that had been arranged had not been a success. They all knew now that they were within striking distance of their destination, and at irregular intervals the ships seethed with boat drills and A.R.P. exercises. The mornings were spent with wireless training, in a formula of communication, or in stripping and cleaning arms, filling magazines and overhauling equipment—all for the most part with a great deal of reluctance.

To Ginger Bowen, it had been a period of boredom interspersed with a series of flaps, all of which had been made more wearisome and frustrating in the encumbered alleyway by the crowding packs, Sten guns and other equipment that lay about the deck with boots, clothing and ammunition.

The sky had been heavy all day, with lowering clouds damping down the swells, so that the sea heaved like glue. From time to time, heavy showers had fallen, only to be followed by sunshine and sweltering heat that left them gasping for clean air. Where Lieutenant Jinkinson's section were huddled, they were unable to see the daylight but they could tell every time it rained by the water gurgling in the scuppers and down some sort of escape pipe just above their heads.

For about the tenth time that day, Ginger listened as the last of the rain gurgled away, ending in a steady drip-drip-drip which he knew now would continue for approximately ten minutes before it finally stopped. Around him, the other men were gloomy and limp. Private Spragg, at that moment out of reach in cells, had not been missed. They had simply closed ranks and filled his place.

Private Leach, however, had by no means finished complaining of Spragg's stupidity. He sat with his back to a pile of hammocks sucking at a brown-stained cigarette end, his brows down, staring at a scrap of paper on which from time to time he made secretive notes which he would permit no one else to look at. Private Snaith was reading a paperback history of the Civil War in England. Ginger wasn't sure what the Civil War in England was about, though he knew it had been a sort of Mods and Rockers affair between a lot of men in kinky lace who wore their hair long, and a lot of men in kinky leather who wore their hair short. Beyond that, he knew remarkably little about the Civil War in England, and Snaith, on the one occasion when he'd tried to make conversation, hadn't seemed disposed to be informative.

Acting Lance-Corporal Jesus-Joseph Malaki, his black face almost invisible in the shadows, sat quietly, staring in front of him, neither reading nor writing, neither happy nor unhappy, fatalistically waiting as his ancestors had done for hundreds of years along this coast they were now approaching. Of all the men in the Starboard Cross Passage, perhaps Malaki seemed most at peace. Privates Griffiths, McKechnie and Bolam were involved in the same old pointless discussion that had been going on ever since soldiers had first put on uniforms, their argument going round and round, boring and repetitive and getting rapidly nowhere.

'She does, you know.'

'She doesn't, you know.'

'She bloody does!'

'She bloody doesn't!'

Nobody paid them the slightest attention. In fact, they were probably never noticed even, and Privates Wedderburn, Welch and Michlam were even playing a three-handed game of cards, though it didn't appear to be very successful judging by the disputes that seemed to spring from it. Though he had never played it in his life, Ginger suspected it was bridge, and he had long since come to the conclusion that if bridge produced as much discord as it appeared to do with Privates Wedderburn, Welch and Michlam, then it wasn't much of a game.

For a while he stared at his companions, then he took out the letter he had written to Sulfika the day before and read it through again. After a lapse of twenty-four hours, it made his hair stand on end, and he found himself grinning as he read the feverish lines.

'Christ,' he breathed, delighted with it.

After a while, the silence in the alleyway grew oppressive. The gunfire had lasted only long enough to rouse them all from their somnolence, and then had stopped. For those on deck it had probably been quite a spectacle, but for those like the group in the Starboard Cross Passage, it had been nothing more than a frustration.

Ginger pulled a diary from his pocket and studied it, working hard at amusing himself. He had once promised himself that he would write it up each day but, every night, when he had sat down to the task, he had found himself staring at the empty pages with a blank mind and a complete inability to unearth anything from the day's events that might remotely be worth recording. He stared at the entries for a moment but they were singularly uninspired.

'Went with Sulfika,' one said. 'All right.' 'Jinkinson is a bastard,' said another. Nothing much appeared to have happened.

Ginger flicked the pages idly, glancing at the dates.

'Guns have stopped,' Wedderburn commented, his eyes on his cards.

Snaith looked up from his book. 'The gunners say it's a prize balls-up,' he said in a low voice. 'Every time they mark their targets down, they get a lot of amendments and have to rub 'em all out and start again. It'll be fine if they're *still* rubbing 'em out as we go in.'

'*If* we go in, brother,' Leach growled from his corner, and Ginger turned his head quickly. Even now, it had never occurred to him that the subtle mood below decks had started from a chance comment of his own, uttered in the nature of a complaint rather than an attempt at sedition.

He was aware that something was afoot, but as he was not

by nature rebellious against authority, except to avoid work, he still wasn't sure what it was.

'Aren't we going in?' he asked. 'I thought we was.'

'You might be surprised,' Leach observed. 'One of the radar operators was saying in the heads that we was being followed by Russian subs.'

There was a shout of derision, but Leach insisted.

'He—said—they—was—Russian—subs,' he said loudly. 'They got orders to watch 'em and report 'em. Nobody was saying anything, but they all knew they wasn't *our* subs. And if they're not ours, brother, O.K., 'oo's are they?'

'Malalan,' Snaith hazarded.

'They haven't got any,' Wedderburn said.

'Yes, they have,' Michlam joined in, more than willing to liven things up with an argument.

'They bloody haven't!'

'They bloody have!'

'O.K.,' Wedderburn said, flinging his cards down in a show of temper that drew looks of approval from Griffiths, McKechnie and Bolam. 'If that's how you feel, play by your bloody self.'

Michlam sneered. 'Jumpy?'

'Who's jumpy?'

'You are.'

'I'm bloody not!'

'You bloody are!'

Ginger watched them all, puzzled. He had been aware for a long time of the increasing tension, and it was beginning to worry him now. Something was in the wind, he knew, but no one in the Starboard Cross Passage seemed eager to enlighten him.

For a while there was silence, then Welch made an attempt to break the awkwardness caused by Wedderburn's nervous outburst.

'Church parade tomorrow,' he said. 'It's in orders. You know what that means: The ball starts just after.'

'We haven't got a padre,' Ginger said.

'Don't matter,' Michlam assured him. 'Skipper can take it. Navy's good at that sort of thing. "Eternal Father, strong to save." Always sing that. "From storm and tempest, fire and foe, oh, Lord, protect us wheresoe'er we go." '

'Much better if it was "The Red Flag",' Leach growled.

Ginger shuffled himself to comfort on the hard deck. Beyond the card game which somehow seemed to have got going again, Bolam and Griffiths were now staring goggle-eyed at a white-backed book with a half-naked girl on the front. They were all trying to relax, grasping at borrowed time with the knowledge that some fateful moment was just ahead in the future.

Ginger pulled his cap down over his eyes and tried to remember Sulfika, and the thought of her slim dark body sent shudders of misery through him. Ginger had always had a reputation with the ladies and his last conquest before leaving England had been along the canal bank near Chichester—where he had been stationed in the Rousillon Barracks—with a strapping girl from one of the villages around who'd been fighting him off for two days. Sulfika, with her simpler morals, had been a much easier victory and much more willing, so that Ginger had almost enjoyed the rare privileges of a husband.

The sudden din of the ship's alarm bell brought him back to sudden reality with a start that almost lifted him from the deck.

It was a noise fit to wake the dead and flung off-watch sleepers from their bunks all over the ship; and started a torrent of men up and down ladders, still dragging on clothing as they ran; filling the wheelhouse with telephone-talkers, messengers and duty officers, and doubling up the crews at the guns. Down in the Starboard Cross Passage it set Ginger and his companions scrambling to their feet and diving for clothing and equipment in a frightful tangle of bodies and equipment straps among the scattered cards.

'We're there!' Welch shouted. 'I thought it was some time tomorrow night!'

Men bolted past both ends of the alleyway and above their heads they could hear the sound of running feet as the crew hurried to their stations, and they all reached for their weapons and hastily began to buckle on their packs.

'We've been spotted,' Snaith said.

'That'll be fine,' Leach snarled. 'Especially with us lot stuck in here.'

There was the sound of watertight doors clanging shut then a long uneasy silence as they all listened. The running had stopped abruptly and all they could hear were the normal sounds of the ship, the deep humming from the turbines, and the creaks and sighs as she shifted in the water. For a long time they sat still, catching the smell of fresh paint and holding their breath and wondering what had happened, then Ginger cautiously put his head round the end of the alleyway. There was no one about but there didn't appear to be any sign of alarm. A sailor in faded blues, moving expertly past the end of the cramped corridor with what appeared to be a bundle of laundry, stared at Ginger, with his helmet over his eyes and girded for battle.

'What's up, mate?' Ginger asked.

The sailor stopped and gazed at him, the planes of flesh on his face tinted by the red lights in the deckhead.

'Ship's cat gev birth to seven little 'uns,' he said solemnly. 'Been expecting it a long time. 'Ad us worried. Captain promised to let us know.'

Ginger slipped back into the alleyway, vaguely ashamed at his alarm, and as the tension slowly relaxed, the men sat down again. The card players picked up their cards once more, unable to do anything but sit where they were and use their imagination about what was happening on deck. Suddenly, the deckhead lights went out, and the dim secondary ones came on.

' 'Ello, 'ello,' Leach said. ' 'Ere it comes, brother. Eyes down for the count. Bombers probably.'

The period of semi-darkness lasted for about a quarter of an hour then the lights came on again abruptly.

'Flap off,' Ginger observed.

The loudspeaker started to crackle and they heard the voice of the Ship's Captain. 'Captain speaking,' it said. 'I'll tell you what that was all about. We have bumped into the United States Eighth Fleet who have been evacuating American nationals from Khanzi. There has been an exchange of signals and the Americans have changed course. They are now out of sight. That is all.'

174

There was dead silence for a moment as the loudspeaker clicked off, then Leach dropped his Sten gun with a clatter to the deck.

'That's bloody marvellous,' he said loudly. 'If the Yanks know we're here, they'll be waiting off the beaches for us. They've been going on about us for weeks. It's time we called this thing off.'

'You do,' Ginger said sarcastically. 'Enjoy yourself. Have a word with the general. I'm sure he'll agree.'

'He'll have no option, brother,' Leach pointed out.

Something in his manner startled Ginger. 'Why not?' he asked.

'Because he'll find himself leading a bloody invasion force that won't invade. That's why.'

For a long time there was silence as half-a-dozen pairs of accusing eyes fastened on Leach. After all his blowhard threats against anyone letting out the secret, it had been Leach himself who had spilled the beans.

He became aware of the distrustful stares. 'Well, it won't, will it?' he said loudly.

Ginger studied the others, aware that he was on the threshold of a discovery but uncertain what it might be. He gave a short laugh.

'Come off it,' he said. 'We've got to, if they say so.'

'No, we haven't, brother,' Leach insisted. 'It's all worked out.'

'Worked out? How?'

'Never you mind. You ain't heard yet, but you soon will.'

Ginger stared at Leach, beginning to frown as a suspicion formed slowly in his mind. 'That's bloody mutiny,' he said.

'It's a strike,' Leach corrected him. 'For better conditions. It's been decided that, what with pay, disagreement over this here operation, and a few other things, it's time we drew the attention of the authorities to our grievances.'

'Who's decided?'

'Committees aboard ships. Strike committees.'

Ginger stared at him for a second. He was never a clever man but he was no fool and he saw through Leach's reply at once.

'In the Army, mate, that's mutiny,' he insisted.

Leach gestured. '*You* should talk,' he shouted. 'You were the one to start it.'

Ginger got to his feet. 'Listen,' he said angrily. 'I've done some bloody funny things in my time, but one thing I 'aven't done is go in for mutiny. I'm not that daft. You can get shot for that.'

Leach jeered. 'Not these days, brother,' he said. 'And nobody can do a thing if everybody's in it. This is political, man, not military.'

Ginger wasn't sure what he meant, but he wasn't having any. 'Well, you can count *me* out,' he said.

Snaith grinned and Malaki's eyes brightened, but just when it seemed that in Lieutenant Jinkinson's section at least the mood might change, Leach grasped at his last argument.

'Christ, man, *you* started it. You turning yellow?'

Ginger had no idea what Leach meant, and he did the only thing his limited intellect suggested to him. He drew his fist back and dropped Leach to the deck like a log.

Immediately, the alleyway exploded into uproar. The cards went flying once more as Welch grabbed Ginger's arms and dragged them behind him, but Ginger knew a trick worth two of that. He tucked his head down and Welch shot over his shoulders, and there was a yell as a flying boot caught Wedderburn at the side of the jaw. A fist flew and, in seconds, everyone in the alleyway was involved, elbows and boots swinging, with the deep resonant voice of Malaki coming from the other side of the turmoil.

'Stop it,' he was yelling at Ginger. 'Stop it, man!'

Then a single shot rang out and Malaki's yells changed to a cry of pain, and as the turmoil came to a sudden frightened stop, there was a clatter of boots along the Starboard Alleyway and Sergeant Frensham stood framed in the end of the cross passage, his brows down, his eyes glittering with disgust.

9

Hodges and Leggo were staring at the chart of the West African coast spread on the table. With them were Group Captain Neville and Admiral Downes and they were studying the marked courses of Hodgeforce and the American Eighth Fleet which had just disappeared into the darkness.

'You know what this means?' Hodges said as he stared at the converging lines drawn by the Fleet Navigation Officer.

'I can guess.' Downes pulled a wry face.

'It means the whole world'll be alerted to what we're up to.'

'If they weren't when *Alamein* sprung *Pijehun* a few hours back. *Pijehun* would inevitably signal King Boffa Port and Scepwe would call in the correspondents.'

Hodges frowned. 'It's only a matter of hours before they'll have *this*, too, as confirmation,' he said. 'There's not the slightest element of surprise left.'

'There never was,' Downes said. 'They've been debating it at UNO for weeks.'

Neville frowned at the chart. 'After what the Americans have been saying about us,' he commented, 'I'm surprised they got out of our way so easily.'

Hodges moved restlessly across the cabin and stopped at the porthole, staring through the streaming glass. The rain storms kept persisting, bringing stifling heat and making life miserable for the look-outs and deck parties. If it persisted, it could even interfere seriously with the landing.

There was a knock at the door, and the Signal Lieutenant-Commander appeared. He handed a signal to Downes who glanced at it and passed it on to Hodges. The general stared at the decoded transcription with a frown, and looked up at Downes.

'You know what it's all about?' he asked.

Downes nodded. 'Yes, I do,' he said.

'It's an answer to my signal of yesterday to the Chief of Defence Staff,' Hodges said. 'Have you read it?'

'I have. Yes.'

'The Leader of the Opposition's refused to withdraw anything.' Hodges placed the signal on the table. 'Where this puts us, I don't know. We're due to go in, in about thirty-six hours' time. Everything's organised, even the final meals on board. I had hoped to be able to cancel it all. This means that I can't.'

Hodges bent over the charts to hide the worry in his eyes and Neville gestured angrily.

'I suppose he's ambitious and sees a chance of office,' he said bitterly. 'Because if this thing falls on its face in front of Scepwe's troops, the Government'll be out of office so fast their feet won't touch the floor.' He pushed at a signal sheet on the table that had come in a few hours before. '*This* is how this blasted operation's been shaped, sir,' he said angrily, picking it up. ' "No gun of greater calibre than four-point-five inches to be fired." I suppose it's important that we can claim we've only killed Khansians with four-fives instead of six-inchers.'

Hodges opened a file and took out another signal. 'Take a look at *this* one,' he said bitterly. 'It's originated later than that. I haven't had the courage to pass it out yet.'

Neville took the sheet, glanced at it, and tossed it down on the table. He stared at Downes, shocked. 'Did you know of this, sir?' he asked.

'They have a habit of going through a ship,' Downes admitted. 'I'd be a poor admiral if I didn't.'

'But, good God, no bombardment!' Neville sounded shocked. 'They're expecting us now to send the chaps in against a defended beach without support. They must be mad, sir,' he said, swinging round on Hodges. 'Those damned politicians are playing for votes and opinions! They've seen what the people at home and in the rest of the world think about *Stabledoor* and they think they can wipe the slate clean by doing the job without killing any of the enemy.'

'I've asked London to clarify,' Hodges pointed out quietly.

'If I receive no answer, I shall disregard it. Bombardment means firing at fixed targets. What *we* shall be doing is giving naval gunfire support, which is different. It's a nice distinction, but I shall stick to it. I'll take full responsibility.' He smiled. 'We have therefore cancelled the bombardment but we shall carry on with gunfire support.'

He paused and looked at Downes. 'Do we still have our Russian friends with us?' he asked.

'We do.'

'Oughtn't we to take precautions?'

'We've taken 'em. I've given orders to the commanding officers of all ships that gun crews and depth-charge parties be kept closed up. We're watching them. There's only one thing . . .'

Hodges knew what was coming.

'. . . If they attempt to interfere . . .' Downes stopped and looked at Hodges, faintly apologetic. 'This is your pigeon, Horace, I'm afraid. Do we poop off at them?'

Hodges paused for a second before replying. 'If they attempt to interfere,' he said, 'we do.'

Downes nodded. 'You know what that could mean, don't you?'

'I do. But my orders are unequivocal. There are no "ifs" or "buts". If anyone attempts to stop us, we remove them."

'Even if it could result in escalation?'

'Even if it could result in that.'

They were still arguing when the telephone rang. Leggo answered it, then he turned and looked at Hodges.

'Well, what is it?' Hodges snapped.

'I'm afraid it's trouble, sir. It's a signal from *Banff*. It seems somebody aboard her has turned up some sort of plot among the troops to halt *Stabledoor* on the beaches!'

Hodges frowned. 'What the hell do you mean, Stuart?'

'It seems there's been some sort of uproar aboard and they've got it out of one of the men involved. Colonel Drucquer reported it. It was passed on to him by one of his officers.'

'Let's have Drucquer over here,' Hodges snapped. '*And* the officer who turned it up, and anyone else who might know something about it.' He turned to Downes. 'Can we arrange that?'

'Of course.'

'Helicopter?'

'Much cheaper for second-class passengers. Highline.'

'Right. Let's have them, please.'

The tannoy system was booming as *Banff* came alongside. She had come up astern, white foam bursting out round her fantail as her ninety-thousand horse-power beat in reverse to cut her speed.

There was a great deal of cursing and the booming of the loud-hailer as the Officer-on-Deck chased his men into action. *Banff*'s rolling and pitching were quicker and more erratic than *Leopard*'s but her approach was fast and confident. At close quarters from his position on the bridge, Hodges could see her hull marked in several places where the undercoating had come through the grey to form ugly red sores among the rust streaks along her sides. In spite of her age and her scars, however, she was being well-handled and gave an impression of tremendous power and efficiency, and he could hear, above the sounds of *Leopard* all around him, the eager throbbing from her engine rooms and the roaring of her blowers, almost like the panting of a hurrying animal. Faces peered through the windscreen of the bridge, clad in oilskins against the beating rain, and there were a couple of cooks, in white, oblivious to the weather, standing on the afterdeck among the clustered khaki of gaping soldiers staring at the cruiser.

Banff had drawn slightly ahead of *Leopard* now and was waiting there, a hundred feet away, easing her speed to match that of the bigger ship. The wash of the two vessels was smashed into irregular wave patterns, the tips meeting awkwardly and leaping up in erratic splashes that were promptly flattened by the rain, the oily sea between the ships a churning millrace as they slowly closed the distance between them until they were only forty feet apart and the revolving radar antennae on the mast of the destroyer threatened to foul the bigger ship's superstructure. Messenger lines snaked across and the men leaning against the rain on the foredeck moved expertly to secure them and haul the highline over.

As the sea hissed and pounded at the steel plates, Hodges recognised Colonel Drucquer standing with another officer on

Banff's foredeck, then the straps were pulled tight round Drucquer's thighs and he swung clear as the blocks creaked and whined on the wire above his head. He dangled awkwardly as he moved over the churning water like a rag doll, his face turned up to the bridge of *Leopard*, looking for Hodges, while the two ships ploughed on through the swells, the bigger vessel heaving gracefully, the smaller one snapping at the water with the irritable action of a young dog.

'Have Colonel Drucquer brought at once to my cabin, please,' Hodges said.

The bosun's chair had already returned to *Banff* for the second officer by the time Hodges had moved through the watertight doorway and begun to descend to his cabin. Along the horizon, banks of low cloud heavy with rain still compressed the heat down on them and the loudhailer sounded like a clap of thunder as the second transfer was completed.

'Stand by to release gear! But please remain close for the re-transfer of personnel!'

The end of the rig was cast off and allowed to fall clear and the destroyer began at once to pull ahead and veer away until she held station slightly abaft the beam and on the same course as *Leopard*.

It was a few minutes before Drucquer arrived in Hodges' cabin and he was able to glance at a sheaf of radio news reports handed to him by Fraschetti and Lyall. Through the open door, he could hear the faint ping of sonar and a steady crackle of morse somewhere down the corridor, mingling with the monotonous calls of the telephone talker from the wheelhouse. Riffling through the reports, Hodges saw that the United Nations was in an uproar over *Stabledoor*, and the United States delegate had refused to speak to the British representative, an unprecedented thing in an organisation where personal dislike, either between individuals or countries, was not allowed to interfere with free communication.

An attempt was also being made by several Afro-Asian countries to make capital out of the crisis by rousing their sympathisers to declare war on Britain, and the coming and going seemed to be reaching the state almost of despair as the prospects of a world conflagration grew stronger. Whatever the instructions of the people in London, it wasn't to Hodges' taste to be the man to pull the trigger that might set it off.

Admiral Downes appeared, his face grim, then there was a tap on the door and Leggo opened it. Drucquer entered. His face looked grave and his uniform was soaked.

'Good evening, Alastair,' Hodges said. 'Get wet?'

Drucquer smiled. 'Only the rain, sir.'

'What's it all about?'

'I'm afraid it's trouble, General,' Drucquer said. 'Worse than we expected. One of the sergeants attached to my people found it.'

'Let's have it.'

'It seems there's some sort of movement afoot to halt the operation by refusing duty.'

Hodges lit a cigarette slowly and held out the packet to Drucquer who shook his head.

'What sort of movement?' Hodges asked.

'I'm still a bit uncertain. But it seems to stem from those pamphlets we turned up. I'm not sure who's behind it but there was a fight on *Banff* and the sergeant walked in on it. In itself a fight might not have raised the alarm—a black eye's not much to worry about—but some fool shot off his Sten gun by accident in the scuffle and an N.C.O. got hit.'

'Badly?'

'It's a nasty place to stop one, but the docs say he'll pull through, although he's lost a lot of blood.'

'Go on.'

'I've got the officer of A.C.T.5 outside. I brought him with me. He's attached to us. It was his sergeant who walked in on the fight and he was the man who talked to the injured N.C.O. He's a good man not given to flapping. He's the chap who turned up that suitcase full of pamphlets at Pepul.'

'Let's have him in.'

White gave a thunderous salute as he came into the cabin.

Hodges thoroughly approved. It still did the heart good, in these days of relaxed discipline, to see a man trot out a salute like a Guardsman. Whatever the army reformers said, whatever the people in Westminster said, the way a man threw up a salute indicated how much pride he had in himself, and it was still a fact that the men who gave the best salutes were usually the most efficient officers.

'Captain White,' Drucquer said.

'Please relax, Captain,' Hodges suggested. 'You'll find it easier to talk. Offer the captain a drink, Stuart. He'll probably speak more freely with a gin inside him.'

Leggo pushed a drink into White's hand as he removed his sodden cap and pushed it under his arm.

'Now,' Hodges encouraged.

'My sergeant, Frensham, heard a shot, sir,' White reported. 'He's a sound man and a good sergeant. He walked into the Starboard Cross Passage where a section of the 17th/105th was temporarily quartered and he found a man suffering from a bullet wound in the groin.'

'Yes. We've heard about that.'

'It seems there'd been an argument and the gun had gone off by accident. Several of the men had obviously been fighting, and the man in question, Lance-Corporal Malaki, had been attempting to stop it. Frensham sorted them out, put them all under arrest, and reported to me. I got from one of the men, Private Bowen, a garbled story about mutiny and it seemed to me I ought to investigate it further. He didn't seem to know much about it—he's known, it seems, as a bad hat and has only just come off detention but I gather from the Military Police sergeant that he's not the type to cause difficulties of this kind. He's just not clever enough to be a barrack-room lawyer. He couldn't tell me much and no one else would. There was a certain amount of sullenness but no direct disrespect towards me. I then got the idea of talking to the wounded man. He was under sedation by this time but conscious.'

Hodges leaned forward, resting his hands on the back of a chair. White took a deep breath and they all heard the passage of air into his throat.

'It seems the wounded man knew about it, sir, though he had no wish to be involved.'

'Perhaps that's *his* story,' Hodges commented dryly.

'In this case, sir, I'd say it was true. He's a good man.'

'Then why didn't he inform his officer?'

White cleared his throat. 'Perhaps because he's in rather an

183

invidious position, sir,' he pointed out. 'He's a West African by birth and he's not found it easy serving with white men in this operation.'

Hodges nodded. 'I can understand that.'

'The sedatives had relaxed him and he was drowsy. He answered my questions. It seems there's a plot—and a pretty comprehensive one as far as I can make out—to refuse to move off the ships when we reach King Boffa Port.'

Hodges glanced at Leggo. 'When is this to start?' he asked.

'As soon as the men are ordered to take their places in the Hippos and infantry landing craft.'

'Before the bombardment?'

'So I understand, sir.'

'Are the naval gunners involved?'

'I believe so, though I wasn't able to find out just how much or what ships. It seems the movement's run through the whole force, sir, though I gather they insist it's a strike, not a mutiny, and that their instructions are to remain orderly and to continue to show respect to officers.'

Downes turned to Hodges and their eyes met. *Operation Stabledoor* depended on surprise, a lot of which had already gone, and if the landing weren't carried out with swiftness and efficiency in the early morning darkness, the whole of Hodgeforce would be found in daylight within range of the shore batteries. Without speed, every single gun could be turned on them while they were stationary and trying to get the men ashore.

'How much do you think is involved, Captain?' Hodges asked.

'More than appears on the surface, sir. I've been aware for some time that something was afoot but I haven't been able to put my finger on it. I knew it was pretty widespread and I stated this in the report I put in to Colonel Drucquer when I turned up the pamphlets at Pepul. I didn't know what it was, however. *This* seems to be it.'

Hodges looked at Leggo who, anticipating his general's wishes, had already picked up a signal pad.

'Make a signal, Stuart,' Hodges said.

10

The Right Honourable Arthur Starke was a worried man. Opposition to *Stabledoor* had grown enormously in the last forty-eight hours. Dockers at Portsmouth and Southampton were refusing to handle any cargoes destined for West Africa, and Whitehall had been turned into a beer garden half a dozen times by students.

The blows he was suffering seemed to grow more heavy with every day. He had enjoyed so much popularity in the past that his sudden descent into odium was twice as hard to endure. As he'd returned to Downing Street only that day he'd seen the painted words on the sides of the buildings in Whitehall, 'STARKE MUST GO'.

There had been more calls for his resignation in the House and he strongly suspected that on the benches behind him dissatisfaction was increasing rapidly at the way *Stabledoor* was being handled, because there was a growing suspicion there that it showed every indication of destroying his party for years to come. As Prime Minister, he tried to turn his face from the signs but he had to admit they were growing.

He made a despairing movement of his hand and looked up at the Home Secretary who stood at the opposite side of his desk. He was hoping for some comfort, but in the bleak eyes behind the rimless glasses he found little cause for it. There wasn't much comfort in any of the faces beyond the desk.

'These demonstrations aren't spontaneous affairs, Prime Minister,' the Home Secretary was saying. 'There are far too many students involved, far more than could possibly come from the London teaching colleges and hospitals, even if they included a few from Oxford and Cambridge. I've sorted out the reports now and it seems some of the arrested came from as far afield as Cardiff, Durham, Sheffield, Lancaster and Aberdeen. There've been more casualties.'

The Prime Minister seemed to wince. 'Oh, God, no,' he mourned. 'What about the child who died?'

The Home Secretary glanced through his papers. In his attitude, the Prime Minister seemed to detect a stiffening towards him. The Home Secretary had always been one of the clique round the Foreign Secretary and more and more it was becoming confirmed in the Prime Minister's mind that, if necessary, the Home Secretary would be prepared to switch allegiance. It had happened before to Prime Ministers suddenly to lose support of their party and to find someone else preferred as a leader, and it would happen again. It was one of the occupational hazards that went with the job.

'It seems now,' the Home Secretary was saying, 'that the girl had an abnormally thin skull which she hit against the pavement. In fact, she wasn't even involved. She'd only gone along to watch, but she got caught up in it and was swept aside by the police who were pretty hard pressed at the time. There can be no blame against them. Quite a lot of things were being thrown and it's no good regarding these students as children. Most male undergraduates these days are over six foot, strong and very fit.'

'It won't alter the fact that charges of police brutality are going to be laid at our door,' the Prime Minister pointed out. 'I understand from the Chief Whip that a question's already been put down and I'll have to be ready for it. I'd be glad to have the details. We can still pull through this crisis.'

He glanced beyond the Home Secretary to the Foreign Secretary, who was clearly anxious to join in.

'Prime Minister,' he said at the levelled eyes. 'Have you seen the result at Rudkin and Hale?'

'I have.' Rudkin and Hale had not only been lost, but a candidate who ought to have won the seat with ease had been flatly rejected.

'Prime Minister,' the Foreign Secretary went on, 'it was a disaster. From having one of the biggest majorities in the country, we've swung to the opposite end of the scale. It was shattering.'

'We can overcome it,' Starke snapped.

'Can we?' The Foreign Secretary's face was sharp. 'It's obvious what it means. The country's not behind us. Rudkin and Hale's just a straw in the wind.'

'We shall be all right,' Starke insisted.

'What if they force a debate?'

'We must see they don't. We can plead security. And even if they do manage it, with a three-line whip there'll be no difficulties.'

'Prime Minister.' The Foreign Secretary was not to be put off. 'I think the Government could fall over this affair. There's a lot of unhappiness in the Party.'

The Prime Minister shrugged. 'Ask the Chief Whip,' he said. 'He'll tell you. I know the backbenchers. They'll come to heel. With a three-line whip we shall be all right.'

The Foreign Secretary shook his head. 'Not this time, Prime Minister,' he said quietly. 'I think there'll not only be a lot of abstentions, but I think there'll even be votes against us. Did you know Marchmant and Harding have written home about the shortages?'

The Prime Minister looked puzzled. The names meant nothing to him for a moment and the Home Secretary enlightened him.

'The two Members who were called up as Reservists,' he explained. 'Marchmant won Tennyson West and Harding's been in at Grassnorth ever since he left the Army six years ago.'

'If they're back in the Army,' Starke demanded, 'isn't there such a thing as censorship?'

'It seems not for lieutenant-colonels, Prime Minister. They both have that rank.'

The Prime Minister considered. '*I* haven't heard about their complaints,' he said shortly. 'Have you?'

'*I* haven't,' the Home Secretary said.

There was something in the way he said it that alerted Starke.

'What do you mean?'

'I hear Carey has.'

'Carey?' For a moment, the Prime Minister was on the point of bursting out into a blazing fury, but he controlled himself. 'They'll pay for this,' he said slowly.

'It's indicative, Prime Minister,' the Home Secretary said. 'There's been a great deal of tunnelling going on under us.'

'People worried about the consequences of fighting,' Starke snapped.

The Foreign Secretary drew a deep breath. 'There's a dissatisfaction with yourself, Prime Minister,' he said with the air of a man with an unpleasant job to do and the Prime Minister guessed at once they'd all had their heads together. 'I have to say it. There's a lot of reaction to the reports of shortages of equipment. Marchmant and Harding have let it all out.'

The Prime Minister stared angrily back at him. 'Two Reservist M.P.s who never expected to be called back to the Colours,' he snapped. 'Troublemakers.'

'Prime Minister, how it got out doesn't matter. The fact remains that it's out.'

'This opposition'—the Prime Minister gestured—'it's nothing but unattached small groups.'

'They're beginning to concentrate now. Under Edbury. Gordon-Gray's thrown in his lot with him.'

'Edbury's in the Lords,' Starke said. 'He doesn't count in the Commons. It's just another ginger group.'

'Prime Minister'—the Foreign Secretary made a deprecatory gesture—'Lord Edbury's an elder statesman. Nothing that he heads could be called "just another ginger group". He's got influence and influential channels to make his opinions known. His committee was formed expressly to voice dissatisfaction with this Government. They'd like a coalition to deal with the emergency.'

The Prime Minister frowned. 'Everybody not running this show,' he said, 'thinks they can run it better than those who are. The back benches are littered with would-be Prime Ministers.'

The Foreign Secretary and the Home Secretary glanced at each other, confirming Starke's suspicion of collaboration, then the Home Secretary spoke.

'I sometimes think it wrong,' he said pointedly, 'that a Prime Minister has to bear so much authority in a democratic world.'

The Prime Minister frowned. 'Someone has to make the final

decision,' he retorted. 'As Harry Truman said, the buck stops here. Are you against me?'

'No, Prime Minister.' The Home Secretary shook his head. 'Yet, I'm not entirely with you. Not now.'

Starke stared angrily at him. 'Those who aren't for me,' he said, 'are against me. You ought to know there's no chance to form *any* kind of coalition, no matter what anybody says. The Opposition hates the idea, yet these people will go on pressing for it. When the explosion comes, it'll hurt those who've been tunnelling more than me.'

The Home Secretary frowned. 'I'm not so sure,' he said. 'The performance in the House last night frightened me.'

The Prime Minister paused, thinking. It had frightened him, too, even though it had had nothing to do with *Stabledoor*. Moreover, a long statement had been presented to him the previous day and, in it, it had been said that if a coalition was refused then there should be a new Prime Minister.

Starke jerked upright in his chair. He wasn't afraid. The Opposition had its own schisms: They'd been against armament and too much for economies to be over-popular. For too long they'd believed that a small army was less wicked than a large army.

Nevertheless, the Opposition Party Executive had been approached, he knew, and the dissenters had even dug up old Sir George Cornelius. They'd even dressed him in his field-marshal's uniform, complete with all his medals, to speak for them in the House. He'd been as incoherent and inaudible as usual but curiously what he'd said had counted for more even than the polished oratory of Derek Moffat who'd followed him. It had been the old warhorse snorting, simple and honest, and it had gone down well.

'The Prime Minister has appealed for sanity,' the old soldier had said bitterly in a final coherent moment. 'The best thing he can do is to set an example by surrendering the seals of his office.'

Carey had followed, his voice heavy with foreboding and looking, the Prime Minister had thought, more like an actor-manager than the Leader of Her Majesty's Opposition.

'If this country is to be saved from the predicament to which the present government has brought it,' he had said, 'we can only pray for a change in the Leadership of the Government. Only in this way can we salvage our integrity and allow the United Nations to safeguard peace. We must have a new administration and a new leader, because the present administration and the present leader have destroyed every atom of faith the people had in them. Since we can't have an election, the things I advocate can only be effected by the honourable Members opposite, and they should ask themselves if they are in agreement with the policy the Government chooses to follow at home and abroad. The error into which we have been led should be set right as soon as possible; and as they, and only they, can do this, I ask them to do their duty.'

It had been sharp political practice and a clear call to rebellion, and it had been heard without the usual barricade of abuse. Carey had concluded with the words with which Cromwell had dismissed the Long Parliament and which Leopold Amery had flung at Chamberlain so many years before. 'You have sat too long here for any good you have been doing. . . . In the name of God, go.'

All through the evening, in the committee rooms over the Chamber and in the echoing corridors, noisy groups of Government backbenchers had gathered to discuss the course of action, a new anxiety lent by the report that the Government was now set firmly on war in Africa. Some had believed that the report would unite the Party, but Starke had known that others were simply hoping to make political capital out of it.

Messengers from Ministers had passed from one group to the next and Starke himself had sent his Parliamentary Private Secretary to ask Members to meet him the next day. Others he had warned of the consequences of their defection and demanded to know their terms. Their reply had been cruel. They had demanded that the Chief of Defence Staff for a start should go, and if necessary the Prime Minister himself. It had been staggering and had come just when he had hoped the situation was in hand again.

The Whips had done their best to halt the storm but the dissatisfaction had gone unspoken for too long and couldn't be dammed, and in the Opposition Lobby, Government Members had mingled with the enemies of years. And there had been enough of them to have raised fears for a time of a

Government defeat; but cheers of relief had started when the Government Chief Whip was seen to be standing on the right, an indication that the Government had won. The figures had revealed a brutal drop in the Government majority, however. Fifty-nine Government Members had voted against Starke and others had only voted for him in the expectancy that their demands for changes in the Cabinet would be met.

There had been uproar as the figures had sunk in, and Starke himself had actually seen two Members, who were normally at daggers drawn across the floor, attempting to sing, 'There'll Always Be An England'. It had all been ill-mannered and indecent and followed the usual fatuous behaviour of the House, but it had taken him all his time to smile at his supporters, and to keep his head up as he had passed through the door behind the Speaker's chair to his room. Even the inquest they were now conducting seemed ill-omened.

'Prime Minister'—the Home Secretary jerked his thoughts back to the present—'we're being labelled as aggressors throughout the world. The United Nations has demanded that we accept a United Nations police force and that we submit our claims to King Boffa Port to the International Court without delay. We used our veto on this last week and I'm not sure now that we were well advised. The Americans are growing very restless.'

'The Americans don't run this country,' the Prime Minister snapped.

'With sixty per cent of British industry financed from New York,' the Foreign Secretary put in, 'I'm not so sure of that, Prime Minister. The man who pays the piper calls the tune and they could wreck our economy if they wished to, by forcing their investors to withdraw.'

The Prime Minister frowned, rebuffed by the remarks. 'I don't agree with you,' he commented gruffly.

The Foreign Secretary was not put off and continued relentlessly. 'I'm sorry about that, Prime Minister,' he said. 'I'm sure the Chancellor of the Exchequer can enlarge upon it.'

The Prime Minister waved a hand and the Chancellor moved forward and opened his brief case. The Prime Minister eyed him with suspicion. He had a strong feeling that, like the

Home Secretary, he too was close to the Foreign Secretary and that they were all working behind his back to ease him out of office. He only partly heard what the Chancellor was saying.

'Sterling area's gold and dollar reserves have declined during the past three weeks by seventy-five million dollars,' he was pointing out. 'That, Prime Minister, is greater by the week than at the time of Suez, and there are menacing signs of a "flight from the pound".'

He unfolded a pink sheet and glanced at it.

'The financial structure of this country,' he said, 'makes us very vulnerable to political events and the impact on our reserves is immediate and substantial. And the world's determined to show its reaction to what we're doing through sterling. There's one other thing . . .'

They all looked up.

'As you know, Prime Minister,' the Chancellor continued, 'we have for a long time been bolstering up our economy with loans from America and Switzerland and the International Bank. I've now been informed from Washington that the United States can no longer see her way clear to continue to lend us money and is accordingly stopping the next instalments. She claims that what she has already lent us was for redeploying our industry and to help us over our monetary crisis, and that we have no right to use it to make war.'

'We haven't used a penny of it to make war!'

'You know that, Prime Minister. I know that. But the rest of the world will accept what the Americans say. They also say they will recommend to the International Bank that they, too, should freeze all loans to us.'

'Unless we stop *Stabledoor*?'

'Yes. The ethical, moral, political and legal issues no longer predominate, Prime Minister. Whatever we like to think, whatever we like to tell the world, it's become an issue of finance that could smash us.'

'The Malalans will never agree to calling the thing off,' Starke said.

'On the contrary, Prime Minister,' the Foreign Secretary interrupted, 'I've just been informed that they may even withdraw.'

Starke looked up quickly. 'Withdraw? From *Stabledoor?*' It was like a blow in the face.

'That's my information,' the Foreign Secretary said. 'The Americans are tempting them with their offer of a loan, and they're under heavy pressure from the African states. I can't see how they can refuse.'

'They can't back out now!'

'They can, Prime Minister,' the Foreign Secretary insisted calmly. 'Indeed, I think they will. The Afro-Asian bloc's strong nowadays and support's growing for them even among those states which have been supporting us. They could crush Braka economically. He needs an American loan and he needs the goodwill of the countries round him. He can't refuse.'

Starke sat for a moment, thinking, then he fought back strongly against the tide of opposition. 'I still feel a *fait accompli* would be accepted,' he said. 'Can't we ask Carey again to withdraw?'

The Chief of Defence Staff tapped his long forefinger on a signal sheet that lay in front of him.

'Prime Minister,' he said harshly, speaking for the first time. 'It's suddenly no longer a matter of finance or approval or speed. I've been listening to what's been said in the hope that it would influence decisions. Since it hasn't, I would like to put my spoke in. Hodges has signalled that *Stabledoor* has a good chance of ending in disaster.'

Starke couldn't believe him, not after all the effort he'd put into the operation. 'Surely he's exaggerating,' he said.

'I don't think he is, Prime Minister. Consider the facts.' The Chief of Defence Staff's face was merciless. 'We know,' he said, 'that Hajaian volunteers are standing by near the border ready to move over as soon as the barriers are removed, and air reconnaissance photographs show Migs lined wing-tip to wing-tip on the airfields in Tasia. We also have information that others have moved down to Atcha, only twenty minutes' flying time from King Boffa Port, which means, in addition to the eighty aircraft we believe they've got, Scepwe will be able to call on an additional fifty operational Migs and some forty pilots capable of operating the older and slower jets they got from us. Against this, Malala can produce a few old French jets and American F84s, twelve Ouragans and twenty-five piston-driven aircraft. Within striking distance, *we* have seventy Storms, twenty-five Hecates and twenty-five V9os. That's not a crushing superiority.'

'It ought to be enough.'

The Chief of Defence Staff looked furious, as though he considered the Prime Minister was blinding himself to facts.

'One minute, Prime Minister,' he said. 'There are also, as I've reported, at least two—we think three to five—Russian submarines shadowing the convoy. The Director of Naval Operations suspects there are at least ten others within calling distance, and what's more, as I've already told you, Hodges' Chief-of-Staff's come up with a whole new set of figures on Scepwe's military set-up that seems to suggest we've been badly let down by Intelligence. We could be humiliated.'

Starke moved restlessly in his chair. 'Surely this is the calculated risk we must take,' he said. 'If we get the troops ashore quickly, all these support forces'll be too late to offer help.'

'*If* we get the troops ashore quickly,' the Chief of Defence Staff said. 'I wouldn't like to be Hodges.'

The Prime Minister knew exactly what the Chief of Defence Staff was talking about. If things went wrong there'd be a search for a scapegoat and inevitably it would be Hodges. It would have to be.

'Have you further information?' he asked cautiously.

'Yes. Looks like out-and-out mutiny to me, Prime Minister, and if *Stabledoor* collapses because of it, you, Prime Minister, are very much involved. Your reputation depends on this as much as mine and Hodges', because your Cabinet, sir, ordered us to set it up.'

It was out now. The Prime Minister looked at the Chief of Defence Staff with something approaching hatred, then he noticed that there was a similar look to the soldier's in the eyes of the Home Secretary and the Foreign Secretary and the Chancellor of the Exchequer, and he realised with clarity that unless he were clever, his days were numbered.

'Foreign Secretary,' he said. 'Have you had any further reports of foreign reactions?'

'Not very happy ones, Prime Minister.' The Foreign Secretary seemed uneasy. 'Our people in Vienna say there's been a bonfire in the Soviet Embassy courtyard for a couple of days. Listening stations report that the Soviet early warning radar lines have been brought up to the highest state of alert, and that the volume of military electronics traffic has trebled across the Warsaw Pact countries. Nuclear weapons have been moved from the north of China to the south, and, although it may be bluff, we understand that fifty thousand officers of the Soviet Reserve have volunteered for service in Africa.'

The Prime Minister looked at the Chief of Defence Staff. 'How much of this does Hodges know?' he asked.

'None. He's probably formed his own opinion but we've told him nothing.'

'Why not?'

The Chief of Defence Staff didn't answer and the implications were obvious. He had begun to hope that *Stabledoor* would be called off.

The Foreign Secretary's quiet voice broke in on the Prime Minister's thoughts.

'Prime Minister,' he said. 'The most serious question facing us is really whether this operation can be morally justified any longer. To prolong it might invite drastic intervention by the Soviets and the United States.'

The Prime Minister felt crushed.

'President Ghaniri has sent a personal message to the American President proposing, with Afro-Asian support, that the United States Eighth Fleet be sent to King Boffa Port at once as the beginning of a United Nations Force, to enforce the resolutions of the General Assembly. Scepwe's said he'll probably allow United States Marines to land, but at the same time he's appealed for volunteers from any nation that, to quote him, "believes in the cause of freedom and justice". He's suggested they should enlist at Khanzian embassies for service in Khanzi.'

'Bluff,' the Prime Minister snapped. 'They can't get to Khanzi with us outside King Boffa Port and you know as well as I do that both the United States, France and Canada have made an announcement that anybody who enlists for service with Khanzi could lose his citizenship. They're determined not to be involved.'

' "Not to take sides" is nearer, Prime Minister,' the Foreign Secretary corrected. 'We've had reports that the Russians have already asked the Turks for permission to pass a naval force through the Dardanelles.'

'The thing would be over before they could get there.'

The Chief of Defence Staff stood up and threw down his papers. He seemed to tower above the Prime Minister.

'Not if Hodges is held up by his own troops,' he snapped. 'And it looks now as though he might be.'

Part Three

1

General Hodges had summoned all his senior officers to his cabin aboard *Leopard* and they sat now round the long table, restless, uneasy and caught by a dozen different apprehensions.

Nobody seemed anxious to stir up more trouble than they had on their hands already, and a suggested attempt to weed out the mutineers had been quickly talked down on the grounds that it would only bring matters to a head more quickly.

To Hodges it seemed that everyone was hoping their reprieve would come not from themselves but from London, but he also knew that, quite apart from what was decided at Westminster, it was still his duty as a commander to make sure that he didn't lose control of his forces long before that.

'Anything we do must be done quickly,' he said. 'And we must decide at once what it is to be. Although all the evidence seems to suggest that though what refusal there is to be is to be orderly and not violent, we still have to accept that an isolated incident could spark off physical resistance which could escalate into something very unpleasant.'

'General'—Dixon spoke—'we don't suspect trouble from the Marines or the Guards. Surely, if they're sent in, the rest of Hodgeforce won't refuse to follow them.'

Hodges wasn't so sure and now, having heard the arguments, he made up his mind swiftly.

'Officers,' he said, 'must be warned what to expect and they must be prepared to arrest all disaffected troops at once, agitators in particular being dealt with immediately. Since we don't know yet which troops are the disaffected ones, there's not very much we can do until they show their hand, but on each ship there are companies of Guardsmen and Marines and tankmen. Reliable men under reliable N.C.O.s and officers must be told off to stand ready at the first sign of disobedience. All seditious troops must be disarmed at once. There is to be no equivocation and no hesitation. They are not to be given the benefit of the doubt.

'Revolver racks are to be emptied where ships carry revolver racks and, since we can't empty the ready-use lockers, officers are to be placed discreetly as sentries over them and over the keyboards where the keys to the magazines are kept. Since we're expecting to use these magazines, officers will have to use their common sense about what to do. Officers are to make an attempt to talk to the men wherever possible. Only the N.C.O.s of the Guards, the Marines and the Tank Regiments are to be informed what is happening and why they are being asked to do what will be requested of them.'

He turned to Leggo. 'Stuart, I'd like you to prepare a statement for the Press. Nobody's asked anything yet but I've noticed some funny looks in the wardroom and I suspect they may already have been warned by the stewards of what's in the wind. Eventually they're bound to ask questions and we must be ready for them. I'd like you to be as vague as possible without telling any untruths.'

Dixon looked up again. He suddenly looked nervous.

'And the invasion, General?'

Hodges sighed. He could just imagine the shambles that would ensue if men were withdrawn from reliable key units to keep an eye on unreliable troops, and the chaos that would result from any attempt to disarm whole sections, while the landing was actually taking place. There wasn't the faintest chance of success for *Stabledoor* but, with his orders as categoric as they were, he also could see no alternative. He drew a deep breath.

'Ship's captains are to be approached discreetly and asked to put store-rooms, lockers, et cetera, at our disposal, in case of mass arrests. There must be no doubt in the minds of commanding officers, and any officers who argue are to be relieved of their commands at once. As for invasion . . .'

He paused. There had been no alteration in the plan from London, and he could hardly resign his command in disgust and let it take care of itself. He saw Dixon's eyes on him accusingly.

'As for the invasion,' he said again. '*Stabledoor* will proceed as ordered.'

In the cells deep in the hull of *Banff*, Ginger Bowen stared with distaste at Leach, Wedderburn, McKechnie and Snaith who were sharing his little corner of the ship's bowels. Not being unfamiliar with his surroundings and far more at home under lock and key than the others, he was far less troubled by the fact that he was under arrest than he was by the fact that he felt for once he had done nothing to warrant being there.

Inevitably, Frensham and Captain White had not attempted to separate the innocent from the guilty, but had marched up the Military Police and a squad of Guardsmen under the biggest sergeant-major Ginger had ever seen, and every occupant of the Starboard Cross Passage was now under guard. Since there were not sufficient cells for all of them and it had been felt necessary to isolate them from the rest of the ship, they had been stuffed into rope stores and chain lockers, and they now sat around, gloomy, depressed and covered with dust and grease.

'For God's sake, man,' Sergeant O'Mara had said bitterly, staring at Ginger as he'd arrived. 'After all I did to avoid it, too!'

Nobody in Ginger's cell felt much like talking and there had been no apportioning of blame, but the distrust was mixed with dislike and a certain amount of despair. They were low enough in the ship to feel the pulse of the propeller shaft and they could see no sign of what was going on above deck. Occasionally, as someone opened a door along the corridor, they felt a draught of warm air and occasionally they heard the sound of men moving outside, but for the most part they were cut off from the rest of the ship—and they felt it.

'Perhaps it's as well it happened the way it did,' Wedderburn said heavily. 'They say the bastards back in London have ordered that we're not to use anything bigger than a machine gun when we go ashore.'

Inevitably the signals to Hodgeforce, passed out quietly by the radio operators in the darkened corridors during a hasty visit to the heads and spread around the ships, had become garbled in their passage through the fleet. And though no one really believed Wedderburn's version, there was no question but that everyone—even at the lowest levels—felt that the heavy hand of politics lay across the operation, depriving it of life and throttling whatever chance it had of success.

Ginger Bowen said nothing. In a way, he wasn't sorry he was where he was. Quite apart from the Guardsman outside the door—who looked at them as though they were something he had picked up on the sole of his boot and seemed more than prepared, if necessary, to use on them the Sten gun he carried under his arm—from what he could make out, whatever it was that *Stabledoor* was intending to do, it had had little chance of success from the start, and it was perhaps a good idea to be out of it in the bowels of the ship when the rubbish started flying. Nevertheless, he felt a profound resentment that he was back in his old haunts without good reason. In spite of his disgust at his earlier punishments, he had never previously felt they were anybody's fault but his own.

Only one of the men in the cell seemed not to have lost faith. Private Leach stirred on the iron bunk where he was lounging, his eyes bitter and frustrated.

'They'll never get the blokes out of the ships,' he said stubbornly. 'Not now. It'll just stiffen the resistance.'

'I'd like to stiffen you lot,' Ginger said bitterly. 'Mutiny,' he went on, his voice shocked. 'You ought to be bloody well ashamed of yourselves.'

Leach ignored him, still concerned for the plan that had been evolved at the meeting on the football field behind the canteen at Pepul. The replacement of the acquiescent captain of *Duck* had presented difficulties among the organisers, and the decision to force the ship to turn back to Pepul had removed most of the brains behind the plot, but he still had faith that the rest of the men in Hodgeforce were behind what had been decided.

Wedderburn lifted his eyes to Ginger, moving them heavily as though he were sick.

'O'Mara said Joe Malaki had been talking,' he pointed out.

'What's it matter?' Leach jeered. 'There are twenty thousand men on these ships, brother. A few Guardsmen can't force *that* lot to go over the sides.'

'I'd go over,' Ginger said earnestly, 'if I had a Guards sergeant-major like that bloke outside poking his Sten gun up my jacksie.'

There was silence at his remark because even Leach realised that, under the same circumstances, even he might conform.

'They'll never make 'em fight,' he said.

They eyed each other for a moment, because they were all well aware of the chaos that would ensue.

'Christ,' Wedderburn said, quite unaware that he was echoing the thoughts of his general. 'What a bloody shambles it'll be.'

2

At his house at Brighton, the Leader of the Opposition was studying the reports that had been delivered to him from the House of Commons. The Home Secretary, the Foreign Secretary and the Defence Minister were, by arrangement, courteously allowing him to keep in touch with events. This was not unusual at a time of crisis but, somehow, Carey had a feeling at that moment that there was more than mere courtesy involved. More and more he felt that a climax was imminent, and he suspected they knew it, too, and were allowing him deliberately to keep abreast of events.

He glanced up at the men at the table by the window. Moffat was leaning over the pile of newspapers, watched by the Shadow Chancellor.

'Starke's wavering,' he said.

'He'll never waver,' the Shadow Chancellor snorted.

Moffat rattled the sheets on the table before him and looked round at Carey.

'*The Times* has it again that you're prepared to join a coalition,' he said.

'Well, *The Times* is wrong,' Carey answered.

'Don't you think, in view of the danger, we *ought* to consider a coalition?'

'Not under Starke,' Carey said. 'He's come round to the idea and sounded me. I told him that we couldn't serve under him, and, in fact, that the country didn't want him.'

'That was pretty brutal, Spencer.'

'It was intended to be. He's a bit of a limpet and we now have a clear chance of office.'

Moffat smoothed the newspapers slowly. 'A coalition would stop the rot,' he persisted. 'It would mean there'd be some direction at last.' He paused, eyeing Carey. 'He's still hoping,' he pointed out. 'He's been in touch with Bryerly, Thompson and Rayner Clark. I heard he's even had a go at Lord Forbes.'

'Elders of the Party,' Carey snapped. 'Men who no longer have any hopes of office if we get in.'

He knew that the men around him saw the crisis to a large extent as an opportunity to seize power after too many years in opposition, and he knew they would be more than willing to try any method to kick open the door. He had himself accused the Government only the previous night of hedging, and of endeavouring to justify its actions in half a dozen niggling ways, and he stared at his own words now in the scattered Press cuttings on the desk in front of him, uneasily conscious that they sounded hollow and even cynical, because the by-election at Rudkin and Hale had shown the way the country was thinking. He was well aware that with a similar swing throughout the country, he could reckon on a solid majority at a General Election.

He pushed the cuttings aside with a quick gesture, telling himself he was anticipating events. Starke was too crafty to allow himself to be manœuvred into an early election—especially with opinion against him. Yet—Carey frowned at the realisation—if he hung on to the last minute, there was a good chance that the country could be destroyed economically for years to come and even of a disastrous possibility of a world at war. It was hardly an auspicious set of events for a new administration to inherit. The pressure would have to be put on the Prime Minister a little.

He moved restlessly in his chair, impatient and resentful. It seemed incredible to him that Starke could continue to survive the outcry that *Stabledoor* had aroused. It was worse even than at the time of Suez. In spite of being repelled by the police, the students were coming back again and again; and no section of the community—even a resilient student section—would go on doing that if they didn't believe wholeheartedly that *Stabledoor* was illogical, immoral and unnecessary. Police reinforcements had had to be called into the capital to help the Metropolitan Force but, with outbreaks elsewhere, only the county forces had been able to spare men, and for the most part they weren't used to city streets and didn't handle riots as well as the

London men, and casualty wards all over the city were filling up, with police and students in beds next to each other. The dockers' strike at Southampton had turned into a minor battle and tear-gas bombs had been used in Bristol. All output had been stopped at Birmingham, Coventry and Middlesbrough because works managers could not promise that what was turned out was not going to be used against the Khanzians; and there had been trouble at more than one pub in the Notting Hill area of London as premises had been wrecked by coloured mobs and white men had been beaten up.

England was sinking into disrepute. Abroad, she stood accused by America, Russia, China, France and a dozen Afro-Asian countries. India had threatened once more to withdraw from the Commonwealth and there was a danger of even Canada, New Zealand and Australia severing the tenuous links that still held them to England.

Weighing matters up, Carey decided that perhaps it would be wiser not to hurry Starke too much. If Starke went too quickly, his successor would inherit not only a great deal of the difficulties but also some of the odium, and he wanted to see the blame set fairly on the shoulders of the men in office first. There must be no taint attached to the Opposition, in case the Party managed to seize power, and no question of joining a coalition while blame still remained unapportioned. If power came, it had to come clear-cut and backed by the whole of the country, and it seemed worth the gamble of waiting.

He sat back in his chair, irritated by the need for restraint when power seemed so near. In front of him *The Times* showed the Prime Minister leaving Downing Street. He looked worried and there were placards visible demanding his resignation. Yet, while he could still command such a substantial majority in the House as he did, there was nothing Carey could do but wait and play his cards close to his chest.

For a moment, he regretted the speech he had made the previous day in the House. Reading it again in the columns of *The Times*, it sounded less like an appeal to restore the country's integrity than an effort to destroy the Government and climb to power on the wreckage. His political instincts had overcome him when he had intended to show only patriotism, and he

would have to be more careful. There must be no feeling in the
constituencies that he was making political capital out of the
crisis. The debate that had followed his speech had been as
bitter, fruitless and arid as ever, and there had been a great
many shouts of 'Traitor' from both sides of the House.
Speeches had been constantly interrupted so that the noise had
increased to a deafening intensity, and it had eventually become
so impossible to hear a thing even from the other side of the
despatch table, that the Speaker, with wave after wave of noise
beating about the Chamber, had risen and left the House to
bring the sitting to an end.

It had been a sad stupid scene and marked the very depths
of parliamentary behaviour, and the Leader of the Opposition
was still suffering from an uneasy feeling that perhaps they
had gone about things the wrong way, when his secretary
came to say there was a telephone call from Greenaway.

He sat up abruptly in his chair. A call from Greenaway could
mean only one thing.

He picked up the telephone and Greenaway spoke at once.

'May I come and see you, Spencer?' he asked. 'I can be there
in a couple of hours.'

'Will any useful purpose be served?' Carey asked. 'I've
refused twice, George.'

Greenaway coughed. 'It's nothing to do with the Prime
Minister,' he said.

'Can't you tell me what it is?'

'I'd rather not over the telephone.'

'Is it to do with *Stabledoor*?'

'Of course.'

'Then I'd like to have Moffat here as well.'

'I'll agree to that.'

Something in Greenaway's manner made Carey suspicious.
'Can't you give me a hint as to what's going on?' he asked.

'I think we'd better leave it till I see you.'

Greenaway's car turned into the drive before the two hours
were up and he was shown at once into Carey's study. Moffat
rose from his seat by the window and they all shook hands.

'Now, George,' Carey said. 'For God's sake, spit it out.'

205

'I think you should be in London,' Greenaway said at once.

'Why, George?'

'Do I have to spell it out?'

Carey's heart leapt. He knew quite well what Greenaway was hinting at but he hardly dared to think about it.

'Why, George?' he asked. 'What's happening?'

Greenaway looked embarrassed. 'There's a feeling among us,' he said, 'that *Stabledoor* must be stopped.'

Carey glanced at Moffat, but neither of them spoke, and Greenaway went on uncomfortably.

'It's well known,' he said, 'that Russian submarines are dogging it every inch of the way, and we know now that Malala's likely to back out. Not only have the Americans and the African states been at them, but we've heard also that Russia's prepared to offer machinery and a thumping big loan.' He lifted unhappy eyes to Carey. 'Nobody wants the sort of war this could become,' he said, 'and they're all—even Russia —willing to offer bribes. Braka will get most of them for himself, but he'll never be able to resist them. He'll back out all right.'

Moffat gestured. 'How about your position in this, George?' he asked. 'I suppose we ought to know.'

Greenaway paused. 'I've already offered my resignation to my constituency,' he said. 'So no one can accuse me of being a traitor to the Party. I've been involved in the events of the last few days more deeply than I like; and as I told you, when they start to look for a scapegoat, it'll probably be me. So I'm resigning. I've done my best to help the Government, but only for the good of the country. I'm sure you both know that.'

The other two men glanced at each other and Greenaway sighed within himself, feeling they were taking in only half of what he said. Politicians had changed since he'd first entered Parliament, he decided, and he was no longer able to keep up with the harder-headed men who were rising to the top, younger men who seemed more fitted by temperament to big business than politics. Patriotism and duty nowadays seemed to be only catchwords.

'Anybody else in this?' Carey asked sharply. 'Anyone big, I mean.'

Greenaway paused. 'Yes,' he said after a while. 'But I can't say who.'

Carey nodded, wondering whether it were the Home Secretary or the Foreign Secretary who had finally lost his nerve and sent Greenaway to see him. Popular opinion was running against the Government and the ripples of uncertainty had spread out from Downing Street through Westminster and Fleet Street. The newspapers were full of speculation already and it was said that Lord Edbury, bringing his weight to bear, had openly started to sound Government backbenchers about their views.

'It's only fair to tell you,' he said, 'that I think now we can afford to shift our position. We're no longer interested in joining a coalition because I think we can afford to aim for the whole lot.'

Greenaway sighed. 'Who said anything about a coalition?' he asked.

Carey looked narrowly at him, suddenly suspicious. 'There's something else, isn't there?' he asked.

'Yes.' Greenaway nodded. 'The Americans have taken a hand. They've been in touch with the Foreign Secretary—though not directly. They're determined to have Starke out.'

'It's no business of theirs,' Carey snapped. 'This isn't an American affair.'

'They feel it is. They claim that since this country's held together by American money, they've a right to put their views. That's all they have put at the moment.'

Carey's temper cooled. 'Go on, George,' he prompted.

Greenaway shrugged. He felt very old suddenly. 'They're anxious to bring the crisis to an end,' he said. 'They want Hodgeforce turned round, and they've been in touch with a few of our backbenchers. The feeling is that if the Prime Minister were to resign—*on any grounds*—they could step in and mollify Scepwe. It would save peace.'

Carey frowned. 'I can't see him resigning, George,' he said. 'He's still young and he's damned ambitious, and he won't want to lose *that* much face.'

'It's been suggested that he might get out of it by being taken ill. If he went into hospital abruptly, all sorts of thing could be blamed on him and, if we could get someone to say he'd had a nervous breakdown, the whole thing could be explained as the work of a man not responsible for his actions, and we could withdraw without loss of face. Something's got to be done. There are likely to be resignations.'

'Thank God someone's got a conscience.'

Greenaway looked up quickly as Carey spoke.

'Don't moralise too much, Spencer,' he warned him sharply, his voice suddenly hard. 'You might well find yourself in the same position some day. These things have a habit of creeping up on you, as I've found out. Before you know where you are, you're committed—and in a way you never intended.'

Carey nodded, accepting the wisdom of the remark, and Greenaway went on.

'There's a belief among us,' he said, 'that we might persuade him he no longer has our support. I was asked to see you, to find out whether you were prepared. I was asked for the same reasons as I was asked last time.'

Carey smiled. 'I'm ready, George,' he said. 'But you'll never pull it off.'

'We've got Sir Wilfred Craig to say he'll put his name to any report on his health. He's the Royal Physician so it should carry some weight.'

The Leader of the Opposition eyed Greenaway for a moment. 'There's just one thing,' he said slowly. 'I asked for a new Government. I didn't ask for a new party in office. Why do they want *me* to be ready? What's wrong with the Foreign Secretary?'

'He can't get enough support. If *Stabledoor* continues, he's prepared to resign. And so is the Home Secretary. But there'll be too many in the Party who'll feel they'll have stabbed him in the back. They'd never form a government.'

Carey felt a surge of excitement. It was like the sudden feel of power. 'Is there no one else?' he asked.

Greenaway shook his head. 'No one with enough stature to take this lot on his shoulders,' he said. He looked shrewdly at Carey, wondering whether he were a statesman or just another politician like himself. 'I'm not sure *you* are. You've not held the office before.'

'I might surprise you, George,' Carey said confidently.

'I hope you will.'

Carey moved away. One had to admit, Greenaway told himself, he had a commanding presence. He had a presence, ability, and a rare gift of oratory. He wondered if it were enough, and if, underneath the Party tactician, there were the sweeping emotions, idealism and passion of a real leader.

'Since you seem to be in some doubt about me'—Carey's words made Greenaway jump and he was startled to realise that his thoughts could have been so transparent—'it might startle you to know that I'm not going along with you.'

Moffat swung round. 'You're *not*?' He found it hard to believe that a man could refuse the chance of such high office.

Greenaway was staring at Carey now, sorely troubled. 'This is no time to play politics, Spencer,' he said.

Carey shook his head. 'I'm not playing politics,' he said, though Greenaway found it hard to believe. 'I have no need to, the way things are.'

'What do you mean by that?'

Carey still had his back to the fireplace, his hands behind him, warming them against the flames.

'I won't be a party to any conspiracy, either by the backbenchers or by the Americans,' he said. 'If Starke goes, he goes in a proper democratic manner, because there's no longer any support for him. I'll not be involved either by the other side or by any foreign power.'

Greenaway looked weary. 'Perhaps we can't wait that long,' he said quietly. 'This thing could escalate overnight. Things are moving fast and with everything set up as it is, we could be carried along simply by the weight of armaments, as in 1914. There'd be no drawing back.'

'I must risk that.'

'For the record?' Greenaway asked bitterly, and Carey looked at him sharply.

'We've been a long time in opposition,' he said, 'and there's a chance now for us to get into office. I've never been Prime Minister, George, and it's an office any man could be proud of. I like to think I could make a good job of it. Perhaps I'd be proved wrong—I don't know—but I think I ought to have the chance to try.'

Greenaway lifted his head wearily, suddenly full of doubt about Carey.

'If *Stabledoor* collapses,' he said heavily, 'you'll be as responsible for the disaster as anyone. You could turn it back if you wished.'

Carey shook his head stubbornly. 'It must be done constitutionally,' he insisted. 'I'll wait until the apple drops off the tree.'

'In spite of the urgency?'

'It's a matter of honour.'

Greenaway looked defeated. 'What a mess the honour of honourable men can make of things,' he said bitterly to Moffat, then, with a movement of infinite weariness, he picked up his hat and coat and left the room.

While Greenaway was talking to Carey, Arthur Starke sat alone in his chair in the Cabinet Room at Number Ten, keeping his long vigil.

In front of him the desk was littered with papers. There was a note from the Chief Whip's Office insisting that there must be a statement by him after Questions the following week, and that there might be a demand for an emergency debate that could not be resisted. Underneath it, there were a group of *Most Immediate* telegrams from African states, all of them showing a shifting viewpoint over King Boffa Port and demanding to know Britain's position. There were also numerous slips of paper fed to him by his Parliamentary Private Secretary with summaries of what they said and suggested replies, and he listlessly wrote 'Approved' across one or two of them and signed his initials, resentful that so many people should be carrying on the normal business of the country, and that so many trivialities should still be offered to him for his advice or approval when so much hung in the balance.

He frowned suddenly and pushed the papers away, irritated and suddenly tired. He was fully aware of the forces that were moving towards his destruction and he felt himself surrounded. He knew perfectly well what was going on inside his own party. The Home Secretary had not left him in much doubt. If his enemies had their way, his career was ended and, unable to accept what was staring him in the face, his mind still searched for a solution.

The hint about being taken ill suddenly had been dropped quite quietly and very simply by the Foreign Secretary, and the Prime Minister knew exactly what they were intending to do with him, because he would have done the same thing if he'd had to. They were proposing to allow the world to think he'd had a brainstorm and that all the events of the past few weeks had sprung entirely from that.

It was a brutal move, but politics, he knew, was a cruel game, and he searched desperately for the solution he was still sure he could find.

He slowly turned over the papers that lay under his hand on the desk, but there was one he'd asked for which hadn't yet arrived.

He sighed and glanced at the map of Khanzi. Already the usual crackpots were trying to get into the area to be ready to count the bodies and quote the numbers at him in the House, just as they had at the time of Korea and Indo-China and Algeria and Suez and Vietnam. Every outbreak all over the world, no matter who was to blame, drew its quota of lunatics ready to claim that a big nation was beating the living daylights out of a small one. Even the Americans who had more than once halted the forward march of Communism had got nothing but insults for their efforts.

The Foreign Secretary entered the room. His face was grave and sombre. Because of the crowd outside the Prime Minister's residence, he had had to enter via Number Eleven and make his way across. Starke looked up as he stopped before the desk.

'I have the report you asked for, Prime Minister,' he said.

His voice was cool and indifferent, as though he could already see the writing on the wall and wanted to be remembered for having registered his protest. The Prime Minister gave him a bitter look. He had no love for the Foreign Secretary who had been quick enough to jump on the Prime Minister's bandwaggon when he was on the way up, and was now covering his retreat in case the Prime Minister fell.

'I've sounded the American Ambassador, Prime Minister,' he said. 'They are quite adamant.'

Unknowingly, the Prime Minister used almost the same words as the Leader of the Opposition.

'It's none of their affair,' he said.

'The way they see it, it is, Prime Minister. Quite apart from the financial angle, and that's serious enough, God knows, they've found themselves running into a blank wall every time they project a new move. There's been a new shift of opinion among the Afro-Asian bloc. All those African states who previously supported us have now about-faced and Scepwe's realised how strong his position is and altered his demands. There's no possibility now of his accepting a United Nations police force from *any* nation while this party remains in power in England.'

The Prime Minister's eyes flashed. 'I won't be dictated to,' he snapped. 'Not by a lot of men recently out of the jungle.'

The Foreign Secretary looked shocked. 'They're members of the Commonwealth, Prime Minister.'

'I sometimes think the Commonwealth would be better off without them.'

'Prime Minister'—the Foreign Secretary looked grave—'a conference has been planned for the week-end at Nairobi. Every African nation, and that includes the Arab nations and all those who previously supported us, is sending a delegate. It's been hurried and I expect it'll be the usual awful mess, but, Prime Minister, they're going there to try to create a United States of Africa.'

The Prime Minister looked up.

'Prime Minister, this is the first real move towards a United Africa, and you know, as I know and everybody else knows, how potentially strong a United States of Africa could be, now that they've begun to industrialise. The first thing they intend to debate is the sending immediately of volunteers to King Boffa Port.'

The Prime Minister rose slowly from his chair and moved to the window. London was grey in the dull spring weather, with the buildings bluish in the haze.

'What we feared is happening, Prime Minister,' the Foreign Secretary continued in a low voice. 'If the Africans unite against us in war, no European nation could stay out of it. The threat would be too enormous. Then the Chinese will come in behind the African states and the Russians and the Americans will never dare to stay out. This is why the United States is insisting, Prime Minister. We all know that unification of this sort will not be good for Africa and even less good for Europe.'

The Prime Minister turned, his eyes tired.

'Suppose we turn Hodgeforce round and send it back to Pepul?' he asked.

The Foreign Secretary shook his head. 'Prime Minister, it must not go back to Pepul. It must come home.'

'It can't come home. Twenty thousand men arriving in England full of complaints and full of reports, and all demanding an explanation—whatever their views—it would destroy us.'

'I'm sorry, Prime Minister, but they're threatening sanctions against Malala if she doesn't drop her demands against Khanzi and I expect that before long a signal will go out to their troops to withdraw. We can't go back to Pepul.'

The Prime Minister moved back to his chair, his actions nervous, his face full of anger.

'I will *not* have the country humiliated,' he snapped.

The Foreign Secretary seemed to be choosing his words carefully.

'The withdrawal of Malalan forces, Prime Minister,' he said as pointedly as he could, 'will leave *us* out on a limb, about to invade a nation that is ready for us and with a whole continent at its back, while we have only half the force we intended to put into the operation, and that remaining half disunited and torn with dissension. Prime Minister, Hodgeforce is heading for a tragedy of the greatest magnitude.' He paused for a moment to let his words sink in. 'Certain members of the Cabinet, Prime Minister, myself included, feel that we could not go so far.'

The Prime Minister turned, feeling like a baited bull. 'Then I will go it alone,' he said.

3

On the bridge deck of H.M.S. *Leopard*, General Hodges stood alongside Admiral Downes and stared through the naval binoculars which a silent commander had passed over to him.

The rain, which had fallen intermittently all day, had stopped at last and the air felt suddenly fresher. The sea was calmer, too, with only a slight swell now and a light wind. It was a still night with stars that glowed brightly through the gaps in the clouds beyond the pitch-black angularity of the ship's superstructure. There seemed to be no sound in the whole fleet except the throb of engines and the hiss of water, and even these sounds seemed blotted out, too, so that only murmured conversations reached up to the bridge deck and the pale moonlight accentuated the darkness beyond its reach.

In the distance, across the black sea, Hodges could see a faint glow appearing and disappearing across the sky, almost like the beam swinging round a radar screen, coming over an edge of purple that ran along the horizon.

'The shadow's Poro Island,' Downes said. 'The light's King Boffa Light. It lies ten miles outside the entrance to the harbour, on Locco Island. That's just beyond Poro, so that places us roughly forty miles from King Boffa Port. In three hours from now, we shall be in position for the run-in.'

'And in Khanzian territorial waters?'

'Well inside. We'll be committed.'

Hodges said nothing and stared at the light again. In spite of the warm night, he felt chilled, almost as though a dose of malaria were creeping up on him. These silent final hours had their own unnatural quality. Below him somewhere, a tin mug clattered in the darkness and he heard a muttered oath. It seemed unreal to Hodges. The arguments, the endless training, the excitement were over, but he was still bowed under the accumulation of too many depressing problems.

He was where a real soldier ought to be, ready to command troops in battle, and in the cabin under the ship's bridge, messages would soon begin to arrive asking for help of various kinds, to which he would have to give immediate decisions.

He felt no joy at the thought, however, because of the harsh sounding of a subconscious alarm that things were desperately wrong with his command.

He'd never been a man to suffer fear much, and he'd never felt overmuch anxiety as an officer at ordering men to their deaths. He had long since accepted this as part of his job, and as a young officer had felt no resentment against those superiors who had ordered *him* into situations which could have resulted in his own death.

He knew he probably had the deaths of many men on his conscience, but he'd always felt they'd been justified by the circumstances because his country had been at war and it had been a case of other men's deaths or the deaths of his own men. He'd not suffered from remorse.

Now, however, it was different and he was full of dread. Black men all over Africa, turning at last from white man's rule, were resenting any suggestion of hostility towards them. For years, long after everyone else had forgotten it, they had kept the chip on their shoulders about their black skins, and they were no longer prepared even to talk to white men who were willing to invade their territory. Only a humiliating climb-down could prevent a calamitous upheaval over the whole continent, and Hodges wasn't sure that humiliation wasn't better than a vast blood-bath.

It was this that chilled him. Radio activity from ashore had revealed that volunteers from other African states had started to cross the Khanzian border on the invitation of Colonel Scepwe. There was still a pretence that they were there to conduct exercises on Khanzian soil, but this was no worse than the pretence he himself had maintained that Hodgeforce was carrying out exercises with the Malalan forces, and it was really only a loophole that had been left for the European and American politicians. The volunteers could finish their exercises and go home at any time anyone wished.

African diplomats from all over the continent were also heading for Nairobi and Hodges knew that this could be the end of white men in Africa, because although with independence, Africans had still accepted them, any attempt to invade Africa by Europeans would mean the operation of apartheid in an opposite direction. There were signs that it was going to affect India and Asia, too. The white man could be forced right back to Europe. Whether or not the fighting escalated into a major conflict, it could have disastrous consequences for the world, morally, politically and financially.

'Hello!' Downes' exclamation jerked Hodges out of his thoughts and he swung round and followed the sailor's pointing finger. The leading ship on the port bow had put on speed and was moving up closer to *Leopard*.

'That's *Uhuru*,' Downes said. 'What the hell are *they* up to?'

'Admiral'—the commander spoke from the back of the bridge—'the Khanzian flagship's signalling.'

There was the clatter of morse from the cabin just abaft the bridge, and a signal lieutenant-commander appeared with a message form in his hand.

'From *Uhuru*, sir.'

Downes took the signal and handed it to Hodges.

'COMEMFO to COMHOJ,' it read. 'EMFORCE ordered to return Pepul at once.'

There was no explanation, no apologies, not even any good luck wishes. They had been expecting it for some time but it came as a shock nevertheless.

Hodges turned and showed the signal to Downes. 'The Malalans are breaking off the operation,' he said.

As he flipped the sheet of paper with his forefinger and turned to watch the convoy, Downes halted the signals officer.

'Make a signal to all British ships,' he said. 'Close up and continue the same course.'

He swung round on Hodges. 'Do you want to talk to Aswana?' he asked.

Hodges shrugged. 'What's the point?' he asked. 'He won't know any more than his orders. We'll have to leave it to the politicians to ask why.'

The starboard column of ships was now turning slowly outwards, following *Uhuru* which, after dropping back into position, was swinging slowly away. One after the other they turned, heading due west, then suddenly their navigation lights came on and they swung round once more away from the darkened convoy, and began to head north again.

'You know what that means, don't you?' Hodges said. 'Whatever happens, *we* shan't be going back to Pepul.'

'That'll be jolly,' Downes said grimly. 'Because if we don't go to King Boffa Port and take on water and supplies, it's going to make things just a little tight. We could make it to Gib from here without a stop, but only just.'

'So far,' Hodges pointed out, 'there's no suggestion that we do anything else but what we are doing.'

Downes glanced at him. 'Surely to God,' he said, unexpectedly bitter, 'those bloody fools at home won't expect us to go ahead on our own *now*.'

Hodges shrugged. He had long since given up thinking about what the people at home, in their massive demonstration of brinkmanship, would do.

'Sir'—the signalman appeared again—'news flash.'

The loudspeaker came to life with the voice of a B.B.C. announcer in mid-sentence.

'. . . Malalan Government. It has been decided in Machingo to accede to the United Nations' request that any contemplated aggressive action against the Khanzian base of King Boffa Port should be dropped at once pending discussions. A meeting is to be held and it is reported from Machingo that a signal has gone out to the Malalan Fleet, which is at the moment at sea south of the Equator conducting exercises with the Royal Navy.'

There was a pause, then light music started again and was stopped at once as the radio room switched off.

'The bastards have tossed the ball into our court,' Downes said.

Hodges stared ahead, noticing that it had started to rain again. It felt cold and sharp against his face, and it seemed to shake him out of his unhappiness. He turned briskly to Downes.

'What would happen, Dennis, if we stopped the convoy here, and waited a while?'

Downes stared at him. 'Are you thinking of that, Horace?'

'I'm not considering anything at this particular moment. It's purely a hypothetical question.'

Downes considered for a moment. 'It would mean that the whole operation would fall flat on its face,' he said. 'If *Stable-door*'s to have the remotest chance of success, we have to be off King Boffa Port before daylight tomorrow morning. We shall be inside territorial waters very shortly, and off King Boffa Port in about three and a half hours. We've either got to go on or get the hell out of it. If we stop here, we're bound to be spotted tomorrow and it'll take a bit of doing to explain what a fleet of a hundred-odd ships is doing just outside King Boffa, armed to the teeth.'

Hodges moved across the bridge and stared towards the distant glow which was already noticeably brighter.

'We'll continue on this course,' he said, 'but I'd be glad if you'd let me know before we enter Khanzian waters.'

Downes studied his face but said nothing, and Hodges endeavoured to explain the way he was thinking.

'I'm considering the possibility,' he said, 'of turning us round. Now that Aswana's gone, you're my deputy and you've a right to know. Particularly since, if I do decide this way, I should be refusing to follow instructions, and you would probably wish to take over.'

Downes stared at him with a drawn face and Hodges went on calmly.

'That, of course, would be throwing the ball into *your* court, Dennis, and you'd be in an appalling position. It's only fair to say I haven't yet decided that way.'

'Thank God for that,' Downes said in a low voice.

Below decks, the troops had lapsed into a glum silence. Everyone knew the Malalan ships had turned away and, although the B.B.C. news flash had not been relayed over the ship's system, it hadn't taken long for it to be passed round the fleet. Radio operators on every ship had picked it up and whispered conversations in the darkened alleyways had been sufficient to see that it spread to every man on board.

Captain White looked at Sergeant Frensham. 'That sets us up as Aunt Sally,' he said laconically.

Frensham frowned. 'What's going to happen now, sir?' he asked.

White shrugged. 'God knows,' he said. 'I wish *I* did. We

218

haven't changed course so it looks very much to me as though they're going to chance it.'

Frensham's eyes glittered. Like every officer and senior N.C.O. on board *Banff* he knew the precautions that had been taken to prevent mutiny. White had taken him into his confidence and Frensham had watched the squads of puzzled Guardsmen and Marines move quietly into position about the ship, not knowing the reason for the change. There had been a lot of grumbling among them because the last-minute moves had disrupted their plans for disembarkation and they knew, as well as any officer, that the result when the time for landing arrived would be chaos. With every disembarkation route through the ship plotted to avoid confusion, units—even supposing the landing went unopposed—would find themselves crossing the paths of other units or even having to force their way into position against the flow of troops heading for the ship's sides. Men had been separated from their heavy equipment and even from their officers, and they all suspected they were going to find themselves on a hostile shore without leadership or the things they needed.

The shifting of the small armed squads had been watched with suspicion by the men of the county regiments it was designed to curb, and Frensham had been quick to note the muttering and the groups of men with their heads together. Even as it had been going on, he had expected trouble in the shape of a scuffle or a sudden move to overpower the small sections taking up their positions at vantage points. The stationing of officers near the keyboards and magazines had not gone unnoticed, he knew, while the clearing of the revolver racks from outside the wardroom had been duly reported, he was certain, by the wardroom stewards. Frensham had been twenty years in the Army and had served through more than one military mistake, and what he saw around him on board *Banff* filled him with horror, especially with the people at home still insisting, in the teeth of the facts, on the operation being carried through.

'Makes you feel bolshie, sir, don't it?' he said to White. 'If they tell me to go in, I'll go, but, by God, sir, I'm beginning to think the same way as them lads in the cells.'

To the men in the cells, the news had come via a disgusted Sergeant O'Mara.

'Well, that does it, brothers,' Leach said. 'That makes us spot ball. They haven't recalled *us*, I notice.'

Ginger Bowen listened to the low-pitched conversation glumly. He was still suffering from resentment that he was under lock and key through no fault of his own, and the look in his eye as he stared at Leach was full of bitter dislike that was rapidly boiling up to the point of physical action.

'They'll never get the blokes out of the ships,' Leach was saying. 'They'll never go.'

'They'll never even get the Guards out now,' Wedderburn agreed. 'They'll soon know what's in the wind.'

'Guardsmen don't know anything,' Snaith said dryly. 'Guardsmen don't think. The officers wind 'em up and off they go like clockwork.'

'But, Christ, brother'—Leach was noisily indignant—'they can't expect men to lay down their lives for their mates against odds.'

Ginger's dislike came out in a low bitter growl that stopped the conversation dead in its tracks.

'You'd never throw down *your* life for your mate,' he said. 'Your wife, yes, but not your life. In any case, you're under arrest and, thanks to you, old Jesus-Joseph Malaki's got a hole in the guts big enough to drive a bus through.'

'Serve him right,' Leach said. 'He should have stuck with us. I expect the black bastard got cold feet.'

Ginger turned slowly, his face full of menace as his fists clenched and unclenched. All his resentment at his incarceration boiled up with his dislike of Leach.

'I shouldn't be 'ere,' he said slowly. 'By rights I shouldn't be 'ere. And I'm blaming it directly on you, Leach. So you just say one more word about Joe Malaki—*or* me—*or* anybody else—that's all, and I'll come across there and ram it straight down your throat. Even if they hang me by the short hairs from the yard-arm. O.K.?'

It was a long speech for Ginger and Leach looked up, his expression changing from startled amazement at the bitter words to sullenness. Wedderburn, McKechnie and Snaith were watching him carefully, waiting for his retort, but for once Leach had none. He looked quickly at them, and then again at Ginger, and then he rolled over on the iron bunk and stuck his hands silently in his pockets.

On the bridge of *Leopard*, Downes turned to General Hodges.

'We're now five miles outside Khanzian territorial waters, Horace,' he said quietly. 'If you're going to do anything, now's the time to do it.'

Hodges turned his head, slowly, almost as though he were sleep-walking.

So the moment had come at last when he had to make his decision. There was no longer any time to equivocate or delay. He knew what Downes meant. With a fleet the size of that moving along silently behind them, they needed room to manœuvre, and he couldn't any longer hold back his decision.

'How long have I got?' he asked.

'Ten minutes,' Downes said. 'Half an hour from now the aircraft take off.'

'Give me that long.'

'There's one more thing.'

'Go on.'

'Radar shows that there are at least five unknown ships following us now, all small, all the size of submarines, and one larger one, the *Chorniye Kazach*, which has been with us all the time. We've also had a signal from the DNI that there are others believed to be within ten miles of us.'

'I see. Thank you. I'll let you know.'

Downes hesitated, knowing how full Hodges' mind must be.

'By the way,' he said at last, 'you don't seem to have noticed, but this rain's becoming rather heavy. Shouldn't you go below?'

'No.' Hodges managed a smile. 'It feels fresh and clean, and I don't.'

'Would you like an oilskin? I'll have one sent up.'

'Don't bother, Dennis. I shan't be brooding much longer.'

Downes nodded then, realising Hodges' need to think, moved to the other end of the bridge.

Hodges put his empty pipe in his mouth and chewed at the stem in the darkness, feeling desperately alone and friendless. He had been hoping and praying for hours that someone in

England would come to his senses and turn the convoy round before he, himself, was forced to make a decision one way or the other. Whatever he decided in the next ten minutes, he couldn't imagine it would look right in history. Across the intervening years, he had a feeling that people would tend to judge the general in command rather than the politicians who had placed him in such a private hell.

He thought of the men below decks and the arrangements that had been made to see that they disembarked at the right time when ordered. Even that problem seemed to have grown out of all proportion. Mutiny or no mutiny, he couldn't honestly be expected to order them ashore with the force abruptly halved. It wasn't even fair to the brave men who had not raised any protest. With his mind stiff with anxiety, to Hodges there wasn't the faintest hope now of *Stabledoor* succeeding. All reports showed that the Khanzians were not only ready for them, with every black man in Africa firmly behind them, but that they had been more prepared than anyone in England had ever dreamed when they had rushed so hastily into the decision to launch the operation. It seemed impossible to him that the people back in Westminster, even engrossed as they were with their ponderous political saraband, would be stupid enough to let them continue. The country was surely sick of politics and in need of government.

Below him, in the wardroom, trestle tables had been erected and the ship's surgeon, in white overalls, with his stethoscope in his pocket and a gauze mask dangling under his chin, had laid out his instruments and bottles of blood plasma. The surgery was ready to receive casualties, and stretcher bearers were taking up their stations at vantage points through the ship. The drugs locker was unsealed and the sick-berth attendants were checking the sterilizers.

Driven into cabins out of the way, the Pressmen waited, smoking and a little edgy, aware of something happening that they knew nothing about and resentful that they hadn't been told. So far, they hadn't asked and Hodges had no intention of telling them anything until he had to.

He glanced at his watch. Two minutes had already gone by with futile thinking. That left eight. Eight short minutes, that could mean life or death to hundreds of men in the convoy around him, disgrace to himself, and humiliation and disaster to his country. Why was it that politicians, in the hothouse atmosphere of Westminster, obsessed with office and the niceties of Parliamentary procedure, never managed to see a soldier's problem from a soldier's point of view? As his mind dwelt on the subject, he began to wonder how many statesmen, having made a war, had ever shown themselves willing to support their views by going to fight in it. None in England, that he could recall, since Cromwell.

Thinking about Cromwell, his mind turned to the prayer of Sir Jacob Astley before the battle of Edgehill in 1642. He'd used it more than once in the course of his army life, once even in orders. *'Oh, Lord, Thou knowest how busy I must be this day. If I forget Thee, do not Thou forget me.'*

It had always seemed a good soldierly prayer to utter before a battle—the sort of prayer that God would expect from a simple man, without frills or requests for special favours, and no fear of death. Hodges frowned, wishing things were as simple nowadays as they had been for Cromwell and Sir Jacob Astley.

He stopped himself abruptly again as he realised he was allowing his mind to be sidetracked into interesting hypotheses, when it should be fixed rigidly on the problem in hand. He glanced again at his watch and saw that the time at his disposal was now only seven minutes. It was amazing how fast time could go when one wanted it to run out slowly.

With the departure of the Malalans, he realised, the possibility of a third world war had abruptly receded. America and Russia might well now not trouble themselves to move their nuclear weapons and align themselves for a greater combat. Perhaps they would be prepared to sit back, contented to let the adventure end in the chaos of its own making, and allow the British statesmen to destroy themselves by their own obstinacy.

For the life of him, Hodges couldn't see that *Stabledoor* had the faintest chance of success. His appeal, through the Chief of Defence Staff, for a change of mind at home had gone unanswered, and to Hodges it seemed impossible that any man could possibly turn down such a request when he knew how much depended on it. Even the appeal to the Leader of the Opposition had gone unanswered.

Considering it, Hodges realised that the Leader of the Opposition was in his own cleft stick. Any alteration in his feelings, any retraction of anything he had said, could well be taken by the rest of the world for a tacit agreement with *Stabledoor*, and the Leader of the Opposition had taken a stand against just this possibility, just as *he* was expecting to have to do within the next few minutes.

Another glance at his watch. Five minutes! The time seemed to be slipping by so fast Hodges was aghast. In the whole of his military career he couldn't remember a single commander-in-chief who had ever made a decision such as he was now contemplating—refusing, on a point of conscience, to follow the instructions issued to him by his government. There had been cases where officers had translated them freely, but none that he knew of where generals in command had refused point blank to carry them out.

On the surface there would be no excuse. But if a man did something of which he would be ashamed for ever, could he be expected to live the rest of his life with his conscience? When the Leaders of the Light Brigade at Balaclava had been faced with a similar decision, they'd disagreed but obeyed orders, knowing full well what the consequences would be. And, although they'd ever since been regarded as fools, militarily they'd behaved correctly, because refusal to obey orders was simply reducing the Army to a state of anarchy; and not long before he, Hodges, had been taking precautions against the men of the 17th/105th doing just that very thing.

What was more, what other chain of events might he be starting by refusing to follow instructions? Although he believed he knew the facts, it could be that other greater events of which he had no knowledge hinged on his obeying orders—even if the orders appeared to be wrong and resulted in the deaths of many men. It had happened again and again between 1914 and 1918 and in his heart of hearts Hodges knew he hadn't a leg to stand on. While he might, as the owner of a conscience, refuse to do what he was instructed, as a soldier he had no option whatsoever but to do as he was told. He had to make up his mind. The moment had come. It was no longer possible to wait.

'Dennis . . .'

Downes turned towards him from his corner of the bridge as he spoke. They both looked haggard with the weight of the decision hanging over them.

'Dennis, I've no option. None at all. We carry on as instructed.'

He thought he heard Downes' breath come out in a sigh and thought he caught a subtle flicker of relief come over his face in the shadows.

'It's on my own responsibility,' he explained. 'It doesn't involve you.'

Downes shrugged. 'It involves me all right, Horace,' he said. 'And though I'm not sure just now what I think about it all, I don't honestly think you could do differently.'

'Thanks, Dennis. That helps.'

Downes made a little gesture with his hand 'You'll never be blamed by me,' he said. 'I'll back you to the hilt.' He paused and drew a deep breath. 'And now,' he ended, 'I suppose we'd better do something about it, and God help us both.'

'Sir . . .'

As they turned away from each other, Hodges heard the signal officer's voice. He swung round. The signal officer was a young man, and to Hodges just then he seemed like a mere boy. Then he noticed the youngster was looking at him, not at Downes, and he crossed the bridge quickly and took the signal. It was in plain language.

'COMCENT to COMHOJ. Hodgeforce will change direction west. Manœuvres to be terminated at once repeat at once.'

A series of elaborate and rigid courses followed, which were obviously intended to bear out the farce that they were on exercise, and Hodges stared at the message for some time before the full import of it sank in. Then he swung round on Downes, smiling. The man on the white horse had galloped up at last.

'Dennis,' he said, and Downes was at his side in a second.

'It's the reprieve, Dennis,' he said. 'It's been called off.'

Downes gazed at him, reading the relief in his face.

'About time someone came to their senses,' he said shortly.

4

The rain that had been dogging Hodgeforce for days had drifted away behind them at last as the ships headed due west; and as they turned and began to limp north towards Gibraltar, the sun rose on a placid sea like a millpond. Fuel was short, food was short, and thousands of men were suffering from being kept too long in confined spaces. But there was no longer any grumbling.

With the rest of the world, the men of Hodgeforce were breathing again without that feeling of constriction that came from fear and indignation and fury.

They had steamed a series of full-speed courses to the west, heading out into the South Atlantic for hours until Downes had been worried about their ability to reach even Gibraltar, then a second signal had reached them, ordering them, with considerable relief, to head north.

The vast pretence had continued. 'Exercise *Stabledoor* terminated,' the signal had concluded. 'Reports requested from all commanding officers.' There had also been a performance of elaborate gratitude towards the Malalans for the use of the port of Pepul for a practice embarkation under tropical conditions, but this was purely for world consumption, to keep up the diplomatic charade that *Stabledoor* had been nothing more than a vast manœuvre put on with the Malalans' agreement, from their port and with the full co-operation of their army, navy and air force.

No one was even faintly deluded. The B.B.C. news had been full of snippets from home that told the story. Faced with the facts, the Cabinet had at last accepted with relief the Chief of Defence Staff's recommendation that the operation be abandoned. The Prime Minister had disappeared into a nursing home, apparently a very sick man unable even to present his resignation at the Palace, and his party had admitted that they could not form a Government. The Leader of the Opposition, having climbed to power over a humiliation he himself had helped to bring about, had agreed to try, and was at that moment, with an air of Divine Right, selecting his Ministers. There seemed little likelihood that he would fail.

Foreign journalists, however, were not deceived, and the air was full of soured commentaries. And judging by the quotations, it was clear that the London newspapers were no more blinded than those of Paris and Berlin and New York and Moscow. Only at the eleventh hour had the resignations of the Foreign Secretary, the Home Secretary and the Chancellor of the Exchequer turned the tables. Nobody was talking, but the intense activity in Westminster was implicit. The Prime Minister had been forced out of office by his own party and they would take years to live down the fact.

To Hodges, it seemed a satisfactory enough ending to an unrealistic adventure. At the United Nations Assembly, the bubbling broth of international hatred had collapsed into nothing more than a simmering brew, with national passions cooling rapidly in an atmosphere of relief.

The generous Americans had announced an immediate new loan to Britain and to Malala, and the conference at Nairobi of African nations, suddenly bereft of its point of resentment, had fallen back on a mixture of jubilation and squabbling. Their guns, aimed at the white man in Africa, had been spiked; and most of them, well aware that they still needed European finance, were willing to forgive and forget so long as the United Nations was prepared to make sure that no such crisis could occur again.

The horizon was full of shattered loyalties and at the United Nations the frostiness between the British and the Americans would not die away until someone found a way to rebuild the transatlantic alliance. In Britain, they were moving swiftly towards an acute political upheaval. Divided, isolated and abused, there was still a feeling beyond the relief that they had been let down by their friends, and that the Americans had interfered unnecessarily in something that wasn't even their business. There was even a joke going the rounds—somehow it had reached *Leopard* by radio—that British diplomats were busy now trying to obtain permission from Washington to allow Starke to leave the nursing home, so that he could convalesce. The bitterness was strong and acrid in the throat.

Starke's party, unable to explain itself in the House, was searching for excuses to explain the diplomatic defeat as a victory which had been spoiled at the last moment. But they were no longer in power and what they said no longer mattered. Ahead of them was a bleak prospect of years of opposition. Their opponents, satisfied to be allowed to put things right, were managing to be restrained and were making no political capital out of their gain. The man who was forming a government, still acting with the utmost honour and rectitude, had allowed no demonstrations of triumph, apparently regarding the recent crisis as too grave for any joy to be drawn from it.

There had been remarkably little comment aboard *Leopard*. Hodges and Downes had seen the force turned west and then moved, without a word passing between them, to Hodges' cabin. Leggo was there and he had poured them drinks without speaking.

'Here's to common sense, Horace,' Downes had said, raising his glass.

'Thank God for it,' Hodges had agreed, as though saying 'amen'.

None of them had questioned the decision, none of them had commented on it. They, who had been at the apex of command, the men with the power of decision, had felt they could leave all that to their juniors.

To Hodges it was a moment of sadness, in spite of his relief. Somehow, in his heart of hearts, he knew the new Government would have no time for him. They had offered to alleviate hardships until enquiries could be made into the question of Services' pay, and in a flurry of signals had let it be known that there could be an amnesty, while making it quite clear at the same time that any further transgression would be severely dealt with under the Army, Navy and Air Force Discipline Acts. It had been received with relief in Hodgeforce, but not one man in the fleet had doubted for a moment the meaning of the last sentence. There would be no further trouble, and the armed squads of Guardsmen had been stood down.

To Hodges, however, it was not the end. They had already heard—by those curious Service channels that pass across the oceans—that Burnaston was not to be Chief of Defence Staff for the new Government, and if someone as powerful and able as he could be jettisoned, Hodges knew they would have no time for him. Probably Downes would go the same way. He knew that retirement wasn't far away, but somehow he wasn't sorry.

An aircraft screamed overhead, gleaming and polished, its long snout catching the light as it turned, and Hodges watched it for a moment, suddenly feeling too old for swift decisions. He needed to see his wife and children again, and he was looking forward to the garden he had taken pleasure in laying out at his home near the coast in Sussex. He just hoped it wouldn't affect his son's career in the Army, and that the women of the village wouldn't be too unpleasant towards his wife.

Downes was watching him carefully, and he knew that Downes knew what he was thinking. Probably, Downes was thinking the same things. Perhaps they'd both come to the end of the road.

Colonel Leggo's attitude was one of unquestioning relief. He had known all along that what they were about to do was wrong, and the only thing he could feel now was gladness that they hadn't done it.

He had been composing joyous messages to Stella Davies for two days now, wondering if he dared approach Hodges for permission to send a personal telegram. He had finally rejected the idea, realising she'd have learnt long since what had happened and would have guessed the problems that faced them all. She'd wait, he decided.

For Colonel Drucquer the decision to call off the operation brought relief mixed with anxiety. He suspected that, after the great lack of necessities that *Stabledoor* had turned up, there'd be a tremendous re-shuffle in the Army. The new Government was pledging itself to look into the mistakes and the shortages and, inevitably, one of the things that would be discussed would be the disaffection among the troops. If it hadn't actually begun in the 17th/105th, it had certainly been found there. The pamphlets which had started Hodges' enquiries had been discovered among Drucquer's own men and the shooting incident which had brought the whole thing to light had been in the same small section. An enquiry would go deep into the trouble, and he knew he'd be called to account for it, though he felt sadly that he could hardly be held responsible. Only a few days before the incidents he'd been in Hong Kong.

He knew there'd be a few compulsory retirements flying about and he prayed that he would not be among them.

There was no feeling of joy whatsoever in Captain White as the ships turned northward. Somehow, he felt they'd been let down. And curiously there was no feeling of pleasure either that he was returning home. He'd enjoyed his return to uniform and, while he loved his wife, he felt somehow that his last adventure with the Army had been a fiasco from beginning to end and one that nobody could be proud of.

Lieutenant Jinkinson was busy airing his grievances and, of the lot of them, he was the most vociferous in his protests that he'd not been allowed to do his duty.

Sergeant Frensham, as usual, said very little. He'd not much time for politicians or for anyone outside the Army. He didn't particularly look forward to going back to his job as an electronics storekeeper. It kept him close to his wife and family but it wasn't much of a job for a man, and he wasn't particularly proud of it and had felt for some time that he needed a better one. Still, he thought, he hadn't descended like so many men he knew to being a commissionaire. That was the very bottom, opening and shutting doors for men who weren't fit to lick his boots and running errands for girl typists. That sort of job could go to those who wanted it, but not to Sergeant Frensham.

On the other hand, considering what had just passed, it seemed that the Army was no longer a place for Sergeant Frensham either. It was a pretty poor exchange for all the glory he'd known in his time.

In *Banff*'s sick bay, Lance-Corporal Malaki lay facing the bulkhead, gloomily surveying a spot of chipped paint.

He could never belong to the others now, he felt. In spite of not agreeing with them, he hadn't wished to be the one to give the game away, but someone—he wasn't sure who—had taken advantage of his drowsiness under sedation and got it all from him.

He wondered if any of the others would have done the same, and somehow, with that strange code of ethics the British had, he had a feeling that they wouldn't. Snaith hadn't agreed with what was going on. Neither had Ginger Bowen. But he felt they'd have died rather than give the others away. It was a strange British attitude that he didn't understand, but he felt that his own instincts were the ones that were wrong.

He became aware of someone standing by the bed and, thinking it was the sick-berth attendant come to attend to the wound in his groin, he turned his head painfully, his dark skin grey-violet with the loss of blood.

It was Snaith who was standing by the bed, however, and he slowly put two or three paperback books on the covers in an embarrassed gesture of gentleness, and grinned sheepishly.

'Hi, Joe,' he said. 'They told me I could come and see you.'

As for Ginger Bowen, he was right back where he started. After the enquiry held by Colonel Drucquer all the others had been released. The affair wasn't ended, of course, because a man had been shot, but somehow it was in everyone's mind that not much was likely to be said about the mutiny, only about the discharge of the Sten gun. There'd be plenty said about that.

Only Ginger, had failed to qualify for the free pardon that the Government had insisted on. As they'd opened the door to let them out, Leach had tossed a final acid remark at him and Ginger's quick temper had caused him to swing his fist in a tremendous frustrated haymaker at his tormentor. Unfortunately, Leach had ducked and it had been Corporal Connell who had received it right under the angle of the jaw. It was a slapstick ending to the affair, but neither Connell, who'd been out cold for three minutes, nor Sergeant O'Mara was disposed to listen to Ginger's explanation and he had promptly been returned to the cells for assaulting an N.C.O.

While it would be untrue to say that his efforts alone had brought *Stabledoor* to its ignominious end, it had certainly been Ginger who had first set light to the fuse under it at Pepul which, with outside pressures in New York and Moscow and Peking and Berlin and Paris, had toppled it off its rails. But, probably fortunately for his character, he never learned how much he'd done to bring a world war to an end even before it had begun. And, suffering bitterly from resentment—against Leach, against Connell, against O'Mara, against the whole military system—he found himself once more painting and polishing fire buckets—this time deep in the bowels of *Banff*.